DIANA NURI

PSYCHO-LOGIST

She heals Victims and hunts Monsters.

To the darkness that teaches us to value the light, and to the light that never lets us forget who we are.

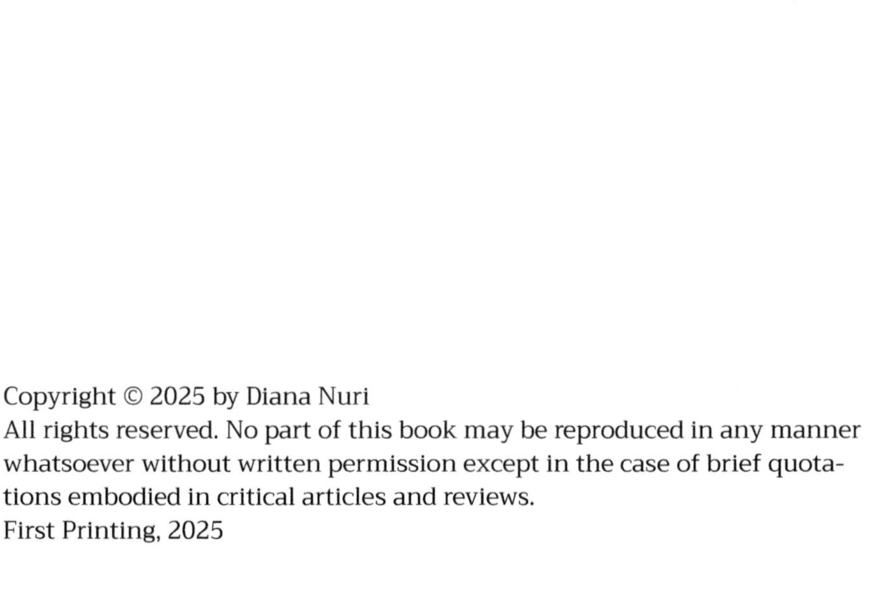

First Printing, 2025

CONTENTS

PROLOGUE

Who is there by our side? Can they be trusted? I do not know. At times, the faces of loved ones are masks that hide demons or, rather, his messengers. I do not know how else to explain why it is the people closest to us that break our spirit and soul. I know from personal experience and from the experiences of people I have helped how difficult it is to recover from this. It can take one person years to recover, while another will never get over it.

What is it exactly that hurts us in this mean-spirited and inhumane approach? It is simple: normal people like us cannot understand how you can trample and injure a person who has not only let you into their heart, but also selflessly opened their soul. When faced with this, we are haunted by the questions of "What did I do to deserve this?" and "How could they do this to me?". The word underlying these questions is injustice. We surrender ourselves wholly and what do we get in return?

A reasonable question arises: how do I protect myself from this? My answer is simple – with love. Not love for someone, though, but for yourself! Learn to value and respect yourself. You will find a reason if you look for it! Many people are so critical of themselves that they forget that they are their own most important person. You have to understand that. You must stand firmly on your own two feet and your self-esteem should not depend on others, especially men. The world is full of them, but you only have one of you. Never let anyone break your unwavering spirit. I believe in you and I believe that you can make your life better. I believe that you can raise your sons and daughters well. Raise them so that they respect not only you and themselves but also the people around them.

As always, with warmth and kindness in my heart,
Diana Nuri.

ACKNOWLEDGEMENTS

Here is my next book with real life stories. Am I happy about this? Absolutely. Is it my doing? I would not say so. My personality was shaped by many teachers, good and bad, and I am grateful to them all. Today I want to mention the main teacher in my life, my mother. She is an amazing woman and unique in her own way. She has always been my compass, my guiding star. Thanks to her, I always knew where I went wrong and where my conscience was clear. Being a highly moral and religious person, she tried to put me on the right path, especially when I persistently strayed from it. Back then, I resisted, was angry at her and incredibly annoyed that she was meddling in my life and not letting me live the way I wanted to. Of course, I am no longer angry, rather pleased that many mistakes have been avoided. Although the mistakes I had already made torment me to this very day.

In adolescence, when our parents fall off the pedestal of perfection, we think that they are stupid and do not understand anything. We, on the other hand, are on fire. We will show them how it is done! As always, the opposite is true. We fall into the same traps as our parents and it takes us a while to admit, and sometimes we never do, that they were right. The older I get, the closer I am to my mother. As I live my life and go through challenging periods, I understand that she once went through the same thing. She tried to raise good children, tried to feed them, love them and much more. Yes, my mother and your mother likely made mistakes, but do we have the right to judge them? We never walked in their shoes. You need to try to forgive everything (what is forgivable, of course) and let it go. I am not telling you to follow my advice, I am just sharing my personal experience. As my own psychological practice has shown, people who harbour resentment in their hearts have more difficult lives. That is all.

The last thing I want to say in this section is:

Dear Mum! Thank you for being an example to me and, to some extent, my idol. I have always admired how you handle any matter and your decent treatment of other people. I will always be grateful for everything you did for me.

I would like to express my gratitude to my family, who has always supported all my endeavours and has been a pillar of strength. How many tears I have shed on your shoulders! I value your presence in my life and wish you only the best.

I would like to mention my son in particular, whose arrival changed me forever. Thanks to you, I became gentler, more tolerant and more driven. Everything I have today, I did for you, my incentive and my inspiration.

Finally, I want to express my gratitude to a person who is beautiful inside and out, who is decent, talented, kind and warm-hearted – Sofia Gutkin. A person without whom my books would not exist as they are now. Sofia is an outstanding professional who translates my works exactly as they are written.

Thank you, Sofia! I am very lucky to have met you.

That is all for today. Look after the good people you meet along the way. As always, I sincerely wish you happiness and peace of mind.

THE BEGINNING

Every morning starts the same way. I get out of bed, take a handful of pills prescribed by my doctor, open the curtains, and stare at the city waking up for a while. I make myself a cup of coffee, not because I want it, but because my brain thinks that its smell will wake me up. I've known for a long time that this isn't true. Coffee leaves a bitter, sticky taste on my tongue, but I continue to drink it nonetheless. I guess this habit is here to stay.

Next, I take a shower, open the door to my large, even huge, walk-in closet, choose one of my expensive suits, put on high-heeled shoes, and go down to the parking lot where my snow-white Porsche is parked. As I start the engine, I smile, because its roar always gives me a pleasant thrill. Then I drive to work and arrive, as always, a little earlier than all my employees and my hopelessly stupid secretary. I like it when no one else is in the office yet.

At 9 a.m., Isabel (the secretary) arrives and, day after day, plops down heavily into a soft armchair, immediately takes out a mirror and lipstick and begins to brightly paint her already bright lips. I hate her red lipstick, and I hate her habit, but I keep quiet because it would be inappropriate for me to get annoyed with her and take out my anger on her. After all, I am a psychologist, the best in town, and I have to control my emotions. As a psychologist, I understand that it's not the red lipstick that angers me, but Isabel herself, or rather her youth and the fact that life hasn't worn her down the way it has worn me down. And to be completely honest, I'm angry that what happened to me won't happen to her. I don't wish that on her. Sort of. But why am I lying? Of course I do! Why did it happen to me and not someone like her? I'm better than her!

I pull down the blinds separating my office from the rest of the space, so I don't have to see Isabel, and sit down in my chair, waiting for my first client of the day. He's always late. I hate that too. Where did I hear that phrase, "punctuality is the politeness of kings"? It definitely doesn't apply to him. There's nothing royal about him. He is rapacious, odious, base human being. He gets rich off the poor, lining his pockets with their money and stuffing his belly with endless amounts of food. He makes me sick just looking at him. And who knows how much effort it takes me not to tell him what I really think of him.

I lean back in my chair and turn to the wall covered with my endless awards for my endless achievements. Who needs them? Not me anymore. The days when my ego played games with me are long gone.

My intercom crackles.

"Miss Heleina is here to see you, Mr. Ridley." It's Isabel's voice.

"Send him in. Thank you, Isabel."

My door slowly opens and this huge ship floats into my office, barely able to breathe.

I smile at him and say,

“Good morning, Mr. Ridley. How are you today?”

“Not great,” he replies, settling down on the couch under the spreading branches of the Ficus tree.

“Interesting,” I think, trying not to look at my client, ‘when was the last time someone watered the Ficus? Some of the leaves are yellow, some have fallen off completely. I hope it doesn't die. I love that Ficus. I've had it for three years.”

“Can we begin?’ Mr. Ridley's question pulls me back to reality.

“Of course,” I reply calmly, sitting down in the chair opposite him.” How was your week?”

He then begins to complain about his life. He tells me that his chemotherapy isn't going very well and that he feels worse after each session.

I know he's scheduled for a liver transplant next month, but I also know for sure that he won't live to see it. I've seen this before. I can see how he's suffering, how much pain and fear he's in, but I don't feel sorry for him at all.

The television showed a protest outside his credit company. Thousands of people were demanding their money back. Some didn't live to see today, others are barely surviving, trying to climb out of the debt hole that Mr. Ridley drove them into without the slightest twinge of conscience. I'm 40 now and I've seen a lot in my life, but I still can't understand how these people can sleep peacefully knowing that someone is suffering greatly because of them. They don't care, they're not ashamed! Not at all. I would be ashamed.

After Ridley comes a housewife who is tired of life. Her name is Eleanor. An interesting name. Eleanor's life is idle. She comes from a wealthy family and married a man who is no less wealthy than she is. She has lived her life without knowing hardship, without knowing what it is like to have nothing to eat and no money to pay for an apartment. She invents problems out of thin air. She has no real, significant problems, so she often comes to me to complain about what she has come up with during the week, namely her unhappy life, as she sees it.

Eleanor is a well-groomed, pretty woman in her 50s. She was apparently not very beautiful in her younger years, so she compensates for this with ultra-expensive clothes and an indecent amount of diamonds. As far as I know, wearing diamonds in the morning is considered bad taste. Although, how would I know, rich people have their quirks.

Eleanor does not lie down on the couch but carefully settles into an armchair. She is tense around me, perhaps intimidated by my authority, and therefore does not act rude, pretending to be aloof, although I have heard the exact opposite from Isabel.

“That woman doesn't consider us human beings,” Isabel snorted once after Eleanor had left.

This Thursday, Eleanor will complain about her daughter. I already know that Sunday is visiting day for the children, and it brings nothing but grief to the parents.

“They asked for money again,” Eleanor complains. ‘It's as if they don't want anything from us except money.”

“How does that make you feel?’ I ask, repeating a question that has become tiresome to me.

“Anger. We've given them so much: the best universities, apartments, cars, trips! They've never worked a day in their lives!”

I sincerely don't understand why Eleanor is surprised. Neither she nor her husband ever took care of their children or gave them the attention they deserved. And if you replace love with money, shutting people up with it, what kind of result do you expect?

And even now, when the children are all grown up, you continue to live your dull life. The father of the family has been living in two houses for many years; in one, he has a young mistress with a new child, and in the other, his old wife with her endless whining. It's immoral, but everyone knows about it.

Eleanor herself, instead of giving her children something resembling love and care, spends her time just as she always has, drinking cocktails with her friends at the club or hanging out at the beauty salon, improving things that no one needs. Certainly not her husband.

Many years ago, I had to change my client base and start working with people from, let's say, "another world." They don't know what hunger is. And today I think that was a big mistake on my part. They are all the most disgusting representatives of humanity. They have no idea about simple human joys, only money, money, capital.

Looking at Eleanor and analysing her children, I come to the conclusion that perhaps some of them would definitely agree to trade the walls of a luxury mansion for a life in a regular trailer, without money and other trappings, but with parents who know what love is. Yes, these children are happier than those. Some of them will become good people, specialists in some useful field, doctors or scientists. They don't have and won't have a rich dad to rely on, but that's okay, because then you only have yourself to rely on, and that's already 50% of success.

I grin and shake my head. Are you talking to yourself, Heleina? No one's arguing, you're doing great.

"Do you think it's too much? " Eleanor asks me.

"I think you should trust your own feelings on that," I reply to her unheard question.

Frankly speaking, I don't give a damn about her questions or her. Or anyone else, for that matter. Immediately, my inner critic pops up and says, "How can you treat people like that? You're supposed to help them, you're a healer of souls!" "But I don't want to help them," I reply to the voice, 'you know why we're here.' I smile again, but for some reason my smile is evil, malicious.

"Thank you, Miss Heleina. I feel so much better now. Shall I come on Saturday after golf, as usual?

"I'll be glad to see you, Eleanor. By the way, I wanted to mention that you look absolutely gorgeous today. You're literally glowing."

"Really? It's new injections," she whispers," from Switzerland. I got them through a connection; they're not easy to come by, but as a special client, they gave me this compliment."

And then she manages to remind me who she is. A special client. I feel sick.

As soon as she leaves, I throw the windows wide open, wanting to get rid of the disgusting smell of her niche perfume. I wonder if she can smell that it smells like cat poop?

"Who else is in for today?" I ask Isabel, pressing the intercom button.

"Mr. and Mrs. Schreiber at 1:00 p.m."

"Got it. I'm going to lunch."

I take the blanket and lunch I prepared yesterday out of my bag and go to the park across the street. I always have lunch here. I like watching dog walkers, children, and their parents. I can give a rough psychological profile of almost everyone just by looking at them. It's probably my favourite pastime.

My lunch is modest, as usual: tine amount of brown rice and stewed chicken. I savour every bite, tasting the different seasonings and convincing myself once again what a wonderful cook I am. I'm a good cook, even though no one ever taught me.

Why do I cook for myself? I'm quite picky about food, which is not true of other aspects of my preferences. My hungry childhood has had an impact on my eating habits. My mother was a terrible cook, and to be honest, she was a terrible mother. Today, I am no longer angry with her, because she is no longer alive, and you can't speak ill of the dead.

After finishing lunch, I cheerfully get up from the bench and go to the office. I am happy to be back there, because now comes my favourite part of my job. My favourite clients, whom I don't have to hate or punish.

Mr. and Mrs. Schreiber are elderly people who have been married for over 50 years. Despite having lived together for half a century, they still haven't learned to give in to each other. They constantly argue about trivial things and then passionately make up, which I find surprising, of course. Perhaps it is love. Returning to their arguments, every time they tell me what they were arguing about, we laugh out loud at how silly they actually were.

I don't think they come to me to solve any "problems." They come to me to feel important, needed, and not alone.

Before the appointment, Mrs. Schreiber applies heavy eye makeup, carefully styles what's left of her hair, puts on her best dress, and sprays on a subtle, pleasant fragrance. I think it's lilac.

Mr. Schreiber is apparently getting ready too. His face is perfectly shaven, and his hair is combed. He also puts on his best suit, which he has kept since his military service.

They are a lovely couple. Overall, they seem happy, but they have their own misfortunes. Their son died in a car accident before he reached the age of 30. He was their light, their joy, and their reason for living. Although more than 20 years have passed since the tragedy, their wound is still bleeding. Time has not been able to heal it. Sometimes they cry for him, and I feel sincere pity for them. With all my heart. In moments of acute pain, I quote passages from the Bible to them; they are religious people, and it immediately makes them feel better. And me too.

By the way, I don't take any money from them. Firstly, they can't afford it, and secondly, I don't want to. I enjoy being with these people. Perhaps we even knew each other in past lives.

After our first session, Mr. Schreiber was very offended to hear that it was free. He wasn't used to that; he is a proud man.

“Let's agree on this,” I suggested. ” I don't want to take money from you because I don't want to insult or offend you. You are like my grandparents to me. And it's not right to take money from loved ones.” Secondly, if you want to repay me in some way, you can do something good at church, for example. And it turns out that the good I put into the lake will create other circles of good from you, then from those you help, and so on. Agreed?

“I don't quite understand, “ muttered the gray-haired man, shifting from foot to foot.

“Oh, what don't you understand?” Mrs. Schreiber exclaimed, grabbing him by the elbow. She’s doing us a favor; we’re doing others a favor, and so on. It's wisdom. Right?” She glanced at me, seeking support.

"Yes, yes. I already knew you were an educated woman, but I didn't think you were so profound."

That day, Mrs. Schreiber winked at me in response and waved as she left.

After this lovely, warm, heartfelt couple, I have another appointment. I don't like them. He's over 60, she's in her 30s. He's very rich, and she's after his money. I can see that she's only with him for the money and she needs to be punished. He can be left alone, he's a good man. He earned his wealth through honest, hard work. It's a shame that he had enough brains to build an empire but not enough to see the rotten core of this whore.

It was her idea to come to me. She wants to convince her new-old husband that he shouldn't give his children any money. She wants it all for herself.

"You see," she says," they've stopped bringing the children to Aiven. They're punishing him for being happy with me, aren't they?"

"Do you think so?"

"Yes. They can't forgive him for finally finding love and understanding. They call me the worst names, and it hurts me to the core."

Looking at her enormous breasts, I doubt that anyone could reach her heart.

"What do you think, Aiven?" I ask the man.

"I already told you that I was alone for a long time after my wife died. Fifteen years is a long time. I never thought I would remarry, and of course I understand the children's fears, but I still want them to see Christy through my eyes. She didn't even know I was rich. It was just love. Pure love. And to forbid her from meeting her grandchildren is inhuman.

Well, well. We've seen enough of that kind of love in crime reports. Oh, you fool. You'll end up like those heroes when your Christie and her young lover come up with a cunning plan to get rid of you and find you somewhere in the desert, or maybe they won't find you at all. What are people capable of for money? This question really bothers me.

What is money? It's the ability to satisfy your needs: food, shelter, buying things. When money works like this, pushing you to do all kinds of terrible things? And why don't people live according to the scriptures written centuries ago? There's a set of rules written there... And there wouldn't be any problems. Or maybe people just can't live according to their conscience, maybe some people just don't have one?

As a professional, I am convinced that people are born good, kind, honest, and pure. They are made bad by adults, who were also corrupted by their own parents. That's how this whole cycle of evil in the universe works.

“Are you even listening to us? “The inflatable doll asks me.

“Christy, I always listen to you,” I reply with a serious face.

“So, what do you advise Aiven? Do you agree with me?”

“You know I can't give you advice. I can help you find the solution that is already inside you.” “Eivan,” I say, turning my head,” your children love you very much, you've said so many times, and I think your original decision to give them time is the right one in this matter. Excluding them from your will, as Christie suggests, is not the best step toward normalizing your relationship with your children, in my opinion.”

He nods his head; he doesn't want to lose either his children or his grandchildren. She presses her lips together. This is not the result she wanted. She thought that since she was paying me, I would dance to her tune and give the old man advice that would benefit her. She's got the wrong person!

As soon as they leave my office, I breathe a deep sigh of relief. I know they won't be coming back to see me. She'll find someone else to help convince her husband to leave the money intended for his children in her clutches.

Those are my last clients for today. I'm glad. I feel tired and want to get home as soon as possible, close the door, draw the curtains tightly, and feel safe.

As soon as I leave my office, I notice that Isabel is sitting with her legs up on the desk. I give her a stern look, and she quickly hides her legs under the desk.

"I'm sorry," she stammers.

Walking down the corridor lined with glass cubicles, I listen to my employees providing psychological assistance. Almost all of them are doing a good job, except for the one in the far corner. I should fire him. But overall, I'm proud of my team. They do a good job, saving people from rash decisions every day. And from mistakes, sometimes fatal ones. This help is free for people, and every day I mentally thank Mr. X, who has been finding sponsors for this activity for many years now.

On the way home, I turn the music up full blast to relax my brain. On the way, I have time to enjoy the city as it sinks into the evening haze. I like the city I live in; it is so beautiful, even majestic. The shiny skyscrapers towering up to the sky do not bother me at all, on the contrary.

As I pass the last two blocks, I finally see my house and my heart skips a beat with joy.

I take the elevator up to my floor, walk down the long hallway, and see my door. There is a beautiful plaque with my name on it, and every time I see it, I smile.

Closing the door behind me, something inside me changes. It feels like I've been chased for a long time and finally found a place where I have nothing to fear. Strange, isn't it? Although, no, I know where this feeling comes from.

After taking a shower and putting on my pajamas, I go to the kitchen to prepare dinner. Since I'm watching my figure, my dinner will be as meager as my lunch was.

While the air fryer cooks my fish, I chop up a salad and listen to a podcast of gossip and news. Yes, it's bad, yes, it's dirty, but it's my guilty pleasure.

After dinner, I put the dirty dishes in the sink, not even bothering to put them in the dishwasher. It's my strange quirk. I hate washing dishes and putting them away. I know that my housekeeper, Gina, will come in the morning and do it all for me. She's a good woman, albeit with her little quirks. She always asks for her salary in advance, and on days when I don't have to work, she sits on my ear and whines about her miserable life, even though her living conditions have improved dramatically since she started working for me.

She came from the Philippines and lived in our country illegally for many years, so she had no rights and worked in the most terrible jobs. Many places didn't pay her, and she was literally starving. When she came to me for an interview, she was meek and quiet, already mentally broken. Yes, I felt sorry for her, which is probably why I took her in. I have never regretted it, well, almost never. Her only significant mistake was when she ruined my favourite suit, which cost $12,000. Oh well.

I lay my head on my pillow and try to fall asleep. I have had a complicated relationship with sleep for many years. I fall asleep with difficulty and wake up at 3 a.m. It turns out that I sleep no more than 5 hours a day, which is bad for my nervous system and my body in general. Although, Churchill slept 5 hours a day and lived to a ripe old age. I wonder if I'll live to be old? With a life like mine, it's unlikely.

WHO ARE YOU, HELEINA PASCAL?

A new day and it's all the same again: medicine, coffee, shower, suit, drive to work, office, Isabel and her lipstick.

Today I woke up feeling anxious. I always wake up feeling anxious, but today it felt different. It felt as if the world had collapsed, as if something irreparable had happened.

Throughout the day, I try to shake off this feeling, but I don't succeed, and I flinch at every sound. When the end of the day comes, I breathe out and calm down. Just a little longer and I'll be home, safe.

I'm about to leave the office when my pager rings and Isabel's voice tells me that the police are here to see me. Ah, there it is, that feeling. It has never failed me. It always works.

Returning to my chair, I tell Isabel that the visitors can come in. Two people enter the office. A woman and a man. The woman looks tired and angry; she obviously wants to go home, just like me. The man is tall, gray-haired, and very composed. I can tell that he doesn't get tired at work; on the contrary, it energizes him.

"Good evening," he says, 'my name is Detective Gishi, and this is my partner, Detective Fraser. Sorry for the late visit, I see you were about to leave,' he concludes, nodding at my coat on the table.

"Good evening, detectives. Yes, I was indeed about to leave. Please have a seat. What can I do for you?" I reply in my usual even tone.

"We'll stand."

Aha, I note, he's choosing the dominant position. Well, let's play.

He looks around the room and continues to remain silent, thinking that this silence will somehow make me nervous, but I have nothing to hide. He is acting very purposefully; this must be his tactic. I also remain silent and watch his every move, studying him. He is the first to give in and finally sits down, looks at me and says the following:

"Miss Pascal, are you familiar with the name Christy Beck?"

"Of course, she and her husband are my clients."

He waits for me to ask, "What happened? Why are you asking?" but I remain silent. He presses his lips together. He understands everything. He's probably a good psychologist too, but I'm still better.

"When was the last time they were at your office?"

"Yesterday."

"You know, Mrs. Beck is missing."

"Hmm, but it hasn't been 48 hours since she disappeared, maybe she'll come back."

"She won't come back. She disappeared under rather strange circumstances. She didn't take any clothes, money, her car, her driver's license, nothing. Everything was left at home, including her fingers!" At that moment, he looks at me, waiting for a reaction.

I raise my eyebrows in surprise.

"Her fingers?"

"Yes, two, to be precise. We suspect she may have been kidnapped. Or something else."

"Why did you come to me?" I ask calmly.

"I wanted to know if Mrs. Beck had any problems with her husband."

"Not that I'm aware of."

"Did she have any enemies?"

"No, none that I know of."

"What can you tell me about Mr. Beck's daughters?"

"What about them?"

"We know that they had a strained relationship with the new Mrs. Beck."

"Are you aware that one of the daughters lives on the other side of the world and the other in a different state?"

"We know, but that doesn't stop them, as they say."

"I don't think the children had anything to do with the disappearance. Judging by Mr. Beck's account, they are respectable Christians and would never hurt anyone, even someone bad."

"Was Mrs. Beck a bad person?"

"I can't judge that. Everyone has different standards of morality."

"Enough, Adam," Detective Fraser interrupted. "Please, Miss Pascal, can you give us any information that might help us find Mrs. Beck?"

“Look for her in strip clubs, casinos, or places where women like her like to spend time. I'm sure that neither Mr. Beck nor his children had anything to do with this.” I understand that you have learned a lot about their family in a short time and surely understand that Mrs. Beck was not kidnapped, let alone murdered.

“No one mentioned murder,” Gishi rejoices at the lead.

“Mr. Gishi, at the beginning of our conversation, I asked you: fingers?” You replied, 'Yes, two, to be precise. We assume she may have been kidnapped. Or something else.' That 'something else' implies certain consequences. I look at him intently and continue, 'You know, I have a phenomenal memory, I remember everything down to the smallest detail. Don't try to play games with me.

He remains silent and looks away in disappointment.

“Thank you, Miss Pascal, “Detective Fraser says to me, ‘we've heard you, if Mrs. Back gets in touch with you, let us know!’ She hands me her business card.

“Of course,” I assure her.

Meanwhile, Mr. Gishi is studying my wall-to-wall filing cabinet, whose shelves are lined with files containing my clients' cases. Each folder is labeled with their last names. Among this huge pile of papers, his gaze naturally finds something to catch his eye. I realize that I have found a worthy opponent.

He is already reaching for the green folder when I sternly interrupt him:

“Please keep your hands off my documents—this is confidential information! You know that don't you?”

He thought I wouldn't notice.

Turning to me, he smiles guiltily and says:

“I'm sorry, it just looked like a familiar surname.”

When they leave, I put on my raincoat but don't leave the office. I look out the window and watch the detectives leave the building. As soon as they appear on the driveway, he turns toward my window and, seeing me, waves. He knows. He senses it. He probably has the same intuition as me. I'm sure he had an authoritarian father who often drank and beat him when he was drunk. Only traumatized children become so sensitive, I know that for a fact.

I walk over to the cabinet and look at the folder that caught the detective's attention. Of course, he recognized the name; it was in all the newspapers. But I have nothing to do with it; I didn't even know him. At least, no one else knew about our acquaintance.

I'm sure that instead of going home (where, by the way, no one is waiting for him, he's lonely), Gishi will go to the office and dig up all the notes mentioning the name on the folder. He'll sit over them all night, drawing logical chains, and then fall asleep on the sofa in the corner of his office. The next morning, after freshening up at the office and drinking a cup of disgusting coffee, he will show up at my office door with more questions.

Morning comes, I put on the best suit in my collection and drive to the office, where I see Gishi at the door. My analysis worked. I've figured you out, which means I can dodge your blows because I'll know where you're going to hit.

I get out of my car, close the door carefully, and walk slowly toward the office door.

“Mr. Gishi,” I say, raising an eyebrow,” I’m surprised to see you here again. Have you found Christy yet?”

He looks at me suspiciously and smiles, replying,

“No, Miss Pascal, not yet, but we'll find her. I'm here about something else. I'm sure you can guess what it is.”

“I have no idea,” I reply calmly, taking my keys out of my purse. «Let’s go to my office.»

Opening the door, I step confidently inside, the click of my heels echoing throughout the room. Once in the office, I turn on the light, settle into a chair, and watch Gishi. He is back at my cabinet, clearly eager to grab the folder from the shelf and look inside. He's boiling inside. His impatience is making him nervous.

“So, what brings you here at such an early hour?”

“You know, yesterday, while I was in your office, I accidentally stumbled upon that folder with the name of a well-known businessman, banker, and so on. The surname is quite rare and unusual, and I was surprised to see it there. As soon as I got back to the office, I immediately checked my assumption and found that the name of the woman on the folder belonged to the wife of this businessman.

“And what surprises you about that?”

“It's just strange that one of your clients disappeared almost immediately after visiting your office, and the husband of another client disappeared under exactly the same circumstances. I should note that both of them lost limbs, but only one of them had all his fingers cut off. I think there's something going on here.”

I smiled.

“You can think whatever you want, that's your right. In our country, thank God, it's not prohibited yet.”

“Well, still,” he continues his attack, ”please tell me, Miss Pascal, do you think there's something suspicious about this?”

“What do you think?”

“I've been to see psychologists before and I'm familiar with these kinds of questions. Let's skip them, shall we? You can probably already see how I think.

"Well, Mr. Gishi, I don't think there's anything there for you to see. I don't understand what you're getting at, by the way. Perhaps these are just obsessive thoughts caused by poor sleep and an unhealthy lifestyle. You may need to have some tests done so I can diagnose your problem more accurately.

He looks at me menacingly. He understands everything, and because he can't get through to me, he's starting to get angry.

"I'm not sick!" he objects. "Miss Pascal, don't play games with me!"

"I wasn't, Mr. Gishi. I have the utmost respect for you and your work. I'm just trying to understand what you want from me. Tell me straight, and I'll answer any question you have."

"How is your psychological assistance fund financed??"

"And what does that have to do with Mrs. Beck's disappearance?"

"So, which ones?"

"Although I'm not obliged to answer that question, if you happen to have a part-time job at the Federal Tax Service, I'll tell you that the fund is financed by patrons."

"What kind of patrons?"

- That's confidential information. I would be happy to tell you about it, but unfortunately, I've signed a non-disclosure agreement.

- Are you familiar with the name Eric Sayber?

- I don't recall. After all these years, it's hard to remember all the clients who have walked through this office.

- He's dead.

"I'm sorry to hear that, but it's something that happens to everyone, even you and me."

"Yes, yes. How long was Mrs. Tara your client?"

"I can't answer that question."

"Are you involved in Mrs. Beck's disappearance?"

"God forbid!" I reply, rolling my eyes.

He's starting to boil over, I can feel it. A little more and he'll run out of my office, slamming the door behind him. His problem is that he's impatient. Apparently, over the years, his father has begun to emerge in him, or rather, his father's behavior patterns. This is not unique to Gishi — copying parental behavior patterns — but is common to all people.

"Miss Pascal, where did you live until you were 14?"

"I think you know that."

"Unfortunately, I don't."

"In Connecticut."

"You were there when you were 14, but what about before that? Where were you before that?"

"The same place."

"And why is there no record of that?"

"I don't know. Those questions are not for me." I continue to answer calmly, still sitting at my desk.

"This isn't working!" he finally says, raising his voice.

"What should work?" I ask, feigning surprise. "Mr. Gishi, you are putting me in an awkward position. I don't understand your hints and I'm starting to feel uncomfortable. You come to our office when no one else is here and try to steer our conversation in some strange direction. You know that I am a respected person not only in our powerful country, but also in other countries! My work is published in all international scientific journals. And here you come and try to lead me into something! I think you'd better leave my office. I get up from my chair as if offended. And you know, come back next time with Detective Fraser. Our conversation is over.

As I had anticipated, he exits abruptly, slamming the door behind him without saying goodbye, while I return to my chair, place my feet on my oak-paneled desk, and examine the folder with the name of my client, Tara. I am familiar with her life story. She is as old as the world itself. Her husband is abusive, she is a victim of circumstance. Nothing new, I see this kind of thing all the time.

I get up from my chair, walk over to the cabinet, take Tara's file, lie down on the couch, open the first page, and start reading.

ONE-WAY TICKET

"Tara, what's taking you so long? Come out already!" Sarah shouted impatiently to her friend.

"I'm coming, I'm coming," came a voice from the fitting room. "I couldn't get the zip to work."

"They offered to help, so why did you refuse?"

"You know that I don't like to change in front of strangers."

"Come on, show me!"

"I'm ready," Tara replied with satisfaction and finally stepped out into the main room, where light fell softly from the high ceilings and the surrounding mirrors reflected it back.

"Oh, my God," Sarah was stunned when she saw her friend.

"Do you like it?" Tara said dubiously.

"So much! It looks great on you."

Tara gazed at herself in the large mirror and smoothed out the hem of the snow-white dress with the light lace sleeves. Tara's wavy and honey-tinted hair was neatly gathered into a simple but elegant bun. She adjusted her veil with a quick movement and looked in the mirror again.

"I think the last one was better."

"Are you kidding? This one makes you look like a white swan! I bet he'll cry at the altar." Sarah said teasingly, knowing that Tara's fiancé was a delicate person.

"Oh, stop it!" Tara replied coquettishly, adjusting the folds on the skirt. "I think it's cute that he's so sensitive."

She continued to spin this way and that in front of the mirror, still unsure whether to choose this dress. Turning around, Tara noticed that Sarah was wiping away tears.

"What's the matter?" she asked in surprise and gave her friend a gentle hug. Tara abruptly saw, in the face of this beautiful dark-haired woman with bright blue eyes, the little girl whom Tara had met so many years ago.

"I don't know, I just got emotional. I remembered when Elliot and I got married. We were so in love, and I thought it would be like that forever, but instead... well, you know."

"Oh, everything is fine with you! You're just imagining things."

"I'm not making this up! I always see the way Oliver looks at you, it's obvious from his eyes, but Elliot? I'm sure he's seeing someone!"

"Stop that right now! He's not seeing anyone. It's like you have nothing better to do than tie yourself in knots. You're both just busy with life so there's no time for romance, but everything is fine with you on the whole. It's exactly the relationship I wanted."

"You got a better one," Sarah stated without envy.

"I got a better one," her friend agreed.

Tara had liked Oliver at first sight. He made a good impression. A tall and well-built young man with rare natural grace. He made even a simple gesture like straightening his cuffs or crossing the room look emphatically elegant. Oliver had inherited an impressive fortune from his father, a well-known businessman, and a fine sense of style from his mother.

His dark thick hair was neatly trimmed, emphasizing his even features and expressive eyes. No matter which suit he wore, he looked like he had stepped off the pages of a fashion magazine. He had a calm but confident smile that captivated you from the very first meeting.

Many believed that Oliver led a social life with no problems or worries. He could afford to stay in the best hotels, buy expensive toys like a speedboat or a new car, as well as decadent gifts that won over the girls. However, behind the outward serenity hid an incredibly vulnerable man. Oliver was not shy about showing his feelings, sincerely rejoicing or being sad if something did not go according to plan. Perhaps it was this sincerity and depth of character that drew others to him. He combined the elegant appearance of a handsome and well-to-do man with a touching vulnerability that he tended to hide.

Before meeting Tara, he preferred short-term flings and noisy parties, but in her, he saw the woman he would do anything for.

Tara had always drawn the eye of not only men, but also women. She had an amazing combination of natural beauty and confidence, gained through years of hard work. Oliver noticed her graceful figure, good posture and toned waist at once. It was obvious that she kept herself in shape. Oliver loved everything about her: the lovely, curly, honey or walnut blonde hair, gently falling past her shoulders; the hazel eyes with a slight golden sheen, which reflected her mischievous nature; and the sophisticated and elegant style, which emphasized her high professional status. His future wife was a self-made woman. Tara told him that she grew up without a father and knew from early childhood that she had only herself to rely on. This was why she pursued her goal no matter what and fought hard to build a career. Oliver respected her for that. Moreover, he was proud of her. He enjoyed going everywhere with her and showing that she was his.

When the wedding day came, Tara was visibly nervous, even though there was no reason for it. Oliver had organised everything. All she had to do was show up. After taking one last look in the mirror, she took a deep breath, winked at her reflection and left the room.

She was stunned when she arrived at the wedding venue. Everything was so magical as to be almost unreal. Tara had not even dreamed of this. The banquet hall sparkled with crystal chandeliers, the fresh flowers created stunning decorations and there were candles burning everywhere, their light reflected in the lacquered dance floor. The orchestra was playing romantic music that took everyone's breath away, and tears glistened in their eyes.

Tara could see the others staring at her and felt like a queen. She was a queen that day. She felt happier than she had ever been. It was with him, with Oliver, that she had begun to feel like that. Tara did not regret for a moment choosing him as her husband. She had never met a more gentle and caring man. He treated her like the most delicate creature. And the surprises he arranged for her! Boat trips in the moonlight, dates on a hot air balloon or dinner on an island with no one else there. Yes, he knew how to woo her. He pursued her wholeheartedly, even though she had not been thinking about marriage at all, because she was focused on her career and other achievements. But here she was, Mrs. Ford, giving up her job and other nonsense for him, for her family. Of course, she missed her old life a little, but this was a new stage, which she had previously been familiar with only through her friends' stories.

They spent the honeymoon in the Maldives. The intensely bright sun was reflected in the clear water, and the snow-white sand seemed to embrace the island like a silk ribbon.

For the first few days, Tara delighted in the blue lagoon and the light sea breeze, which brought the smell of salt and algae. But after several evenings, she realized that lazy beach holidays were really not for her. There was absolutely nothing to do here and she was already tired of looking at the marine life, eating, sleeping and drinking in the restaurant in the evenings. Tara preferred long walks through the medieval streets of European cities, but Oliver was responsible for planning their holidays. Tara did not want to upset him and pretended that she was enjoying it all.

When the honeymoon was coming to an end, Oliver arranged a romantic dinner by the ocean. The red sunset was reflected in the waves, and stars were beginning to twinkle in the darkening sky. Candles laid out in the shape of a heart burned on the sand, and the aroma of exotic dishes wafted from the table.

"To us," Oliver said, raising his champagne flute.

"To us," Tara replied, feeling the pleasant coolness of the drink refresh her throat.

Things proceeded the same as usual, that is, delightfully well. Oliver did not want to return to the bungalow after dinner and suggested to his wife that they continue the evening in the restaurant. Tara was already tired and wanted to get some sleep before the difficult journey back but decided to give in to her husband. After all, when would they be here again?

There was some kind of entertainment program on at the restaurant. Women in fancy headdresses were dancing around. There were magicians, people with guitars, and a lot of noise in general. After the entertainment was over, the MC invited people to the dance floor. Oliver was already pretty drunk by this time.

"Should I order you some food?" Tara offered.

"I'm fine," Oliver replied, slurring his words.

Tara did not insist. She was already stretching her arm out and motioning to the waiter to bring the bill, when an older man, old enough to be Tara's father, approached their table.

"I can see that you're holidaying here," he began amiably. "and I'm guessing that this is your beautiful wife. Would you mind if I asked her to dance?" The man asked.

"Why not?" Oliver smiled. "Invite her!"

"I'm sorry, but we're already leaving. I'm not in the mood to dance at all. We have a plane to catch tomorrow so we need to get some rest."

"Tara, go and dance, and we'll leave straight after."

"Please," the man begged.

"All right, Tara agreed reluctantly and followed him to the dance floor. She had been dancing with the stranger for only a couple of minutes when she felt someone yank sharply on her hair.

"Hey," Tara shouted, turning around. Oliver stood behind her, staring at her with glassy eyes.

"Go home!" he ordered.

Tara did not understand where this tone had come from, so she stood rooted to the spot.

"I said," he ground out. "Go home!"

"Excuse me," Tara turned to the other man. "My husband seems to have drunk a little too much and is expressing his desire to go to bed in such an unusual way."

Smiling to the man in goodbye, she took her husband's arm and headed for the exit. On the way home, she berated Oliver for his disrespectful tone and loss of self-control, while he kept muttering to himself.

Once inside the bungalow, Oliver tossed his shoes in a corner and tried to undo the buttons on his shirt. He was not having much luck and pulled hard on the shirt, making the poor buttons ricochet all over the bungalow.

"What's wrong with you?" Tara burst out. "Oliver! I'll order you some food."

Oliver did not answer and kept mumbling incoherently.

Tara poured some water from a carafe and went to the balcony door where her husband was standing.

"Here, have some water," she suggested and brought the glass to her husband's lips. He turned away. "You need to drink," she insisted. "What are you muttering about?"

"Whore!"

"What... did you say?" Tara asked.

"I said what I said!" Oliver snapped.

Unable to stand such an insult, Tara flung the water in Oliver's face. In response, he slapped her across the face with his big, heavy hand.

She clutched her cheek, tears streaming from her eyes. "What's wrong with you?" she screamed.

"Whore," he repeated. "Wiggled your arse enough?"

"I won't stay with you for another second!" Tara said and started to pack her things.

Oliver rushed up to her and said through gritted teeth, "Just try to leave and see what happens!"

Tara was frightened but broke out of his grip anyway. Slamming the door as hard as she could, she dashed towards the ocean. She kept looking behind her, afraid that her husband would follow her, but this did not happen. Tara was scared by these events. Her cheek felt like it was on fire. Sitting down on the shore, she finally gave in to her emotions and burst into tears.

"What was that?" she thought as she sobbed. "How did my happiness collapse in an instant?"

A jumble of images flashed through her mind: the restaurant, the older man, dancing to music and Oliver's sudden rage. She wondered what she had done wrong and searched for an excuse for her husband. "Maybe he's just drunk? Maybe I really did hurt him somehow?" Tara herself could not understand why she was trying to defend him in her thoughts.

"How can I forgive this?" she asked herself. "I can't. What about the wedding? What will everyone else think? How? How did this happen? Things were going so well!"

She had no answers. Just moonlight on the water and the night around her. Which had suddenly turned cold and merciless, here beside her on this deserted beach. This seemed to be the end of her perfect union. At least, that was what she thought in that moment.

Having decided that she would not remain with Oliver, she got up from the cold sand. On the way to the bungalow, Tara suddenly remembered her mother telling her once, "You have to leave right away. If he hits you once, he'll hit you twice. Don't forgive him."

"Who had she been talking about?" Tara muttered, trying to remember the context.

The reek of alcohol hit her nose when she entered the bungalow. Oliver was passed out on the bed in his trousers and torn shirt. Tara thought that she would solve this problem tomorrow and lay down on the sofa by the balcony. She fell asleep immediately, although the flurry of thoughts continued to disturb her sleep.

When Tara awoke in the morning, Oliver was nowhere to be seen. The room was tidy and looked as if nothing had happened last night. Unfortunately, it had. Tara felt sick to her stomach. She imagined a heavy stone placed on her chest, which made her feel a little queasy. She felt even worse when she glanced at the open suitcase with their things all neatly packed.

There were 4 hours before they had to catch the plane. Tara pulled herself together and went to freshen up. She could hear a commotion in the bungalow from the shower. She knew that Oliver had returned, but she had no desire to face him.

After drying her hair, she opened the bathroom door and saw her husband. He was kneeling in the middle of the living room with a giant basket of roses.

"Tara," he said apologetically. "I'm sorry. I beg you to forgive me. I don't remember last night very well. I obviously drank too much. I just remember staggering home, and I have a feeling that I hurt you."

Tara was silent. Oliver, seeing that his wife was not reacting in any way, crawled up to her on his knees and clutched at her legs, begging for forgiveness. He said that he was sorry, that it would never happen again, that he did not remember anything. Tara pulled away from him and finally spoke. "You hit me."

"No," Oliver said, refusing to believe it.

"Yes. And you yanked me by the hair in front of everyone."

"Tara, my darling, please forgive me. I know this is unforgivable, but please try to forgive me somehow. I don't know how I can keep on living if you don't forgive me. I can't do this without you. Please, let's make up and forget all about it. Please."

He looked so pathetic that Tara took pity on him.

"I brought you breakfast, my love. Sit down, I'll pack the rest myself. Relax."

He was so caring and courteous. Tara thought that this, here, was her Oliver, the man who had stolen her heart. Yesterday's Oliver would not reappear, she would not let him drink anymore so it would never happen again. Oh, Tara.

She was still heartsore on her return home, but as the days passed and Oliver continued to fawn over her, what had occurred felt more and more like a "misunderstanding". She did not tell her family, much less her friends.

Life went on as usual. Tara and Oliver enjoyed their new status, went on dates, caught up with friends and visited museums and the movies. Tara gradually arranged their new house, buying furniture and choosing interior designs. Oliver spared no expense for this, and Tara really enjoyed these tasks.

As soon as she and Oliver moved into a spacious country house with green lawns and a cozy terrace, her husband began to constantly talk of children. Oliver grew more persistent by the day. He kept saying that the house was too quiet and that he wanted to hear children's laughter.

Tara, on the other hand, knew that she was not ready to be a mother yet. The very thought of it scared her. Oliver knew about her doubts but seemed to ignore them. He pressured her day after day, forcing his dreams of a large and close-knit family on her.

"It's our priority, Tara!" he insisted. "That's why I asked you to quit your job!"

Tara felt a protest growing inside her with every sentence he uttered, but she loved Oliver too much to openly argue with him. She was also afraid of hurting his feelings, because he seemed genuinely inspired by the idea of becoming a father.

Tara's mother, when she learned that Oliver was insisting on children, could not restrain herself from a truthful tirade, which upset her daughter.

"Tara," her mother said back then. "don't be in such a hurry to have kids. You have plenty of time. Do you really need all these sleepless nights, snot and teething problems right now? Children are a serious trial, including for the marriage. I'd like to remind you that you haven't known each other for very long and haven't had time to test each other. Who knows what might come up next?"

"Mum," Tara grew irritated, "why must you always be so negative? What might come up? You know that he's a good guy and he loves me! I'm lucky to have him and he's always fussing over me!"

"That's all very well, darling, but I've lived long enough to have seen all sorts of things!"

Tara hated it when her mother started these conversations and saw a trap everywhere. Yes, of course, she understood and even saw that most of her mother's predictions came true, but still, the very mention that life or a person could turn nasty really dampened her spirits.

A year of married life passed. Tara was still in love with her husband, just as he was in love with her. Everyone noticed the chemistry between them and envied them.

"That's only for now." her friends said. "Live together for another year, then have children, and you'll see! The romance will disappear without a trace."

"It'll be different for us," Tara insisted.

When she told Oliver about this "generous" advice later, they both laughed, once again convinced of the nastiness of human nature.

"To think, I've been friends with them since school," Tara concluded with disappointment.

"Ah, forget about them. They can go to hell! You have me, your true friend! We don't need anyone else. It's just you and me. All I can say about your friends is that they didn’t pass the happiness test. Don't tell them anything from now on. They're jealous of you."

"I guess so," Tara agreed.

Gradually, she began to talk to her friends less and less often. Tara disliked sharing all the things Oliver did for her with them. Indeed, he became the person she would tell everything, even things she should not have shared with her husband.

After a year of married life, Oliver knew his wife inside and out. He knew about her fears, her worries and her childhood traumas. Tara forgot about her mother's advice that under no circumstances should she completely hand herself over to her husband. She bared her soul to him without a second thought. She did not notice when she began to lose herself and her own opinions. Now she only said things that Oliver liked.

"I don't recognise you," her mother scolded her. "Is this how I raised you? You've completely fallen under his influence!"

"If you keep saying that, then I'll just stop calling you!"

"Tara," her mother continued, "you can't continue in this way! You should have your own opinion."

"Well, I do. Is it my fault that we look at the world the same way?"

"I have a feeling that he's manipulating you. Why did you stop talking to Sarah?"

"How do you know about that?"

"Her mum called me and that's how I found out."

"I see. So, you're gossiping behind my back?"

"No one is gossiping. I just learned that you stopped talking to the person you've known for most of your life, and I want to know why. Did something happen?"

"Nothing happened. But ever since I got married, I noticed how much she dislikes my stories about my family life. All these jibes and hints that the fairy tale will end soon. I got sick of it."

"I see. Are you sure that's what it was? It's just, knowing Sarah, it's hard to believe that she would do such a thing."

"I'm sure. There's nothing more to discuss."

"What do you do all day? Aren't you bored at home?"

Tara rolled her eyes. Luckily, her mother was a thousand miles away and could not see it. "You'll say I'm doing nothing, of course."

"Tara, am I not being nice to you? Have you reverted to your prickly teenage phase?"

"I know what you're getting at, Mum! I'll say that I'm taking care of the house and garden, and you'll say, "Maybe you should do something useful instead? Take a course, for example." And so on."

"Yes, I will, because I'm your mother. I don't want you to be left with nothing, no money and no long-term work experience at the age of 40."

"Great. Goodbye, Mum. I bet you'll be pleased if all your nasty imaginings come true!"

Tara hung up without waiting for an answer. She did not respond to subsequent calls from her mother.

The more time passed, the more confident Tara became in Oliver's decision to have children. She could now see a happy future with a child. She imagined them walking in the park with a stroller, bathing the baby and decorating their first Christmas tree.

The anniversary of their first date was approaching when Tara discovered that she was pregnant.

"You didn't even want to go on a date with me!" Oliver joked. "And now look, you're expecting a baby with me."

"It was impossible to say 'no' to you! You were very persistent."

"That's true. Are you unhappy about it?"

"I'm happy now."

They went shopping together, picking out a pram, baby clothes and the wallpaper for the nursery. Everything was so rosy and wonderful. Tara was happy right up until their baby was born.

There was a sudden change in Oliver, which horrified Tara. He became rude to her, even going so far as to insult her. Tara could not figure out the reason and tried to find one. She felt betrayed and deceived during this period. She could not understand why a man who had wanted a child so desperately had suddenly become cold and withdrawn.

"Honey," she began, "have I offended you in some way?"

"No," he replied calmly.

"Did something happen at work?"

"No, everything's fine."

"But I can see that it's not fine. Please tell me what's wrong. Maybe you feel depressed after the baby's birth? I've read that it's a lot of stress for both men and women. You realise that your life now revolves around..."

"Stop this nonsense," he cut her off. "You should focus on your actual duties! How can you look after a child if you have time to read such rubbish?"

Tara fell silent and continued to be tormented by these thoughts. There was not a trace left of the previous fairy tale. Oliver was just as cold towards the child, perhaps even hostile.

"Oliver," Tara begged. "can you please take the baby, I haven't even showered today."

"He's your job! I've done mine for today," he replied, staring at his phone.

"I can't keep an eye on him 24/7, I need my own time!" Tara tried to explain.

"I'm paying for this house, I'm paying for food, I'm paying for you and your needs. What more do you want? Should I start watching the baby too? What will you do then?"

"I just want to take a shower and eat in peace."

"You should have done that while he was asleep."

"But I was sleeping too!"

"You shouldn't have slept, what else can I say? And don't bother me, I'm busy!"

Tara's life turned into endless Groundhog Day. Every day was the same. Sometimes, she could not even remember which day of the week it was. One day, Tara rang her mother and could not resist telling her about what was happening at home.

"Could you take some time off work and come help me? I'm not coping."

"Of course, darling. I'll call you tomorrow."

Tara's mother showed up at her door three days later. Although Oliver was surprised by his mother-in-law's arrival, he greeted her with a charming smile and big hugs. It was only after Tara's mother went to her room to settle in that he grabbed Tara's arm and revealed his true reaction to the unexpected arrival.

"Why the hell did you invite your mother here? And without even telling me!"

"First of all, let go, you're hurting me. And second, I knew you'd be against it."

"This is my house, and I get to decide whom I want to see here and whom I don't! Get it?"

"It's my house too," Tara protested weakly. Oliver only laughed sarcastically in reply.

During the two weeks that her mother stayed with them, Tara felt like a human being again. She finally got enough sleep, cleaned herself up, and felt important and needed. Her eyes were sparkling again. Oliver also changed while her mum was around. He became as attentive as before, bringing Tara flowers, kissing her and giving her compliments. Tara thought that her life had taken a turn for the better.

"I'm sorry you're leaving," Tara said sadly during her last evening with her mum.

"Me too, darling, but what can we do? I have to get back to work, you know that my patients need me."

"I know. I just don't want to say goodbye."

"You can come and visit me anytime you want."

"Yeah."

"Is everything okay with Oliver?" Her mother switched to a whisper.

"Yes, I think so. I don't know what it was before. Something must have gone wrong at work."

"Maybe and maybe not. Well, I want you to remember that you always have a place to return to."

"I know, Mum," Tara sighed.

"I'm not harping on again," her mother warned her. "I'm just saying that you have a home."

"Thank you."

As soon as the door behind her mother closed, Tara's life returned to its previous state. She was alone with the baby again, while Oliver disappeared at work. There were days when he did not come home at all.

Tara could finally breathe when the baby was three months old and his colic began to resolve. One day, she put their son to bed early, put on a dress, ordered dinner and waited for her husband. She hoped to spend the evening together and try to restore what had been lost. Once again, Oliver came home in a bad mood.

"Why are you so dressed up?" he was surprised, examining his wife from head to toe.

"I decided that we should have a romantic dinner."

"I see. Can we just have dinner, without the romance?"

"No," Tara was hurt and went back into the kitchen.

When Oliver sat down at the dinner table, she brought out a fragrant baked duck. Glancing at the beautifully decorated dish, he nodded in satisfaction.

"Well done, you tried hard today."

"Actually, I ordered it," Tara smiled.

"You should make it yourself next time," he replied, going to the bar. "I think we can have some wine today."

"Pour me some too." Tara asked.

"Aren't you breast feeding?"

"No, we switched to formula a week ago. I told you."

"No, it's the first time I'm hearing about it."

"I definitely remember that you were sitting on the couch, and I was rocking Stevie."

"No way. I would've remembered if you told me. It doesn't matter, let's just sit and eat."

The dinner passed pleasantly. It was their time, just like before. Oliver even shared news from work. Tara did not notice when they finished the second bottle and then the third. She felt dizzy after not drinking alcohol for so long and went to collect the plates.

"We're still sitting!" Oliver protested.

"I've had a little too much, I need to get some sleep before Stevie wakes up."

"Well, I was thinking of fulfilling my marital duty," Oliver replied as he came up to her.

"At least let me put the plates away." Tara smiled.

"Leave them!" he ordered, snatching the dirty dishes from her hands.

He performed his marital duty in a rude and humiliating manner —right there on the table. It did not last long, but Tara felt awful and, even worse, dirty afterwards. It was the first time such a thing had happened to her, and she had never expected this from her husband. As she cleared the table, stone-cold sober already, a nasty chill swept over her from the memory of her husband.

The next morning, she resumed her chores and tried not to remember what had happened the previous night. She convinced herself again that it had only happened because Oliver had drunk too much. After all, no normal person, and Oliver was a normal person, would do such a thing to his wife, especially without her consent.

Oliver came home earlier than usual. Tara did not come out to meet him, remaining in the nursery with her son. Suddenly, there was a knock on the door and a huge teddy bear appeared in the doorway as soon as she said, "Come in". Tara did not even smile.

"Who lives in this kingdom?" Oliver thundered in a voice not his own. "Do the princess and the little prince live here?"

"Not here," Tara tried to mimic his voice.

"I know they do," Oliver said gently, peering out from behind the bear. "Tara," he said, sitting down next to his wife, "I went too far yesterday. I'm sorry. I used too much force. Are there any bruises?"

"I don't even know what to say," Tara replied, looking away. "I have marks on my neck."

"I'm sorry. Truly. I don't know what came over me. You know I'm not like that, right?"

"I know."

"I brought you something," he said mysteriously, taking an object out of his pocket.

Tara knew where this maroon box had come from and had some inkling that it was not just expensive, but very expensive. Inside the box lay a pendant studded with sparkling diamonds.

"You shine the same way to me," Oliver said, kissing his wife on the neck.

After this unpleasant incident, everything was fine again. It was like a second honeymoon, except that it ended as quickly as it had begun. Oliver became angry and irritable again and made awful comments about Tara's appearance.

"You need to lose weight ASAP," he said, showing her his phone. "See what Alice looks like? And she has two children. What do you do all day? Don't you have at least 5 minutes to do some sit-ups?"

Tara found such statements incredibly hurtful. She felt more and more insecure after every such insult. It now seemed to her that she did not deserve her husband. This had never happened to her before.

Oliver's constant mood swings were affecting Tara's mental health. The alternating hot and cold were slowly but surely turning her into a downtrodden animal. Every time she saw Oliver's car in the driveway, she peered nervously through the windshield, trying to make out his face and guess his mood.

In fact, Tara noticed that her husband had a strange habit. When he was in a bad mood, he deliberately hurt her and brought her to tears. As soon as Tara started crying, Oliver felt strangely happy and became the same as when she had first met him.

The longer they were together, the more often Oliver's aggressive outbursts occurred. They happened for all kinds of reasons: the soup was not salty enough, the baby was screaming too loudly, the house was dirty, and so on. There was nothing to find fault with, yet Oliver always found a reason. Tara still tried to stand up to him and prove the opposite, but things only got worse whenever she said anything.

One day, Oliver rang her unexpectedly and announced that he was coming home with an old friend.

"Make something quick," he said, as if it was no trouble at all for Tara.

She had no choice but to follow her husband's order. Tara put the baby in a highchair and started cooking. She decided not to make anything fancy, just bake chicken with potatoes in the oven and prepare a green salad. By the time Oliver arrived, the table was set and a steaming dish stood in the centre.

Oliver introduced his friend to Tara as soon as he set foot in the house. "Honey, this is my college friend, Bud."

"Nice to meet you," Tara smiled.

"And you. I've heard a lot about you." Bud smiled sweetly and shook Tara's hand.

Tara poured the men a drink but did not really join in the conversation. She was already tired and did not feel very well.

"Where are the appetisers?" Oliver asked.

"I didn't many any," Tara replied, serving the best pieces to their guest.

"I told you we were coming," Oliver said irritably.

"You know that I'm busy with the baby. Be grateful that he was quiet, and I could make this at least."

Oliver said nothing but gave her a baleful stare.

"Where did you work before, Tara?" Bud asked.

"At an advertising agency."

"Oh, how interesting. What position?"

"Marketing Director."

Bud pursed his lips. "A serious position for a woman. Is that where you met Oliver?"

"No, he saw me in a cafe I used to frequent. Then he found my profile and wrote me a message."

"Romantic, huh?"

"I suppose," Tara replied dryly. "Are you married, Bud?"

"Oh, no, no way! I'm never getting married again! I was once and that was quite enough. Women are nothing but gold diggers and more trouble than they're worth!"

"I'd be curious to hear the other side. It usually takes two to tango." Tara felt offended on the other women's behalf. "Perhaps you were simply unlucky."

"What other side?" Bud started to get worked up. "She'd tell you anything to get even more than she got."

"Tara, mind your own business!" Oliver said, frowning.

"I am. I only said that maybe his wife has a different view on the matter."

Tara did not like Bud. It was probably obvious, although she tried her best to hide her feelings. His talk reeked of obvious resentment and hatred of the opposite sex, and he kept mentioning that a woman's job was in the kitchen and raising children.

"You're lucky with your wife, Oliver. She doesn't open her mouth unless she has to but looks after her husband and family. She stays home. I'm sick of this newfangled, "I'm a person, I have a career and all this nonsense." It's ridiculous! How long have they been feminists? There was no such talk 100 years ago!"

"Don't you think that feminists didn't exist because women didn't have well-paid jobs and were completely dependent on their husbands? They were forced to stay silent and endure."

"Dependent like you are now, Tara?" Bud smiled maliciously.

"I wouldn't say that I'm dependent on my husband. I can always find a job and leave him if necessary."

Bud laughed, while Oliver stared at his wife.

"Okay, let's drop this topic. Tell me about your hunting trip in Africa!"

Bud began to describe how he and his friends had hunted a lion. These cruel people in large SUVs drove the poor animal back and forth until it was utterly exhausted.

Tara imagined it vividly, feeling like she was the lion who had been scared to death. She felt a pain in her chest and indescribable pity for the poor animal.

"I put the whole clip in him!" Bud laughed and Oliver laughed in reply.

All this made Tara felt sick and she left the table without saying goodbye.

"I see your wife isn't very friendly," Bud concluded.

"She's just tired," Oliver said defensively. "All day with the baby."

"Why don't you hire a nanny?" Bud suggested. "Although, you know what, don't. Otherwise, she'll get some free time and start going to places like my ex! Remember what that bitch did?"

"Don't think about it, buddy. Forget her like a bad dream."

Leaving the men, Tara went upstairs, took a shower and, after checking the child's breathing, went to bed. She woke up because something heavy was restricting her breathing. In the darkness, she saw a dark figure bending over her. The figure was growling.

"How dare you open your mouth in front of my friend? Bitch!"

"Oliver," Tara tried to pull away, "let me go. Oliver, please."

He let go of her neck but grabbed her by the hair and struck her across the face with all his might. Tara thought that her brain shook from the impact. Her husband did not stop there but continued to beat her. Tara could not even scream, for their son slept next to her. She was crying quietly and trying to calm her husband down. When she managed to escape his grip, she got out of the room and ran down the stairs. Oliver ran after her. Tara hid in the library and froze. She could hear Oliver running around the house and shouting her name. Her heart was pounding, and it seemed to her that this pounding would betray her position.

The house soon fell silent. Tara slid down to the floor and, hiding her face in her knees, wept bitterly. Her body ached and her head was buzzing. Touching it, she discovered that there were large patches of hair missing. She began to cry even harder.

"I can't forgive this," she whispered. "I can't!"

After making sure that there was no danger, Tara quietly left her hiding place and crept upstairs. As she passed the dining room, she saw Oliver asleep at the table with an unfinished bottle of whiskey.

Morning was not far off, and Tara needed more time to pack her things. Locking herself in the bedroom, she began to gather only what was necessary. She decided to leave the jewellery, shoes, handbags and everything else that Oliver had given her. Her whole life fit into two suitcases. It could have been more, but Tara decided that this would be enough for the next little while.

Their son woke up at 7 am. He began to cry pitifully, which brought tears to Tara's eyes too for some reason. This was how her marriage was ending and her dreams of a happy family life. Just like her mother, she would no longer have a husband, and her child would no longer have a father.

After feeding and washing her son, Tara began to dress him. It was a long way to her mother's house and there was so much more to do: tickets, taxis, bottles for the road.

"Tara," came a voice from behind the door, "why did you lock the door?"

She did not answer. There was more pressure on the door. Her heart sank.

"Tara!" Oliver shouted, pulling sharply on the door handle.

"Get lost!" she replied.

"Tara, open the door! Please."

"I said, get lost. Get away from the door! You're scaring the baby!"

"Tara, what are you doing?" he asked gently.

Anger churned inside her. She put her son in the crib and flung open the door. It made Oliver stagger.

"What am I doing?" she shouted in a broken voice. "Me? Look at what you've done!" She pushed her hair away from the top of her head and showed her shiny, bruised skull to Oliver.

"Tara," was all he could say.

"I'm not Tara, I'm nobody to you. Just like you are to me. I'm going to stay with my mum and file for divorce."

He threw himself at her feet again and began to kiss them. Tara felt sick.

"Don't come near me," she pleaded, beginning to cry again. "Don't touch me."

"Tara, forgive me. I shouldn't have done that. Forgive me. I won't do it again, I swear."

"Let me go."

"Forgive me, baby. I know that I'm a complete jerk. What I've done is terrible, but try to see it from my point of view. Bud and I were supposed to strike a deal, but because of the way you talked to him, he decided to terminate the contract. We lost a lot of money. Why did you speak to him like that? Couldn't you see that he's not good with women? You should have just kept quiet."

"So, it's my fault that you almost killed me yesterday? Look at my arms," she said, holding out her hands, "they're blue!"

He took her hands and began to kiss them.

"Forgive me, please. I don't know how to beg your forgiveness. Please don't leave me. I'll die without you. I'll shoot myself. I must have been overwhelmed by my past again, when my dad did the same thing to my mum. I'm sorry. I just can't control myself."

"I have to leave. No ifs and buts. Let me go, please."

Oliver crawled away from her but remained on his knees and with his head bowed. Tara would have felt sorry for him if she did not remember what he had done to her a few hours earlier. Turning away from him, she continued to pack her bags.

"Okay," he agreed, "go visit your mum. But please come back."

"I can't promise you that."

"Please, Tara! Tell me that you'll come back! I'll make an appointment with a therapist. I'll do anything to make sure this doesn't happen again. Please, please."

Tara was silent. She sat down on the bed and stared out the window. "I want to go home," she said wearily.

"I'll take you to the airport. Take only the one suitcase. If you need anything, you can just buy it. Here, take my credit card."

"I have my own."

"Please take mine. You know it has a bigger limit."

She held out her hand without looking at him.

On the way to the airport, he apologised again but Tara did not really listen. She was still in shock, and something had broken inside her. She snapped out of her stupor when he kissed her goodbye at the check-in desk. "Gosh," she thought, "anyone looking at us probably thinks that we're the perfect couple and he's the perfect husband."

The flight home was easy. The baby slept the whole way, waking up only to feed. Her mother met them on arrival.

"Tara," she called out as soon as she spotted her daughter, "is everything okay?"

Tara could tell from her mother's expression that she was alarmed by Tara's unexpected arrival and rushed to reassure her.

"Yes, we just decided to surprise you." Tara lied, deciding to tell her mother everything later, in a more comfortable environment.

On the way home, her mum kept asking leading questions to find out the real reason for her daughter's visit. Besides, she could see that something was obviously wrong.

"Why is your face so puffy?" she asked. "Were you crying?"

"No, Mum. I ate pickles yesterday, plus the flight, so I'm all puffy."

"Aren't you hot in the turtleneck?"

"No, actually, I feel a bit cold."

"Tara, darling, please tell me the truth. Has something happened?"

Tara turned to her mother and said, staring into her eyes, "Everything's fine, Mum. Really. I just wanted to be home, that's all. Things are fine."

"Well, okay. Oliver's not hurting you?"

"No."

That was the end of their conversation.

Once home, Mum took the baby so her daughter could rest after the journey. When Tara entered her bedroom, she was struck by a wave of pain. She remembered spending the night before her wedding in this room. Everything seemed perfect back then, and what did she have now? Is this how it would be from now on? Would she have married Oliver if she had known about his "issues" at the time? Who would have thought that her impeccable husband would turn out to be an alcoholic and abuser?

Burying her face in the pillow, she began to cry. There was a gaping wound in her chest, it burned and would not let Tara breathe, let alone live. The young woman did not notice when she fell asleep. The incessant sound of her mobile woke her up. It was Oliver calling. She dropped his call, but a couple of minutes later, there was a knock on the door. It was Mum.

"Darling, are you asleep? Oliver's on the phone. He wants to talk to you."

Tara was forced to get up.

"Has your phone gone flat?" Mum whispered, covering the phone's receiver.

Tara nodded and took the phone from her mother's hand. "Hello," she said.

"Were you asleep, baby? How was the flight?" Oliver spoke as if nothing had happened. His voice was the same as usual: sweet, gentle and affectionate.

"It was fine."

"How's Stevie? He didn't bother your during the flight?"

"He was asleep."

"Are you tired? You sound so..."

"How am I supposed to sound?" Tara was surprised.

"Baby, I understand. I don't even know what to say. I've ruined everything. I promise you, I swear that I'll never stoop to something like this again. Please forgive me."

"You know, I want to be alone. Don't call me for now. I have a lot to think about."

Oliver promised that he would leave her alone for a while, and they said their goodbyes.

He did not keep his promise. He would call several times a day, forcing Tara to talk, and sent her endless messages, as well flowers, fruit baskets and other nonsense every day. Moreover, he showed up at his mother-in-law's house a week later.

Tara's mother cooked a quick dinner and they had a nice evening. As soon as Oliver went to put the baby to sleep, her mother came up to Tara and said, "I can see that something happened between you. Quick, spit it out!"

"I don't know how to tell you all this."

"Tell it like it is. Stop playing games with me!"

Tara was about to tell her mother the whole truth when her husband appeared in the kitchen.

"Do you girls need some help?" he asked cheerfully.

"Oliver, we're having a private conversation here," Tara's mother said rather sharply.

"Okay, I won't interrupt."

Tara was shaken by his arrival and could no longer speak, feeling as if her husband was still standing behind her. No matter how hard her mother tried to get a word out of her, Tara remained silent.

At night, Oliver entered Tara's room without knocking.

"Make some space for me, will you, baby?"

"There's not enough room for two here. Plus, we agreed that you'll sleep in the nursery!"

"I've missed you."

"Oliver," Tara began, sitting up in bed, "do you realize that you're not letting me breathe at all? I didn't get a moment to myself or with my mum!"

"Why's that?" he was surprised.

"Your endless calls and messages!"

"Tara, I'm miserable without you two, and without you in particular. Yes, maybe there was too much of me lately, but only because I was beside myself with worry. All my deals have fallen through, I can't do anything right because of the state I'm in. I can't sleep, I can't eat, I can't work. Let's go home?"

"No."

"Tara, baby, please, let's go. I promise, everything will be the same as before. You know that everything I do is for you and Stevie. I don't need any of it myself. My life is meaningless without you, my love."

Again, there were promises, vows, plays on her pity and empathy. Tara felt guilty by the end of the conversation. It sounded like the business and their family affairs were falling apart because of her. Because she had left, leaving Oliver in such a state. She felt sorry for him and flew home with him the very next day.

For a while—or rather, for the first two weeks after Tara's return—Oliver kept himself in check and behaved appropriately. Before long, however, he became irritable and rude again, although there was no physical abuse. Tara was certain that she would not let him do that again. There was still hurt in her heart. She had not forgiven him and did not let him near her until one day, when they were invited to a friend's wedding. Oliver was the best man as his university friend was getting married.

Oliver was all charm that day, and he looked incredible. Tara gazed at him and remembered their own wedding day. The feelings overwhelmed her. She looked stunning too. A new dress, new hair colour, and she had finally lost the extra weight. Oliver noticed it all and did not leave his wife's side all day. He was attracted to her.

When it was time for the best man to make a toast, he stood up and, tapping his glass, addressed the audience.

"In this tiny and yet enormous world, inhabited by billions of people, it's so hard to find the one and only person who will become not only your rock, but most importantly, your wife and best friend. I'm happy for you, buddy, for you were lucky enough to meet Laila. I was just as lucky once upon a time!" He glanced at Tara and winked at her. "The most important advice I'll give you is try to ignore each other's shortcomings and remember that you met for a reason. Therefore, do not destroy what was bestowed upon you by God. Let's raise our glasses!"

Tears welled up in Tara's eyes for some reason. "He's right," she thought, "billions of people... By God. Did God send me this man? A shortcoming? What am I supposed to do with this shortcoming? He can be rude, he must get tired, but he is doing all this for me, for us. He's battling this world so that we may have everything."

Once again, Tara did not notice herself getting hooked. She believed that the past "misunderstandings", as Oliver called them, would not happen again, and they would live a happy life. Perhaps, someday, if her husband changed careers, he would become calmer and stop taking out his fatigue on her.

They walked around the hotel after the event, holding hands. It was so romantic. Oliver was carrying Tara's shoes and looking at her with glowing eyes. They had an unforgettable night, after which they found out that they were going to have another child.

Oliver was over the moon with happiness, but Tara felt terrified. Memories of her previous pregnancy were still fresh in her mind, and she was afraid that Oliver would act horrible towards her again. She was also scared of the weight gain. She had such a hard time losing the weight after Stevie, starving herself and exhausting her body with workouts.

"Are you sure that this is what we need right now?" Tara asked her husband.

"What are you talking about?" he was indignant. "Of course we do! People struggle to have a baby for years, and we got lucky on the first go! Consider it a gift from heaven."

"I'm just worried that it might turn out like last time."

"I told you, nothing bad will happen again. I won't insult you anymore. Let's speak no more about it."

The pregnancy was surprisingly easy. Tara looked forward to meeting the new baby. She imagined them pushing the child on the swing, walking and enjoying life. Besides, she was glad that her son would have a brother or sister, just as she had dreamed of during her childhood.

They went to learn the sex of the baby together. Oliver was a little nervous. When the doctor said it was a girl, he even cried a little.

"Another princess in the house!" he said.

The same day, Tara ordered things for the baby and imagined dressing her up, braiding cute plaits and doing other girly things with her.

There was no hint of trouble until the phone rang one day.

"Mrs. Ford," said an unfamiliar voice on the phone.

"Yes," Tara replied.

"I'm sorry to tell you but your mother... your mother passed away this morning."

Tara could not believe it. "You must have the wrong number – my mum is fine. I spoke to her recently."

"Mrs. Tara Ford, I know this is hard to accept, but there was an accident. We couldn't save her. I'm very sorry. You need to come."

"No, I don't believe you," Tara said and hung up abruptly.

She then dialled her mother's number, but nobody picked up the phone. Tara paced the room like a wounded animal and kept trying to reach her mother.

"No, no, they're lying," she mumbled. "Come on, pick up the phone! My God, what if they're not lying? What if it's true?" The young woman stood still, her arms hanging limply by her side. When the phone rang again, she did not even check who was calling. She could not think straight.

"Tara, it's Alba," Tara's aunt was calling her. "You need to come here, darling. We've received terrible news."

Her aunt was telling her about the accident, at times interrupted by sobs, but Tara did not seem to hear her.

"Tara, can you hear me?"

"Yes," the young woman replied and, ending the call, collapsed on the bed.

Somehow, she flew to the funeral, attended it and spoke to other people. It felt like it was happening to someone else. Tara was too shell-shocked to even cry, as if she could not believe that her mother was really gone. Forever.

The pain hit her later, when she was alone in the house. Mum's scent still lingered and her things lay everywhere. A cup of unfinished coffee stood in the office. Tara howled like a she-wolf.

"No, no, no," she screamed. "Come back! Please, Mummy, please. Mummy."

She uttered the word over and over, as if her mother would hear her and open the door with her key, come in and say, "I'm not dead! It was another woman who looks like me and has the same name. How funny that you buried me." She would laugh merrily, and Tara would press her head to her mother's warm chest and smell her floral shampoo and vanilla perfume again.

Curled in a foetal position on the floor, clutching her mother's scarf to her face, she fell asleep. Tara dreamed of her mum, who stroked her head with a soft, warm hand. Waking up to a persistent ringing, it took Tara a moment to comprehend her new reality, and she burst into tears again. She dragged herself to the shower and tried to tidy herself up. It wasn't until she was dressed that she picked up the phone and saw that she had more than a hundred missed calls from Oliver. She called back and heard, "Why aren't you answering?" He sounded angry.

"I was asleep," she replied.

"What do you mean, asleep? Do you have any idea what you've put me through? I'm besides myself, wondering if something has happened to you or the baby! I had to call all your relatives!"

"I'm sorry. I just, I just couldn't. Don't you see? I thought I'd call you, but it was all such a blur and then I was left alone and..." she began to break down into sobs.

"Tara," his voice softened. "I can't understand your pain, but you've got to pull yourself together and come home. I can't look after Stevie, I must go to work. You've been gone for so many days already."

"Okay, honey."

"All right, come on. We'll see you tonight."

He hung up the phone. Tara started packing quickly. She thought that she would feel better back in her own house, next to her husband and son.

Oliver did not even meet her when she arrived. Exhausted, she set foot in the house, and he thrust the child into her arms and rushed off to work without kissing her goodbye. Tara spent the whole day with Stevie in her arms, holding him tightly, as if the warmth of his body could heal her grieving soul. It did not help. Nor did she get anything from Oliver. He returned as grumpy as always, and when he saw that she had not cooked anything for dinner, he flew into a rage.

"I know you're grieving and all that," he raised his voice. "But life goes on here! I run around all day at work, I'm tired. I haven't had anything to eat, and what do I see when I get home? This!" He was shouting as he pointed at the empty table.

"Sorry, I'll order something," Tara began to apologise.

"You know that takeaway food gives me heartburn!"

"I'll make you some sandwiches."

Tara woke up that night from a growing pain in her lower abdomen. It worried her. She considered the sensations, then picked up her phone and went to read the forums. Some wrote that this was normal, others that it was a cause for alarm. Reassured by the positive comments, she calmed down and, turning on her side, tried to fall asleep. The pain was still throbbing inside her, but she managed to fall into a doze.

Tara woke up exhausted in the morning and found that the pain was still there, which frightened her. When she reached the toilet, she saw that she was bleeding, just a bit.

"Oliver," she called out to her sleeping husband.

"What?" He sounded annoyed.

"Oliver, I'm bleeding. I think we should go to the hospital."

They dressed quickly and had to take Stevie with them. On the way, Tara kept calling her treating physician, but as bad luck would have it, she did not answer. Tara was examined as soon as they reached Accident and Emergency. The ultrasound showed that their baby's heart was not beating. Tara could not believe that this was happening to her. She was taken from the emergency room to the operating theatre. She learned after the operation that their daughter was gone.

"It must be God's will," an old nurse reassured Tara. "Be strong, my dear."

"Mum," Tara whispered and, turning her head to the side, began to cry.

Oliver was allowed to visit her the next day. He was displeased and showed no sympathy.

"Well, how are you?" he asked. "I've brought your things, a charger and a comb."

"Thanks, honey. How's Stevie?"

"He's fine. Same as always. When are you getting discharged?"

"I don't know. Maybe in five days."

"I see. So, I'm supposed to babysit Stevie instead of working?"

"You're making it sound like it's my fault that this happened!"

"Isn't it?" He looked her dead in the face.

"Are you serious right now?" She could not believe it.

"I am. You knew that all these hysterics over your mother could affect the child. Didn't you?"

"My mum died! Your mum is alive, and I don't wish her any ill, but can you imagine how you'd react if you found out that your mum was gone?!"

"People die every day. Who knows how many people have died while we've been talking."

"I can't believe you're saying this! When did you become so callous? You used to be completely different."

"Not this again," he sighed. "Okay, I'm going."

He left without saying goodbye, leaving Tara in an even worse state than before. Now she wondered if it was her fault that their daughter had died. The emotional pain grew exponentially. She staggered up from the hospital bed, went to the window and, leaning her head against the cold glass, stared at the street. Tara looked at the road and the people but did not see them. Before she knew it, she began banging her head against the glass and calling for her mother. A nurse found her in this state. Tara was clearly out of her mind, and the nurse had to call for help to return the thrashing girl back to bed. The patient calmed down only when she was given a sedative. In fact, the doctors had to use it several more times to keep Tara calm. She spent the following days after the breakdown in a stupor. She could still feel the emotional pain, but it was dulled.

A doctor came to see Tara on the day of discharge.

"Good afternoon, Mrs. Ford. How are you feeling?"

"Neither good nor bad." Tara replied.

"I know that you have been through a lot lately, and a miscarriage is a huge loss for a woman. Everyone processes it differently. What I'm trying to say is that I think you should see a psychologist. It will be difficult for you to cope with this on your own. I've already spoken to your husband, and he agrees with my opinion. You will also have to take some medications to maintain your strength and energy as you go about your day."

Tara did not reply, staring blankly out the window.

"Tara, can you hear me?"

"Yes," she replied. "Medications."

"I'll give you something for the first week, and then I want you to come back and see me, okay?"

"Yes."

Oliver led Tara out of the hospital, holding her by the hand like a little girl. He sat his wife in the car and drove her home.

Entering the house, Tara smelled the delicious scent of food. It turned out that Oliver had called his mum, and she had taken care of both the house and the boys in Tara's absence.

"Are you back at last?" she asked without saying hello. "Finally. Come on, wash your hands and sit down at the table. We'll have dinner."

Tara could hear the stupid conversation between her mother-in-law and her husband at dinner. As always, her mother-in-law gossiped and said nasty things about other people. Tara had not liked it when her life had been going well, nor did she like it now. "It's a good thing the drugs are still working," she thought and continued eating the soup her mother-in-law had made.

After dinner, Tara went to her room and got into bed without getting undressed. As the days passed, she continued her dull life, eating and sleeping. After a week, her mother-in-law came into her room.

"Tara," she began, sitting down on the bed. "I'm sorry, but it's time to pull yourself together. You're not the first to lose a child and you won't be the last. I'm sorry about your mum too, of course, but it happens. You have a husband and a son, and you need to think about them. Besides, I can't move in with you so that you can continue your endless grieving."

If Tara had not been taking the sedatives, she would have jumped off the bed and given her mother-in-law a piece of her mind, but right now, she lacked the energy or the desire to do so.

"Do you know, Mrs. Ford, that your son is a rapist?" Tara said for some reason.

Her mother-in-law laughed.

"Yes, yes, I'm not kidding," Tara continued. "He beat me and then raped me. Sometimes he didn't beat me, just raped me. In the most disgusting way."

The laughter stopped immediately. Tara stared at her mother-in-law, trying to read the woman's mind.

"You know, my dear," her mother-in-law finally said. "I also suffered from Oliver's father, but as you can see, I'm sitting here alive and well. He didn't kill you, after all. What did you think would happen? That you would score such a handsome man—who gives you whatever you want: diamonds, houses, cars—and you would give him nothing but your beauty? Nothing in life is free, and such is your payment for this," she gestured to her surroundings.

To say that Tara was shocked would be an understatement. Her mother-in-law's words sounded like madness. A pity that she would start thinking the same way afterwards. The older woman's poisonous seed had been well and truly planted.

While her mother-in-law remained in their house, Tara went to therapy. It did not help because the psychologist was incompetent. Tara did not feel a sense of relief after seeing him. On the contrary, she felt sadder and sadder. It may also be that the medications prescribed by the doctor did not relieve the pain, but made Tara feel indifferent to life and death.

One day, waking up in the morning, as always, with a heavy head, Tara looked at the pills on the bedside table and, for the first time, did not take them. After that she began to come back to herself. For the first time since her discharge from hospital, she noticed that Oliver never came near her and spent most evenings with his mother. Stevie also felt like a stranger and even cried when Tara picked him up. He also preferred being with his mother-in-law than with her.

"When are you heading home?" Tara asked her once.

"As soon as you're healthy again," her mother-in-law said with a nasty smile. Why nasty? Tara knew that her mother-in-law did not like her. She thought, like all such mothers did, that Tara was no match for her son. Women like her usually did not raise sons but husbands for themselves. Ugh, how disgusting, Tara thought.

Oliver came up to her soon after this conversation.

"Why are you trying to kick my mother out?" he asked, grabbing Tara's arm painfully.

"Let go," Tara snapped. "I'm not kicking her out, I asked when she was planning to return home."

"This is her house!"

"Well, this is the first time I'm hearing about it. Fine, in that case, I asked her when she was going back to her first house."

"You ungrateful pig. My mum took care of all of us, performed your duties, and you're sending her away?"

"I'm not sending her away, I just asked her. Stevie only wants to be with her, but I'm his actual mother."

"Well then, consider what kind of mother you are if your child doesn't want to be with you."

"Maybe you should just live with her then?"

"Maybe we will."

He slammed the door, leaving Tara feeling bewildered. Her mother-in-law's presence was clearly having a negative effect on her husband. Tara suspected that her mother-in-law was turning Oliver against her. She had to get rid of the older woman.

Fortunately, this happened without Tara's involvement. Oliver's mother left of her own accord when she started missing the news and gossip of her neighbourhood. Tara breathed a sigh of relief when the door slammed shut after her. Oliver saw Tara's joy and was not happy about it.

Life went on as before once they were alone again. Oliver was always away, so it was just the two of them, but Tara preferred it this way. She wanted to catch up on the time she had lost with her son. They walked and played a lot, and Tara taught him how to pronounce words correctly. He sounded very cute and funny. Stevie could not obscure the pain from losing her mum and baby, but he made it a little easier, at least during the day. Tara allowed her feelings to bubble to the surface only at night.

Oliver's business continued to grow, and their family wealth increased. Tara was not particularly happy about this. She already owned so much jewellery that she had nowhere to wear it. Oliver began to drink more often due to stress. Tara grew afraid at such times, but her husband still held on, stooping only to insults so far. Then he remembered that she was the murderer of their baby, that she stayed at home and did nothing while he worked all day long, and that she did not love his mother. Tara was hurt by his words every time. The guilt over her daughter's death was already firmly ingrained in her head. Their young son already knew all the curse words that Oliver tossed left, right and centre.

By the time Stevie turned two, the atmosphere in their house had not changed. If Oliver had at least apologised after their fights previously, he stopped doing even that. Apparently, he believed that since he was the breadwinner, he could behave as he pleased. He often did not spend the night at home, and when he did, he smelled of women's perfume. Tara tried making a scene, but he would put an immediate stop to it.

"I told you, I was at a business meeting. The partner's wife was there and it's her perfume."

"Where did you sleep last night? And don't tell me it was at the office!"

"Yes, at the office. Look at the cameras!" he would shout. "Should I show you the video?"

He jabbed the phone in Tara's face so confidently that she never asked him to actually play the recordings from his office.

One night, while Oliver slept, his phone began to vibrate loudly. Tara had become a light sleeper since her mother died and woke up at the slightest noise. She slipped quietly out of bed, went to Oliver's phone and picked it up, deciding to find out who could be texting her husband in the middle of the night. The phone was locked. Tara gently pressed her husband's finger to the display and the phone unlocked so that Tara could see all the messages. Of course, there was nothing good inside. In addition to work-related texts, Oliver had numerous message threads with other women. Moreover, there was a permanent one among them, with a long history of communication. It turned out that her husband led a busy life outside his family. There were numerous intimate photos and dirty details of their sex life. Tara was infuriated, even enraged. She woke Oliver up and threw the phone at him. "Deborah, huh? She can't wait for you to touch her again!"

Oliver was half asleep and did not immediately realize what had happened.

"You won't come near me, but you're okay with Deborah? Flowers for her but insults for me and having to wash her lipstick off your shirts?"

"Have you been going through my phone?"

"How could you? How could you? I'm your wife!"

"Have you been going through my phone?" he asked, standing up and raising his voice.

"Yes, your phone wouldn't stop ringing!"

"If you touch my phone again, then I'll wring your neck, got it?"

"Don't worry, I won't touch it again. I can't live like this anymore. I don't love you, and I will no longer pay for this life like your mother had suggested."

Oliver rushed at her and punched her in the jaw without the slightest hesitation. Tara tasted blood.

"You're a monster and a rapist!" she uttered calmly, spitting blood in his face.

"Why, you bitch!"

Knocking his wife to the floor, Oliver kicked her as hard as he could all over her body. His strikes were so sharp and fast that Tara could not even stand up. She did not notice when she started screaming. Their little son came running. At first, he thought that mom and dad were playing, until he saw the blood spreading across the floor.

"Dad!" he screamed shrilly and rushed over to cover his mother. "Stop it, stop it!"

Perhaps it was the only thing that saved Tara. Oliver finally spat on Tara's hair and left the room after calling her "scum".

Stevie cried over his mother's almost lifeless body for a long time.

"Go to bed, please," she moaned. "Now!"

"But, Mum," he began.

"Please. Go on. I'm okay."

Tara lay on the floor for a long time after her son left. She was afraid to move, afraid that Oliver would come back and then nothing would save her. As soon as morning came and Tara heard the front door slam, she stood up, got dressed and, without washing off the blood, went to her son's room.

"Get up, honey. We have to go somewhere together."

"Mum, what's wrong with your face?"

"Just pretend that it's make-up."

"You're lying, it's blood," her son began to cry.

"Honey, if you start crying now, then we won't be able to go to the place I really need to go. And if we don't go there, then Mummy won't be well. Do you understand? I'm going to put on my sunglasses and tie a scarf around my face, and then I'll wash it all off, okay?"

"Okay."

Jumping into the car, Tara rushed to the nearest hospital and, after having the bruises recorded, went to the police station. No, she would not take this anymore. She had had enough.

Oliver quickly found out what was going on. His friends worked for the police, and their money was invested in his company. He calmly entered the house, calmly locked Stevie in his room and went to the master bedroom, the door of which was shut. Oliver was a big and strong man, so it was not difficult for him to break down the thin door. Meanwhile, Tara was packing her things. When Oliver started breaking down the door, she panicked and tried to calm him down, although he probably could not hear her very well. When the lock gave way and the door swung open, Tara saw her husband. His face was blank. The execution continued. He strangled her and beat her head against the floor. He didn't yell or make a sound, only leaning down from time to time to hiss in her ear, "Did you go to the police station to embarrass me? To ruin my reputation? My business?"

"I'm leaving you," Tara screamed with the last of her strength.

"The only way you're leaving me is feet first!"

After smacking her head on the floor one last time, he went to her handbag and dumped its contents on the floor. Having found what he needed, he went to the dressing table and took out a lighter, which they used to light candles during romantic evenings, and set it on fire. Tara was so battered that she could not even lift her head to see what Oliver was burning. A little later, Oliver threw it in Tara's face. Only then did she see her passport and identification card.

Tara wanted to fight him further and she certainly would have left him, if not for one thing.

"If you ever do something like this again—sully the honour of our family or stick your nose where it doesn't belong—I'll put you in a mental hospital. I'm not kidding. You'll never see Stevie again. Never. You know me, my dear, and if I set a goal, I'll achieve it no matter what. You'll rot in there. They'll pump you full of tranquilisers every day because I'll say that you were violent, and you'll live your life as a vegetable. And Stevie? He'll be raised by another woman, my new and normal wife. An obedient wife, unlike you."

After that, Tara stopped fighting. She tolerated everything, even things that any self-respecting woman would not tolerate. Oliver bullied her in every way he could. Tara's will had been broken. She endured everything just to stay with Stevie. The abuse lasted for years, until something happened in her life.

Oliver was invited to some bigwig's party. Tara was told to wear her best dress, but none of the dresses fit her. She had lost a lot of weight and was covered in bruises, so she could not show any skin. She drove to the mall to buy new clothes. She did not want to go shopping and went into the first one she saw.

"Can I help you?" A consultant hurried up to her at once.

"I need a black floor-length dress that covers my arms and preferably covers my neck as well. I don't know if you have something like that?"

They found such a dress, although it was green rather than black, but Tara did not care. While paying for the purchase, she suddenly felt someone's gaze on her. Looking up, she did not recognize her childhood friend straightaway.

"Excuse me, is your name Tara by any chance?" the woman asked as she stepped closer.

Tara burst into tears right at the checkout. Sarah ran up to her and hugged her. Yes, it was her.

"Honey, calm down. What's wrong?"

Both visitors and staff tried to calm the poor woman down. She had broken down from this one simple question. But who could have known what lay beneath this question? What lay beneath it was Tara's old life, where her mother was alive, where she had her friend Sarah, where she had a job and she was someone, not just an appendage to her husband, and where no one beat or humiliated her.

Taking her friend aside, Sarah sat Tara down on a stool and brought her some water. Calming down a little, Tara gazed at her dear friend. "Sorry, I don't know what's going on with me."

"Quite a lot, it seems. Come with me to our back room."

"Do you work here?"

"Yes, I'm the store manager."

They finally hugged once they were alone. Sarah forgot her resentment over Tara's betrayal of their strong friendship and asked tenderly, "Did something happen to you?"

"Yes."

"Do you need help?"

Tara burst into tears again. Bit by bit, she told Sarah the story of her life and her marriage. Sarah could not believe that her once successful, bright and cheerful friend had turned into this miserable and pitiful woman.

"He said that he'd take our child."

"He can't."

"He has connections."

"There are things we can do too, you know! Do you have any savings?"

"No, he doesn't give me any money. All I have is his card, which he keeps an eye on."

"I see. Did you get a new passport?"

"Yes, but he won't give it to me. He keeps it in a safe and I don't know the password."

"We'll help you. I've got to ask Elliot for advice. We'll figure something out. Do you have a phone?"

"Yes, but he checks it all the time. He won't like it if he finds out that I'm talking to you."

"All right, then come back here in two days and I'll decide what can be done in the meantime. Agreed?"

With that, they said goodbye. Anxiety bubbled inside Tara, mixed with joy and hope. No, no, she would not let herself hope. What if it all came to naught?

She returned to the store two days later. Sarah was nowhere to be found, and Tara began to think that her friend had tricked her. She even imagined that Sarah had betrayed her and brought Oliver here. Her anxiety spiked so much that she was about to run away when she heard Sarah's voice. "Tara, you've come! Come on."

"Where?" Tara tensed.

"To the same place again, our back room. What's wrong? You're shaking."

"I'm afraid."

"Don't be afraid, I'm on your side."

In the cramped room, Tara looked around, as if her husband could be hiding in there.

"Listen to me carefully," Sarah began, "this is all the money we were able to gather in two days. It's not much, but it'll be enough to start with. You can't go home, he'll look for you there first, so you'll go to the town of N to stay with Elliot's aunt. She's a lovely, kind woman. She's a lot older, but she'll be able to watch your son while you're looking for work. Next, this is the lawyer's number. He's a good divorce lawyer and he'll help you both with the divorce and getting sole custody. Remember what he told us: your husband must not learn your location under any circumstances. You must be very careful. Do you understand?"

"Not under any circumstances," Tara repeated.

"Good. Tomorrow, when Oliver leaves for work, get your son ready and go to the bus station. Don't bring a lot of things with you, just a bag for the first few days. Well, that's it. Oh, one more thing! Here's my phone number, call me when you get there. We'll come and visit you later."

"I don't know how to thank you," Tara wanted to cry again.

"There's no time to cry, so pull yourself together! You can do that later. Why didn't you find me sooner? Never mind, there's no time for that either. We'll talk about it later. Now go."

The next day, as soon as Oliver left for work, Tara packed a bag, made Stevie sandwiches for the road and called a taxi. She left her phone, jewellery and everything else at home. She also left her engagement ring on the table with a note that said only one thing: The End.

After going with Stevie to the cinema for extra cover, they took a bus and reached the bus station. It was a sunny day, and Tara gazed up at the blue sky. It was so beautiful, with the birds flying high overhead. Tara looked at them and wondered if she was as free now. She approached the ticket office, handed over the money and named her destination.

"Do you need a return ticket?" the cashier asked her.

"No, one way only."

As the bus left the city and Tara stared out the window, she suddenly heard her mother's voice. She said, "I don't want you to be left with nothing, no money and no long-term work experience at the age of 40." Tara smiled inexplicably.

"You were right about that too, Mummy," she whispered.

Years later, Tara remarried a good and kind man, not in words, but in deeds. He was a simple factory worker with no great ambitions, but he loved her to the moon and back. She never heard a bad word from him nor saw a bad deed. Yes, her life was ordinary now, without all that her first husband had given her, yet she was truly happy. She never thought about Oliver unless she had nightmares about him. She would wake up in tears and her husband would comfort her. Sitting in his arms at night, she fervently thanked God that it was just a dream. Just a dream.

***

Putting the folder aside, I think for a moment and sigh heavily. Every instance of violence against a person begins with this pattern. Emotional rollercoasters, gaslighting, total control, instilling guilt, one blow after another.

What I usually tell victims: “When you encounter the first signs of violence, whether physical or emotional, pack your things and run. People who abuse you will not change. Don't play the rescuer and don't think, 'I'll change them,' 'our love will overcome this,' and so on. It won't. They won't change. If you don't want to ruin your personality and your life, leave without looking back. No second chances. Love yourself! Find something to love about yourself. You are a respectable person, and no one has the right to walk all over you. Period.

I pick up the folder again and look at the descriptions I wrote about the people in Tara's life.

A psychological portrait of the characters and the mistakes they made.

1. Tara – main character

Characteristics:

- A tough person, striving for independence

She grew up without a father and learned to rely on herself from an early age.

She achieved success in her career without anyone's help.

She developed a backbone through years of perseverance and struggling for a place under the sun.

- Vulnerable to being wooed and "fairy tale happiness"

Despite her strong will, Tara craved warmth, tenderness and support. Oliver, with his lavish gestures and obvious "care", filled the emptiness caused by the absence of a father and the constant struggle for survival.

· Willingness to sacrifice herself and her goals

Tara made concessions after the wedding: she gave up her career, moved into a new house and became a housewife.

The fear of hurting a loved one led Tara to agree to decisions she wasn't comfortable with (moving, having children straight away, leading a reclusive lifestyle).

· The gradual descent into a dependent relationship.

Subconsciously, Tara felt that she was losing her independence, but she was afraid of arguments and conflicts.

When the first signs of abuse (insults and physical violence) appeared, Tara made excuses for Oliver's behaviour: he's tired, he's drunk, "it happens to everyone".

She tolerated and forgave his behaviour because she suffered from typical victim's syndrome: she was afraid of losing her child and family and believed in a "better future" and that her husband would change.

· Psychological breakdown

The loss of her mother and unborn baby girl was a heavy blow, which increased Tara's sense of guilt and helplessness.

After experiencing numerous episodes of violence (including sexual, physical and emotional), Tara almost lost her own identity and became isolated from friends and family.

However, meeting a childhood friend gave her the chance to find support. In the end, Tara decided to escape and start her life anew.

Main mistakes:

· Ignoring the red flags

She attributed the early warning signs—rudeness, humiliation, jealousy, control—to her husband's "stress". She tried to find excuses for his behaviour instead of setting strict boundaries.

· Isolation and loss of personal support

She agreed to leave her job, stopped talking to her friends and abandoned her own interests.

The fewer external sources of support she had, the more she came under her husband's influence.

· Dependence on an idealised image of relationships

To the last, Tara believed in a fairy tale that did not exist. This prevented her from accepting reality and solving the problem sooner.

· Unwillingness to seek help in time

She did not admit to her mother that her husband was beating her.

2. Oliver – Tara's husband

Characteristics:

· Narcissistic traits and a tendency to manipulate others

The prince from a fairy tale at the start, bestowing gifts and romantic surprises.

At the same time, behind the outward courtesy hid the need to control everything: Tara's life, her career, her body and the people around her.

Lack of empathy for other people's feelings: he believed that "everything should be done my way".

· Aggression as a way to assert himself

He showed extreme cruelty in stressful situations, including using physical violence.

Violent episodes alternate with "honeymoon" periods: he begs for forgiveness and showers his wife (the victim) with love to keep her by his side.

Using guilt to manipulate his wife (jealous outbursts, claiming that Tara is to blame for their problems and even their baby's death).

· Immaturity and puerility in relationships

Pressuring Tara to have a child as soon as possible, thus tying her to him, yet ignoring his parental duties.

Inability to admit his own mistakes, shifting the blame to his wife and others ("You provoked me", "It's your fault that I lost the deal").

Using his wife's financial dependence to control her and crush her resistance.

Main mistakes:

· Choosing violence as a behaviour model.

Did not try to work through his own childhood trauma (he obviously witnessed domestic violence);

He repeated his father's behaviour by physically and emotionally humiliating his partner.

· Creating the illusion of an ideal relationship

He talked about a big and close-knit family but destroyed his wife in reality.

He got married while not being ready for a genuine partnership and mutual respect.

· Manipulation and gaslighting

Consciously isolated Tara from her friends and career, undermined her self-confidence and instilled feelings of guilt. "It's your fault that I lost my temper".

He did not seek professional help even though he was aware that he lost control of his feelings and emotions.

· Duplicity

He maintained the façade of an ideal husband while behaving completely differently when alone with Tara.

He did not acknowledge the real problem, which only reinforced that part of his personality.

3. Tara's mum

Characteristics:

- Caring, pragmatic and with a wealth of life experience.
- She warned Tara about the possible hazards in marriage and advised her not to rush into having children and to maintain her own opinions and independence.

Main mistakes:

In her relationship with her daughter, the "harsh truth" she delivered caused Tara to resist and refuse her advice. It would have been much better to have a constructive conversation with her daughter.

4. Oliver's mum

Characteristics:

- A woman who previously put up with her husband's aggression and accepted this scenario as the norm.

Main mistakes:

- A habit of justifying violence (since she had lived with it herself).

- She basically encouraged her son's tyrannical lifestyle by telling Tara that "nothing in life is free".

5. Sarah (Tara's friend)

Characteristics:

- Sensitive and emotional. She continued to care about her friend and tried to help her when she suspected that something was wrong.

Main mistakes:

- Distancing herself from Tara (it was Tara's fault or rather, Oliver's, who turned his wife against her friends), which meant that she missed the moment when a loved one needed her help.

6. Bud (Oliver's friend)

Characteristics:

- Obvious resentment and distrust of women.

Doesn't hide his dislike of women, calling them "gold diggers".

- Tendency to judge people harshly and rely on stereotypes.

Convinced that a woman's place is in the kitchen.

Makes fun of women's independence and careers.

There is a general rejection of modern values: equality, feminism and career advancement for women.

- Demonstrates aggression and cruelty.

He tells a story about a lion under the guise of manliness, and the description "put the whole clip in it" sounds like a symbol of ruthlessness. He considers such cruelty normal. This indicates problems with aggression and empathy.

- Shows loyalty to Oliver.

It is clear from their conversation that they are united by the common idea of "inconvenient women".

- Compensation for his own inferiority complex

The eager use of stereotypes and the derision of women can be an external defence against feelings of his own vulnerability—perhaps Bud was hurt in a relationship or experienced some form of trauma. Now he is trying to assert himself at the expense of women by denigrating them.

Main mistakes:

- Generalization and transfer of a negative experiences to all women.
- Lack of empathy and respect.

· Use of an aggressive hierarchy.

Hunting wild animals illustrates the desire to dominate: "I am stronger, and I can destroy".

· Inability to build partnerships.
· Lack of self-reflection.

What conclusions can we draw from this story?

Firstly, neither Tara nor Oliver established clear boundaries around personal space or what was acceptable during the first months of their marriage. Tara allowed her husband to make decisions for her, leaving work and giving up social connections "for love". Oliver, on the other hand, believed that he had the right dictate terms.

Secondly, the cycle of abuse: euphoria, crisis, explosion (violence), remorse, euphoria again. Tara forgave Oliver when she witnessed short-term tenderness and hoped that "this time everything would change".

Next, Tara underestimated the seriousness of the situation. For a long time, she believed that the physical violence was an accident that could be explained by work stress or alcohol.

What we can note here is that Tara formed the illusion of an inevitable victim. She believed that she had to endure and solve everything on her own and remained isolated until things came to a head.

Oliver, on the other hand, believed that since he was the breadwinner" he could do whatever he liked.

Tara's story is an example of how even a strong personality can fall into the trap of a toxic relationship. Years of hard work and independence did not save her from abuse, for there were no internal brake lights and the support for loved ones.

Oliver is an example of a dangerous model, where outside respectability and the "perfect image" are combined with deep psychological problems, inherited trauma and the inability to establish healthy communication.

The main lessons to be learned:

1. Any instance of physical and emotional violence should be perceived as a serious threat and not a temporary deviation.
2. It is important to maintain personal boundaries, social connections and financial independence.
3. An early response is vital: a conversation with loved ones, contacting specialists (psychologist, crisis centre or lawyer).
4. Society's condemnation ("what will others think?") should not outweigh one's own health and safety. They may discuss it today and forget it by tomorrow. Think of yourself first.

These mistakes, made at the very beginning, lead to serious family dramas, sometimes with a tragic outcome. **Look after yourself!**

My phone rings, and I get up from the couch. I'm already feeling tired. Maybe meeting Gishi has affected me? Or maybe it's another dive into Tara's story? I felt so bad for her, for the post-traumatic stress that had haunted her for years. It's good that her story has a happy ending; others sometimes don't manage to survive, let alone save their children.

Finally reaching the phone, I press "decline." It's Eleanor. I don't want to hear her voice, I don't want to listen to her stupid problems. I desperately want to be home, but I have a full schedule today, which upsets me. At the moment, my soul is empty. I can't give anything to my clients, I don't want to. I've been bored with them for a long time, but I can't give them up either; I need their money for the fund.

Isabel enters the office without knocking.

"Why didn't you knock? " I ask sternly.

"Mrs. Eleanor is here," Isabel replies, her eyes wild with fear. "She's covered in blood!"

I go out into the reception area and see Eleanor. I can see that she's not herself. Her eyes are darting around, her lips and hands are trembling. She is wearing a beautiful white blouse with a large bow at the neck, and the only thing marring her appearance is that she is splattered with blood.

"Good morning, Eleanor!" I say to her as if nothing has happened.

"Heleina," she smiles. 'I called you, but you didn't answer. You probably already know? You know, right? Everyone probably knows by now. I did something, Heleina!' She's already shouting. " I did something!"

I calmly put my hands on her shoulders and ask her to calm down. I lead her into the study and close the door, signalling to Isabel not to do anything.

After sitting Eleanor down in a chair, I learn that this morning, while getting ready for brunch with her friends, she unexpectedly went to the safe, opened it, took out a gun, and went to her husband's bedroom. They sleep in separate rooms, so I'm not surprised by this. She knocks on his door and, after he shouts "come in," opens it. Her husband is still in bed; he came home around 5 a.m., and she heard his car pull into the driveway. She knows where he was and with whom. She goes to the head of his bed and stares at his face for a long time, as if trying to remember him for the last time, then points the gun at his head and empties the magazine. She then leaves the bedroom, closes the door behind her, throws the gun on the floor, and runs down the stairs.

"I can still get away!" she says to me.

I shake my head.

"What should I do, what should I do? What will people think of me? Am I a murderer now?"

"Eleanor, it doesn't matter what people think of you. What matters is that you finally stood up for yourself. You defended your honor and dignity, which had been trampled into the dirt for years."

"Really?"

"Yes. You must save face. There's no need to hide. You need to go to the police station now and make a full confession.

"But I don't want to go to prison! Are you crazy?"

- Believe me, it will be better this way. You can stay at home on bail until the trial, of course. And you know, you'll be fine at home now, because he's gone. And there will be no more humiliation. Besides, you still have his money.

- Yes, I'll hire the best lawyers!

Our conversation continues for some time, she asks me to call the police, and 10 minutes later, people in uniform enter my office.

Eleanor is calm now, she doesn't resist. She is ready for the consequences of her decision. Is it hers?

SHALL WE PLAY?

After Eleanor killed her husband, days passed, then weeks. It was all over the news, and I was tired of hearing about it. People were ready to dwell on this case endlessly. Everyone in the park and at work was discussing the details of this family drama.

Even though Eleanor turned herself in to the authorities, she will still go to prison. No lawyer can win this case, and stories about him being an abuser and a tyrant won't help her.

Their children will receive a pittance from the inheritance by their standards. The will was drawn up in such a way that virtually all property and funds go to charities and other social organizations. Mine included.

Of course, I had to testify about how she ended up in my office, but after questioning, I was immediately released home, as they found nothing suspicious.

Gishi hasn't contacted me since our last conversation, but I know for sure that he's not sleeping. He's still digging.

I am still working and seeing clients. The other day, I found out that I lost one of them. Mr. Ridley died. As I predicted, he did not live to see his liver transplant. His lawyer contacted me and said that my foundation had been bequeathed $5 million. I plan to use this money to help people who were affected by his schemes. Of course, it's a drop in the ocean, but still.

Today is my day off. During the summer months, many clients go on vacation, and I have to work less. Although I don't like my clients, and some I frankly hate and despise, without them I would probably be worse off than with them. I don't like to relax, because then I have to spend time alone with myself, listening to my endless stream of thoughts, rummaging through the past, which is painful and disgusting to remember, and gnawing at myself for the sins I have committed. I'm still not sure if they are sins, because in 90% of cases I always find excuses for my actions.

Since I have nothing to do today, I'm going to the supermarket to buy groceries and cook meals for the week. I usually go to the supermarket first thing in the morning so that no one is there.

As soon as I arrive at my destination, my phone rings. It's Isabel. I already know that something important has happened. She never disturbs me without a reason.

"Miss Heleina," her voice is agitated.

"Good morning, Isabel," I answer as usual.

"The police are here. Miss Heleina, I think you need to come!"

"What do they want?"

"They're confiscating your documents."

"All right, let them. You know we have nothing to hide."

"They've forbidden the employees to answer the phone."

"That's not good. I'll take care of it, everyone stay where you are."

"What should we do with the papers?"

"What can you do? They have a warrant, let them take whatever they want."

I hang up the phone. I cancel the groceries, start the engine, and drive to my trump card. I don't call his receptionist; I know he's busy and they'll probably give me a date and time to visit, but I don't need a date, I need to see him now.

When I pull up to the old building, I show my pass to the security guard and drive onto the grounds.

"Oh, Miss Heleina! Nice to see you," his advisor says to me. "Is something wrong?"

"Yes, an unpleasant situation. The foundation's work has been suspended for unknown reasons. The staff has been forbidden to take calls."

"He's in a meeting right now. Can you wait a little while? I'll let him know as soon as he's available, okay?"

I don't wait long. Before I even finish my cup of coffee, He comes out of the swinging door. My close friend, a former client whom I helped solve not only personal problems but also work issues.

"Hello, dear," he says, kissing and hugging me. "Come in."

Entering his office, I sit down in a tall leather chair. He sits down across from me at his desk. He looks serious, and I realize that he already knows something he's afraid to tell me. Knowing him and understanding him, I laugh out loud.

"Harold," I say, calming down, 'you look like something terrible has happened!

"Heleina,' he smiles guiltily, 'charges have been brought against you.

"What?' I ask, still amused.

"Mrs. Scholz. Do you know her?

"Of course! She's my client who recently shot her husband."

Seeing that I'm not upset at all, he relaxes.

"Is that why you came?"

"No, I came because I need the fund to continue its work!"

"Oh, that's easy. I thought you came for protection."

I smile faintly. Sweet Harold.

"You think I can't protect myself? And besides, it's all nonsense. You have an election coming up, I wouldn't put you in that position.

"You know I'll always try to help you.

"I know, my dear friend! But this isn't the case. I'm not interested in anything but the funds work, and I'll take care of the rest. No charges have been brought against me. And I know who's behind all this.

"Who?

"An old, useless detective. He wanted to rummage through my files, so he's doing everything he can to do that. Making up reasons.

"Is there anything in them? In those files?" He's getting tense.

"No! There's nothing there. And even if there is, he'll never guess what it says about you. That's what you're worried about, isn't it?"

"Sorry for showing such a self-serving interest", he apologizes.

"Don't say that. It's not self-serving at all—I completely understand. So, what about the fund?

"I'll make a couple of calls, and the fund will be able to operate."

"You promise?"

"I promise."

"So, how's Buffy, kids?"

"Everything's fine. Peace and quiet."

"And Jessica?" I smile slyly.

"Shh!" he says, putting his finger to my lips. "Our 'dog' Jessica is fine too. She recently had some beautiful puppies. Girls."

I wink at him and get up. As I leave, I give him a big, sincere hug.

On the way to the office, I think what a good guy Harold is, a real man. He's done a lot for our town. It's a better place because of him. Sure, he didn't always use the best methods, but in a fight, anything goes. Especially when it comes to the common good. He did it for their benefit, not his own. I know for sure that he's not a thief like the others.

When I pull up to the office, I see all my employees on the lawn. They look dejected. I walk up to them, smile broadly, and say:

"Why so glum?"

Dozens of eyes look at me, and I realize that they are all trying to read me. They are scared, and I understand why.

"Get up, guys," I command. 'We can start work in 30 minutes."

"Are you serious?' someone asks me." They've turned the place upside down!"

"So what? Don't we have enough hands to clean it up? Get back to work."

When I get to the office, I don't recognize it. The barbarians have indeed turned everything upside down. Well, Gishi, you'll pay for this. The game is on. If only you knew who you were messing with!

Before I have time to finish tidying up the office, I get a call from Harold. We can get to work. Hooray!

As soon as the employees' workplaces are back to normal, I finally go into my office. I have a smile on my face because I see my empty cabinet. Not a single folder. I know what's going to happen next, and I'm curious to see how it will all end. I want to compete with Gishi because I've been bored for a long time, and now there's some spice, some excitement.

I'm not called to the police station, my phone is silent. And it will remain silent for now. I am sure that in the coming days, his entire department, and he himself, will be scanning notes about my clients, digging into their dirty secrets, and possibly mine as well.

Five days have passed since my office was searched. Finally, my phone rings and a pleasant female voice invites me to the police station. Gishi himself doesn't call me. He's probably saving his energy to attack me in person. It makes me laugh.

On the way to the station, I imagine what awaits me there. I am ready for any questions; they don't know yet how smart and cunning I am. Gishi thinks nothing of me and my life, but I have been thinking about her for about 30 years. He won't be able to catch me.

When I arrive at the station, I go to the reception desk and say that I'm expected. I give my last name, and the police officer makes a phone call. After the conversation, he asks me to sit down and wait until someone comes for me.

Detective Fraser comes to get me. She's kind and friendly; it looks like she's the one playing the good cop.

I am led into a windowless office where Gishi is already waiting for us.

"Miss Heleina," he says," I'm glad to see you."

I realize that he is not glad to see me at all, but rather that over the next few hours all his assumptions about me will be confirmed, which will be further proof of his professionalism. He was never praised as a child, which is where all this desire to go out of his way to be noticed, to be confirmed that "I'm good," comes from.

On the table in front of him are my files, on which his hand rests carefully and even gently. This is his sacred treasure, proof that I am not who I claim to be. He keeps looking at me and then at the folders, trying to read my thoughts, the slightest movement of my eyes or eyebrows. But I remain impassive. After all, I still have nothing to hide.

"Good morning, Detective Gishi," I say, sitting down on a chair.

He presses his lips together.

"You probably already know why you're here, don't you?"

"I have no idea."

"Come on, your client goes missing, then it turns out that the husband of one of your clients goes missing under similar circumstances, and then another client of yours kills her husband. Isn't that a lot for one psychologist to handle?"

"I still don't see the connection."

"Then it turns out that another client of yours committed suicide, even though he had a good life, a home, a job," he continues, as if not hearing me.

It's worth noting that he's acting cocky, like he's better than me, which is the biggest mistake people like him make. Where's your ego taking you, dear Gishi? Never underestimate your enemy, never put yourself on a pedestal.

Once, in my younger years, when I was a child and trying to escape the reality of my life, I read books, many books. So, I remembered for the rest of my life a phrase by a famous Russian writer,

Chekhov. He said that an intelligent, that is, an educated person should always doubt themselves.

"Interesting, Heleina, why do you remember this phrase, but you don't follow it yourself?" my inner voice asks me.

Gishi takes out the top folder and, opening it, continues the interrogation:

"Are you familiar with this folder, Miss Pascal?"

"Yes."

"Here you're describing a family and, strangely, you've written it in the first person. Who is Tom??"

"He's the stepfather of one of my clients."

"What's her name?"

"I can't say, this conversation took place when I was still working on the psychological helpline."

"Do you have a recording of this conversation?"

"With all your professionalism, you surely know that there are no records."

"Yes, yes. Why don't you have any records?"

"There was a fire in the office."

"There are no reports of a fire at your office."

"Yes, it was a small fire. We didn't call for help or file an insurance claim."

This is followed by some silly questions, to which I give short answers. I know that Gishi already knows everything; he doesn't have any facts, but he's 100% sure of everything. He can't seem to get me to say what he wants me to say. He simply has nothing to go on.

- You said you lived in Missouri?

- No, I said I lived in Connecticut.

- You don't remember where you lived before you were 15? - he tries to confuse me.

- Not until 15, but until 14. No, unfortunately, I don't remember much of my life before the age of 14, just a few fragments.

- Do you remember your real parents?

- No, I only remember my father, I don't remember my mother at all.

- You know, the story in this folder keeps bothering me. I think it's definitely about you.

- What led you to that conclusion?

- Your notes led me to it. It says here that your alleged client—he makes quotation marks with his fingers—was wounded in the stomach, a knife wound. It was Christmas morning, which narrows down the search. I ran the databases and found the names of all the injured children. There weren't that many. And you know what I found out for sure?

"What Mr. Gishi?"

"That your name isn't Heleina Pascal," he concludes triumphantly, thinking he's caught me out.

"Yes, not Heleina. I used to have a different name, but I don't know what it was. My adoptive parents gave me the name Heleina when they took me from the orphanage."

Gishi thought I would continue to beat around the bush and didn't expect me to answer that way. He's sorry that he's wasting all the clever words he prepared for me.

"You probably want to know my real name," I say with a smile.

His eyes change expression. He quietly begins to hate me for stealing his triumphant investigation.

"Your name is Diana Nuri. You were never American; your family emigrated from Italy when your mother remarried. The man who became your stepfather was named Ray Charles Myers. That is why you are not in the United States database."

I break into a smile.

"What an interesting story."

"What's more, his daughter, or rather his stepdaughter, disappeared without a trace after being taken to hospital with a stab wound, and Ray Charles himself was found dismembered in his home five years later."

I cross my arms and bring them up to my chin. I look serious. I even shake my head disapprovingly.

"There's one thing I don't understand about this story, Miss Pascal. With your status and global reputation," he mimics our last conversation, "you didn't think to get rid of the circumstantial evidence proving that you are not who you say you are?"

"With all due respect, Mr. Gish, where is the evidence?"

"Here..."

"Where's your evidence? " I don't let him finish.

"It's right in front of you, Miss Pascal!" He starts to get worked up. "And I'll prove it to you right now."

He pulls out another folder, and I realize that the hospital sent him the file with the girl's injuries. Gishi starts reading:

"On the left side, in the ovary area, there is a long, deep wound, 2.7 inches long." He looks up at me and asks," Do you have a scar, Diana?"

I smile again and raise my eyebrow slightly, asking,

"Please don't call me by someone else's name, that's the first thing. And second, if you want to look at my body, I can show it to you without any problem."

I quickly pull open my shirt and expose my stomach to Gishi and Fraser. Fraser says, "Oh, my God," and turns away, but Gishi continues to look.

"What happened to you?" he asks me, pointing to my scarred stomach.

"I told you, I don't remember. According to my hypnotherapist, these wounds were inflicted on me by my real family, who abused me in every way possible." Somehow, I managed to escape from them and ended up in a convent, where I was later taken in by my adoptive mother.

I button up my shirt and sit back down in the chair. Gishi and Fraser exchange glances and get up from the table.

"We'll be back in a minute," Gishi says as he leaves, glancing at the open folder with my client's file and slowly closing the door.

I guess his train of thought has been interrupted. He needs to approach it from a different angle. The question of who I am has been answered, but he will have others.

I know he's watching me through the camera, but I'm as relaxed as possible. He won't read me. I also know that he left the folder open on purpose. He wants to get some kind of reaction from me.

I don't look at the folder; there's nothing new in there for me, and I know this story by heart. After all, it's the story of my life. Gishi is heading in the right direction. The only question is, who will prove to be smarter, him or me?

TO TURN BACK TIME

My hopeless mother remarried when I was six years old. Well, by generally accepted standards, she was not hopeless: she did not drink, smoke or hang out with the wrong crowd. Furthermore, she was a hardworking person with two jobs. Not that the family ever saw the money from these jobs, but that is beside the point.

I will never forget the fateful day when a strange man appeared in our close-knit, or so it seemed to me, family.

I did not like my new stepfather from the start. Perhaps I could sense that things would turn out badly or perhaps there was a different reason. It is also possible that I simply did not want to share my mother, whom I rarely saw with anyone else. By the way, neither my grandmother nor my grandfather, with whom we lived at the time, liked this man. I often think back to that day and wonder if I could have influenced her choice. I could have screamed, cried or thrown a tantrum. Would it have helped, though?

Soon we had to move away from my grandparents. The newlyweds found it awkward to live under someone else's roof since they wanted freedom and independence. We moved into an apartment that the factory, where my mother worked day and night, had assigned her. Strange that she was not afraid to leave me with some "mister". She probably did not suspect anything bad or maybe she did not care. Although, as experience would show, she was an irresponsible woman when it came to children.

At first, my stepfather, whom I will call Tom, tried to seem like a decent person and even gave me a pair of beautiful tights once. But once he gained more power over my mother, he revealed his true nature. He was a monster. A real-life monster. I am sure that people like him should not exist. If such mutations do occur among people, they should be urgently removed from society. Even more so, they should not be allowed to marry and have children. But who am I to judge? Just a soul.

Tom first used his fists on me when I was about seven. Before that, he only beat my mother, who did nothing to resist and did not try to protect herself. It is strange how a beloved daughter, raised in care and comfort, could become a victim of violence. Unfortunately, no one is immune to this. Back in those days, when people tried to preserve a marriage no matter what, it would have been impossible to raise a fuss. Many suffered who knows what. That was what my mother thought. Although this is probably just another excuse I have for the stupid woman. Undoubtedly stupid! After all, who would let themselves be hurt and then let the same person hurt your child, your own flesh and blood? She allowed it, and more than once. For some reason, she believed that Tom would change one day. After all, he did not want to hurt anyone, we were the bad ones, we pushed him to it, but it was not his fault. How wrong she was. People like that do not change, and if he hits you once, he will hit you a second time, only harder. This will continue for years. Of course, he will apologize at first, but then he will stop doing even that. And one day, when you least expect it, he will not hold back and knock your precious soul out of your already broken body.

Well, let us return to when I was seven. We were in the kitchen when Tom punched me in the ear. The reason was trivial – I had spilled some jam. Just a little bit. I was sitting at the table in a white top, and it took me a moment to realize where the unbearable pain had come from. No one had ever hit me before – especially a large adult man, and with his fist, too. My vision went dark, and my head felt like it was going to explode. I clutched my head in both hands and screamed as loudly as I could. Tom did not like that either. He rushed up to me, clamped a hand over my mouth and said, "If you don't shut up right now, I'm going to squeeze your head so hard that your skull will crack like a watermelon."

I kept yelling. My mother tried to defend me and asked him haltingly to let me go, but after he glared at her with his red, furious eyes, she turned back to the sink and washing the dishes. This was the first time she had betrayed me. There would be many such betrayals in the future, and they all hurt as much as the first time.

That evening, they watched TV as if nothing had happened. My mother hugged the one who had hurt me, her precious and only child. Other parents probably valued their children a lot more that mine did. I was never worth much to her. So what if he hit her? It was how he raised children. Maybe she would grow up a decent person. What a travesty!

Home alone the next morning, I pulled on my coat and hat and, without thinking twice, went to my grandparents' house. I told them about what was going on at home. It turned into a terrible scandal. My mother convinced them that everything I said was a lie and that our life could not be better. Of course, I was punished, by my mother this time. She beat me with her heavy leather boots and I huddled in a corner, unable to do anything but cry bitterly. I was no longer allowed to visit my grandparents, and contact with other relatives was forbidden. I found myself completely isolated. I was all alone with no one to help me or believe me.

This was how the new chapter of my life called "endless violence" began. It really was. I was beaten for everything, even food. One day, I took a couple of eggs from Tom's shelves. I did not know that he had his own shelf for personal items. After boiling these eggs, I went to do my homework, unaware of the impending punishment. Tom came home from work early, and my hair stood on end as soon as the key turned in the door. I did not know yet what I would be punished for, but I had learned to sense it somehow. He noticed the missing eggs quickly, probably because he had counted them. Funny, is it not? I was not laughing. He struck me with his fists on my head, my face, anywhere he could reach. "For what?" the question echoed in my head. "For two eggs? Really?" I learned my lesson. I did not take food from home again and was always hungry. The meals my mother cooked me after her endless, useless shifts did not last for long.

You may ask: was there really no one to help me? The only person who cared about my fate was my teacher, the kind and wonderful Mrs. Cottam. She even used to feed me, doing it as subtly as possible so that I did not feel humiliated. She came to our house once to check how her best student, and I was her best student, was living. I was mopping the floor that day while my stepfather lounged on the couch. He met my teacher in dirty and stretched boxer shorts, not even bothering to cover himself. Mrs. Cottam tactfully ignored my stepfather's appearance and got straight to the point. She said that not only was she proud of me, but the whole school was proud of me, because I was smart beyond my years. She said that a diligent girl like me needed special care and attention, and so on. In no case should such a young girl be forced to carry a heavy bucket of water and wash the floor. My stepfather tried to listen to her at first, but got angrier and angrier each time she praised me. It was not even the arrival of an uninvited guest. He was annoyed that this flibbertigibbet was trying to tell him what to do.

"Who the hell does she think she is?" he shouted after she had left. "If this trollop ever comes to my house again and tries to teach me how to live and raise my child, I'll wring her neck. Tell her that I said so!"

My brother was born when I was nine and another one arrived when I was ten. I had three years left to live, but I had no inkling of what the future had in store for me. I thought that as soon as I turned 16, I would go far, far away and build a new and happy life.

Naturally, I became the children's babysitter. Who else could it be? The older boy was very sweet and I loved him with all my heart, while the younger one demanded constant attention, always whined and was unhappy with everything. I hated him with a passion. As soon as he started crying, the adults would come at me swinging. My mother had become a monster herself by that time and tortured me constantly. She took out the humiliation she suffered from Tom on me. My soul was crying and so was my body. I really wanted to die and often imagined my mother crying over my grave and regretting treating me so unfairly while I had been alive. I also imagined my life if my father had lived. A happy life, where he would have loved me and taken me on the merry-go-round or to the park. He would have bought me ice-cream and gazed at my content and cheerful face bathed in sunlight.

I scroll through the film of my life, nearing the end. I often watch it and think about how it could have turned out if not for the eternal 'but'.

It was a typical, frosty Christmas morning. The children woke up and ran to the Christmas tree to open their presents. They were noisier than usual and I struggled to calm them down. Naturally, my mother burst out of the bedroom at the sound of their screeching and started hissing at me. She said that I was not looking after the boys properly and that we would all be in trouble if Tom woke up from this racket.

"Can't you look after the kids for once?" I suddenly grew emboldened. "If I remember correctly, you gave birth to them, so why am I always responsible for them?"

My mother had no answer to this.

I was putting the kettle on when I heard the deafening sound of breaking glass. Running out into the living room, I saw that my mother, who had apparently fallen asleep on the couch, had failed to stop the boys from attacking the Christmas tree. One of them had yanked on a garland, fell and pulled the tree down after him. They howl so loudly in fright that, of course, they woke Tom up.

He walked into the living room, staggering after yesterday's party. His head was buzzing, and the children's cries only made him feel worse.

"Who did this?" he asked harshly.

"Tom, they didn't mean to," my mother stammered.

"Who said you could speak? I asked, who did this?"

The culprit began to cry even harder.

"Shut up and go stand in the corner! Now!"

After the little boy went to stand in the corner, Tom grabbed my mother by the hair and hissed, "Why am I being woken up on my day off? Are you not keeping an eye on them again?" he tossed my mother on the floor and growled, "Clean this up!"

I saw that she had fallen on the broken toys, which hurt her badly. Her blood spread rapidly under the tree.

I ran up to my mother and gave her a towel to mop up the cuts. That could have been the end of it since the holiday was already ruined but knowing Tom, it was just beginning. My mother should have run but...

Thuds were coming from the kitchen – clearly Tom was looking for something. I was treating my mother's wounds at the time and did not notice when the enemy appeared behind me.

"Where's the bottle?" he asked hoarsely.

"What bottle?" my mother replied, playing the fool.

She knew where it was but would not give it to him for some reason. Why?

"You know what bottle! Bring it here! I'm not playing these games with you."

"I won't!" baulked the stubborn woman. "You'll get drunk again, and my boss and his wife are coming this evening."

"They're coming to see you, so you can sit with them. Bring me my bottle."

My mother just shook her head. He grabbed her by the shoulders, pulled her to her feet, and punched her in the nose as hard as he could. When she fell, he started kicking her in the stomach. The children began to cry, scream and throw themselves at their father, but he did not spare them either. They got hit too, with fists and feet. I ran to the kitchen and, grabbing a dirty knife from the sink, rushed over to save my mother and brothers.

"Get away from Mum!" I shouted in a voice that was not my own.

My stepfather looked at me and something danced in his eyes. "Well, come on!" he said, opening his arms as if for a hug. "Come on!"

I stood rooted to the spot as he came at me. I backed away until I struck the wall, unable to do what I wanted or say anything. The survival reflex did not work in me. I remember kicking him, I remember trying to push him away from me, but I do not remember the knife entering my chest. My eyes were frozen with pain, and I felt hot blood running down my legs. I heard my mother's screams echoing from what felt like a great distance.

I was still alive when the ambulance arrived, but I could sense that I was dying. My agony did not last long. My heart stopped and my soul was freed before I reached the hospital.

I could find no peace for a long time, wandering around familiar places and visiting my home. Life there had not changed at all and continued on as before. My mother kept working and the boys were left unattended at home. They often cried, and I would stroke their heads. I thought that they could see me.

I was at the trial, too. My stepfather sat stony-faced in the dock, showing no remorse or regret. He did not think he was guilty, just as my hopeless mother did not consider him guilty. It would have been hard to surprise me, but I was surprised when I heard her defending him. Nevertheless, he was sentenced to life imprisonment. This brought me no satisfaction since it would not bring my life back. Yes, it was joyless, but I kept believing, which means I could have changed it all for the better.

The years passed and the boys grew up. Their lives did not work out. My favourite brother, forever neglected, cold, hungry and angry, fell in with a bad crowd. He started stealing and then became involved in more terrible activities. He ended up dying in prison from an overdose. Unfortunately, I never met him for he was destined for a different fate.

The younger brother ended up in a psychiatric hospital. He was diagnosed with a multitude of disorders, and to my sadness and sorrow, there was no help for him. Perhaps he had inherited them from his father, or perhaps it was the atmosphere he had grown up in. It is hard for a young, immature and innocent child to live in the environment that we lived in.

My mother remarried. She occasionally shed a few tears for each of us but lived well on the whole. I guess I am happy for her. I never wished her ill.

My gentle soul gets up from the fluffy armchair and goes to the record player. She finds her favourite record and starts watching a film that could have been a spectacular version of the previous one.

And so, we are back at the Christmas tree. The boys wake Tom up again. He gets up, shouts, grabs my mother, and her hands are bleeding again. He asks her for the bottle and she gives it to him. While Tom is busy, she comes up to me and whispers, "There's a stocking in the underwear drawer, take it and hide it in your room. Get dressed and dress the boys. We're leaving. Don't take anything else."

I nod and hurry to follow her instructions. A moment later, we are at the bus stop. The boys are quiet, as if they understand that now is not the time for games.

We spend the day with our grandparents, then buy tickets to another city the next day and leave. My mother understands that we need to get far away from someone like Tom.

Life is not easy in the new city at first. Mum is always working so I have to do all the chores, but I am no longer afraid to be home. Although I often dream at night that Tom finds us and kills us all. This does not happen the first year or the second or the third.

I try to finish school as an external student and write articles for the school paper. I have a lot of friends and people love me. I am loved at home too. My mother keeps apologizing for subjecting us to that life and feels like she was not herself back then. Like she was a different person.

Years pass and I am walking my oldest son to school for the first time. It is such an emotional moment, and there are tears in my eyes. My husband is standing next to me, holding our little daughter in his arms. The sun is shining on her head and her hair glitters gold. I feel so happy right then. Of course, I experience moments of frustration but, on the whole, I think my life has been a success. My family's life has worked out too. My mother remarried – to a good and decent man this time. He is calm, caring and hardworking, and with him, my mother's house has finally found its true master. My brothers also lead a good life. My favourite brother has grown into a wonderful man, but he is in no hurry to start a family because of his career. On the contrary, my younger brother prefers family life and is not very ambitious. He has a wonderful wife and equally wonderful children. We often see each other on special occasions, as well as on the weekends, and every time, there is laughter in the house.

What happened to Tom? Regrettably, or maybe not, he died many years ago. I know that he drank too much, and his heart gave out. He died alone.

This could have been the story of my life. Perhaps it was? I am starting to forget.

A psychological portrait of the characters and the mistakes they made

1. The child (main character)

Characteristics:

- Childhood vulnerability

A girl who grew up in a family where her father died early, and her mother remarried.

She experiences a serious lack of attention and love: her mother works but there is no money in the house, and she lives with her grandparents' part of the time.

She is very sensitive to any form of violence – she had not experienced beatings before but then suddenly encounters them.

- Feelings of abandonment and betrayal

Her mother does not protect her, moreover, she shows aggression toward her daughter in an attempt to please her husband (Tom).

The child feels that her closest person (her mother) abandons her in favour of the "outsider".

· The hope for salvation and the desire to survive

Fleeing to her grandparents, desperate attempts to tell them about what is happening.

The desire to "turn 16 and leave" shows that the main character, despite the long-term abuse, did not give up, but was looking for a way out.

· An inner world of dreams and fantasies

She invents an alternative reality, where her father is alive, her mother takes care of her and her stepfather does not exist.

This helps her to survive the pain and to stay in her right mind.

· Abuse and lack of support

None of the authorities, except her teacher, try to help her. This results in the main character's death at the hands of her stepfather.

Main mistakes:

Since we are talking about a child, it is hard to talk about mistakes due to the girl's limited life experience, but I will list them anyway.

· Trying to deal with the situation on her own

She should have looked for a trustworthy adult outside the family circle (a teacher or neighbour) and persistently contacted police and social services. The child cannot protect herself, so her "mistake" is forced. It is the fault of the people around her.

· Confronting the aggressor

She tries to confront her stepfather (Tom) with a knife, but she is clearly not strong enough.

She should have tried to run away and sought the help of neighbours and other adults. But the child's decision is dictated by panic and a lack of knowledge of how to act in critical situations.

· The hope that her mother will come to her senses

The child believes to the end that her mother will suddenly start defending her.

With this level of violence, it is important to understand that her mother is incapable of performing her parental duties and urgently look for another source of protection.

2. <u>The main character's mother</u>

Characteristics:

· Irresponsible attitude towards children

She does not care about the safety of her daughter or her sons.

Joins in the abuse perpetrated against her daughter by beating her with boots and supporting her husband when he gets violent.

Gives birth to two more children but dumps the responsibility for them on her daughter.

- A victim who becomes an accomplice

She suffers from Tom's beatings herself at the start, but instead of resisting or running away (for the sake of the child, at least), she condones his behaviour.

She gradually "learns" the model of violence and begins to abuse the child too, turning into a monster herself.

- A false belief that "he will change"

She believes that Tom will become a better person and refuses see that abusers do not change. This is their behavioural pattern.

- Fear of being alone and social dependence

She is afraid to be left without a man.

She works two jobs, but there is no money in the house – most likely, the husband controls the finances.

She isolates herself from her relatives to avoid going against Tom's will and to preserve the marriage.

Main mistakes:

- Failure to ensure her child's safety is a key mistake, leading to the child being systematically abused.

She could have left Tom or sent the child to live with her grandparents.

· Saving the marriage at any cost

Faith in the "traditional" model – marriage must be suffered and preserved. "You shouldn't air your dirty laundry in public." The result is her daughter's death and the ruined lives of her younger children.

· Passive acceptance of the victim role

She does not go to the police or ask for help from her relatives. The mistake is compounded when violence is extended to children.

· Condoning the abuser

"It's not his fault", "They drove him to it", "He's stressed" all form a vicious circle of abuse.

She could have run away and asked for help from the police or a crisis centre at the first sign of violence. I will say this again, at the first sign! She could have saved her daughter when she saw her husband hit her for the first time.

3. Tom (stepfather)

Characteristics:

· An abuser with sadistic traits

Uses physical violence against his wife and child (hits them on the head, threatens to kill or torture them).

Financially controls his wife.

Perceives violence as a normal form of interaction – resolves any conflict by force.

· Megalomania and the desire to dominate others.

He demands complete obedience from his wife and beats her for the slightest mistake.

· Pathological jealousy/intolerance of children's behaviour

He views even the children as the "enemy" if they get in the way or make noise.

He shows sadism (threatens to split her head like a watermelon, beats her for stolen eggs).

· Alcoholism and uncontrolled aggression

He often drinks to excess, which worsens the aggressive behaviour.

He does not express remorse after the murder of his stepdaughter and sits silently in court.

I will not list his main mistakes, because the man is a criminal. I think we all understand the behavioural patterns of such individuals. I just want to point out that such people are only strong with those who are weaker than them. If you ever come across a person like that, stay away from them and keep them away from your children. Stay alive and be well.

4. Grandmother and grandfather

Characteristics:

- They love their granddaughter and do not accept the new husband
- They do not approve of their daughter's choice from the beginning
- They do not protest enough and do not insist that the granddaughter stay with them after the scandal.

Main mistakes:

- They do not interfere much in what is happening in their daughter's family
- Accepting the daughter's "attitudes or beliefs". Perhaps if they had believed the granddaughter and not the daughter, who convinced them that the child was lying, the story could have turned out very differently.

5. Mrs. Cottam (the girl's teacher)

Characteristics:

- The only adult who takes genuine care of the girl by feeding her and visiting her home. She tries to convince her stepfather that the girl deserves to be treated kindly.

Main mistakes:

- Insufficient use of law and order.

She realises that the child is being beaten and starved but does report this to the police and child protection services.

She limits herself to a conversation, despite the systematic violence.

- Ill-considered visit

She appears unannounced, without considering the possibility that this might provoke the stepfather's aggression.

A social worker or police officer should have been involved in this visit.

6. <u>The younger children</u>

Characteristics:

- They are born in an environment of constant fear and aggression
- The older sister acts as their mother.
- They are deprived of basic safety and normal conditions. As a result, one becomes a criminal and dies of an overdose, while the other ends up in a psychiatric hospital.

***

That was the story of my life. And if I managed to survive after He almost killed me, then I can survive under any other circumstances. Yes, I will never have children because of my injuries; my female organs were removed. Although, on the other hand, why would I want children? I already had them once, even if they weren't mine, but I raised them partly. And yes, Tom, or rather Ray, died in tragic circumstances. Here I feel a touch of sarcasm. I don't feel sorry for him. If I had had the choice to do it or not, I would have done it again. He deserved what he got. And my mother also deserved to die, even though I had nothing to do with it. By modern standards, she died quite young. I know she had cancer and died a painful death. No one came to see her. If she had chosen me instead of him, she would have died loved and cared for, not like a stray dog.

Do I feel sorry for my brothers? Of course. They are victims, victims of one man, although I believe my mother should also be included in the list of those responsible.

THE SUN HIDDEN BEHIND THE FOREST

Gishi returns to the office. He looks lost, no longer so confident, but he still has some cards up his sleeve.

"Miss Pascal," he says wearily, "Mrs. Scholz has testified against you." She claims that you put her under hypnosis.

"I will repeat what I told you, Mr. Gishi—where is the evidence? Bring charges against me, and I will defend myself. I don't even need a lawyer for this case. Imagine a jury gathering and who they will believe? A woman who has never worked a day in her life, who has lived the best life that millions of other women, no worse than her, have been denied, suddenly realizes one fine morning that her husband has been cheating on her for years, has a mistress with a child, and decides to kill him. That's the point, that's the motive. You know it, and I know it. What hypnosis are you talking about?

- You receive money!

- Nice try, detective. But I would like to point out that it is not me who receives the money, but the foundation. And if you look at our statements, documents, and so on, you will see that I receive the same amount as my regular employees.

"Why do they all transfer money to your foundation?"

"Who are they?"

"All your deceased clients."

"Because my foundation does a lot of good work on a clean and honest basis, and all our wealthy clients want to help us in some way. Perhaps this is their way of atoning for their sins before God. We don't take money from ordinary citizens because sometimes they don't have anything to pay us with; they don't even know how to feed themselves or their children.

- Every month, your organization receives money from a company registered in the Cayman Islands.

- Yes, as I already told you, this is assistance from influential patrons.

- You won't give us their names, of course?

- That's none of our business. No.

- Why?

- Because I'm not under investigation. Press charges. Are we done here?

- No, you'll have to stay here a little longer.

Just as I expected. He senses everything and already knows everything. He knows about the account in the islands, he suspects that I am involved in the disappearance of Christy and Oliver. He knows, but he can't do anything to me. And so, of course, he'll keep me here until the legal detention period expires. Although, what kind of detention is this? I came here myself.

"Who is Eric Sayber?"

"I don't remember."

"We found this folder in your office," he takes out the bottom folder, opens it, and pulls out my notes.

"Are you involved in his death?"

"I told you, I don't remember anything like that."

"Would you like to take a quick look?"

I shrug and hold out my hands. To be honest, I don't need to read it, I remember everything perfectly. But I can't refuse to take it for appearances' sake. The folder contains many of my notes and notes made by Mr. Saybers himself. I begin to read.

The Sun Hidden Behind the Forest

I am sitting behind the old desk with my legs resting atop it. My father's .38 revolver, a pen and a blank piece of paper that will remember my last words lie on the desk. It is difficult for me to put everything I want to say in a few lines, so I look out the open window, trying to force my memory to replay my life for the last time. From the beginning to the very end. My gaze rests on the photograph of us when we were still young and happy. A tall, slender, curly-haired young man with emerald green eyes looks back at me. He grins at me with his brilliant smile, his whole life still ahead of him. She stands beside him, a petite brunette with alabaster white skin. Her gaze seems cunning, a bit like a fox, but that is misleading. I remember the sweater, which she had knitted herself.

Where should I start? Perhaps all the way back in my childhood?

My mother never loved me and neither did my father. I did not feel any love. I can say this calmly now because I am an adult man who has lived his life, but to be honest, I was able to process it only a couple of years ago. I have been a parent for a long time, and it is fair to say that I have been as terrible as my predecessors, perhaps even worse. What I know for sure is that children absolutely need love. But that is not the point. Somehow, when I was seven years old, I already knew that my mother had tried to get rid of me when I was still in the womb. Why was she so desperate to get rid of me? Her marriage was quite strong at that time and besides, there was already a child in the family, my sister. I always thought that the problem lay in me, that I was bad or wrong, since they so clearly did not want me. I am skipping ahead again. Let us go back to the beginning. Despite my mother's many attempts to get rid of the foetus, I was born on a hot day in July. I did not scream like a newborn should and how could I? I was not breathing. The umbilical cord wrapped around my neck had cut off all oxygen, rapidly turning my face blue. Everyone thought I was dead, but the doctors managed to resuscitate me and I started breathing. If you think about it, you will say that such a persistent person was destined to be born, perhaps to do something worthwhile, because I fought so hard for my life and God saved it for a reason. To my great regret, however, I did not achieve anything worthwhile and brought only disappointment to the people around me.

I have thought a lot about my mother, and I am in no position to judge her. Do I even have the right? Moreover, she openly did not want me and did not owe me anything, as she often said herself. Later, of course, she demonstrated something akin to love, but it was hard to tell if that was what it was. I remember that she worried about me whenever I ran off, but I do not remember her ever hugging me or saying anything nice. Poor, miserable children of parents who have never been taught to love! You hear it shouted from the rooftops these days, for it turns out that love needs to be learned. But back in those days, no one thought about it. And psychology and related personality sciences were not as well developed as they are now.

I often compared my life to that of my best friend Aslan. He was not smothered with attention either since his mother was always working, and he was on his own most of the time. But he had other relatives besides his mother with big hearts, equally big hugs and other attributes of a normal family life. My family, on the other hand, was never very affectionate, limiting themselves to dry, restrained handshakes and equally dry and indifferent questions about what one planned to do today. Nobody cared about anyone else. Well, I am exaggerating a little, or rather, lying outright as usual. I had my sister Ariadne. She loved me. Even though she was only three years older than me, she became the real mum I should have had. She loves me still, even though I have caused her a lot of grief.

As I said before, I often ran off. I scampered away to neighbouring estates and returned home late. My mother searched for me everywhere and smacked me hard when she found me. Nevertheless, I would do the same thing the next day. I have realised only now why this plan appeared in my head every time – I was trying to gain her attention, to ensure that she needed me and that I was important to her. A pity that this was not the form of attention that my tender soul really sought.

I do not remember exactly when I became a compulsive liar. Probably when I realized that the truth would be followed by fists, while a lie allowed me to go to bed untroubled. It became so deeply ingrained in me that even now, I answer a completely innocent question with a lie first. The fear is so deeply rooted in my soul that it refuses to come out by any mean. Although perhaps I do not have a soul, if you believe the people I once lived with. God knows,

I did not mean them any harm. I have never doubted that this is the truth.

By the way, I completely forgot to mention the period of time when I was sent to a children's home. Strange that my mind hid these memories from myself for many years. Only recently, the psychologist whom I abandoned after the second session opened this Pandora's box and the horror of it now pops up in my head, keeping me awake at night. So, the children's home: I was sent there because there was no one to look after me. My father was offered a manufacturing job in another city, and he left to build a new and wonderful future before disappearing without a trace. Without a moment's hesitation, my mother packed a bag and rushed off in search of him. My sister, who was now at school, was left in the care of our grandmother, but they did not want to leave me there because, as my mother said, I was a problem child. At first, my grandmother took me home on the weekends, where I felt warm and full, but when Monday came around, I was taken back to the children's home. Actually, I was dragged back. I kicked and screamed, cried and begged as hard as I could, but my grandmother was a firm woman. In any event, I found myself back at the government facility. I felt so lonely, hurt and upset. They all betrayed me, including Ariadne, over and over again.

I lived there for six months. Perhaps that was when my heart became cruel and callous. I do not know, and considering what I am about to do, I will never know.

My mother came to collect me. I had not seen her for so long, yet I did not have the slightest desire to run to her or hug her. As I found out much later, she had been absent for a good reason – she was saving her marriage. My father, finding himself free and unencumbered by a wife and relatives, went wild and completely forgot the reason for his arrival. There was a group of young men at the factory, parties and girls, and they spend every evening after work amusing themselves. Mum found my father in someone else's apartment, drunk, in the arms of a stranger. That woman probably still remembers my mother, who pulled out nearly all her hair. She pummelled my father too, but a couple of days later, he cleaned himself up and rejoined the family. Mum seemed to have forgiven him, and moreover, never brought this period up again, as if it had never happened. Why did she bring him back? Was it still customary to hold on to one's marriage? Maybe she truly loved him.

I scraped through high school and somehow got into university but did not last long there. I was stupid and hot-headed in my youth and could not keep my mouth shut when necessary. I suffered many times because of my big mouth, and my first major mistake took place during my second year at university. For some reason, the economics lecturer took an instant dislike to me. He tripped me up in every possible way, lowered my marks and made cutting remarks. My patience ran out when he gave my term paper back to me to revise for the tenth time. I was so drained by this man that I told him exactly what I thought of him, while also grabbing his shirt. Perhaps this was exactly what he was trying to achieve. I was expelled the very next day, without a trial or investigation. Looking back, I think that I should have endured no matter what, keeping my mouth shut and teeth clenched, because I needed the education, not him. Or maybe things turned out the way they were meant to. I am no longer certain of anything.

I tried to work after my expulsion, but I never seemed to find a place that suited me. In the end, after working less than a week at a new job, I quit once again and enlisted in the army. I liked the army life at first, it was fun and I was in a good squad. However, a little later I saw something that I never wanted to see. Although we were all healthy, adult men, we were not spared the schoolyard bullying. Strong guys chose weak ones and picked on them in every way they could think of. Ha, strong ones! I write this as if I was not one of them myself. I participated in the bullying, moreover, I came up with many of the ideas. Where did this anger inside me come from? Envy, most likely. These "weaklings" were better than me in some ways, smarter perhaps, or stronger in spirit. I was clearly infuriated by something they had and that I lacked. I am ashamed to not only write about what happened next, but to even think about it. All my life, I have been haunted by the image of a guy who hung himself with his own belt. He wrote that no one was to blame, but I knew that we were the reason for his departure: animals, whose strength lay only in numbers.

After that incident, I retreated into myself, shunning my old mates and waiting for my contract to end.

I got a job on my return home. I was hired as a simple electrician, but I had no complaints. It was more than enough for me, given that I had never received a proper education. Admittedly, it hurt to run into my former classmates and hear about their success, but the feeling passed quickly. After such meetings, I returned to my life, where things were not so bad. If I compared it not to the people aiming for the top but, say, to the boys in my neighbourhood, then my life was turning out great. I was just like everyone else, perhaps even better in some ways.

I continued to live with my parents, which did not bother me either. Everything was fine until the day when I met her. This was when my life changed and maybe I also changed for a time.

One day, Aslan dragged me to a party at his girlfriend's place, whom I had not yet met. The dorm she lived in was on the other side of town and I was reluctant to go. As soon as we arrived, Aslan disappeared somewhere, leaving me all alone, and I felt awkward. The place was swarming with already drunk people, which annoyed me even further. I was about to leave when my eyes fell on a girl in a pink sweater and black jeans. Her black hair, glistening in the lamplight, fell gently over her shoulders. She was arguing so heatedly with someone that I immediately wanted to find out the details of the dispute and take her side.

"Oh, there you are!" shouted Aslan and punched me in the shoulder, having managed to somehow get hammered in such a short time.

"Who's that?" I asked him.

"Where?" he asked.

"The girl in the pink sweater."

"Ha," he looked amused. "do you like her? Come on, I'll introduce you!"

"No, no," I tried to resist, but Aslan was already dragging me towards the stranger. Coming closer, Aslan hugged the girl and looked at me mischievously.

"Eric, meet this charming future teacher and my girlfriend, Nelly."

"Nice to meet you," I mumbled with a sinking heart.

She was even more beautiful up close. The thick black eyelashes framing her amber eyes fascinated me. I wanted to gaze into them forever. Besides being beautiful, she was also incredibly smart. Talking to her, I learned that she was in her third year and studying on a scholarship. She also worked as a nanny and a cleaner in a shop alongside her studies. That was how hard-working she was.

I noticed that evening that Nelly was in high demand and realized that she was a popular girl. Everyone wanted to talk to her and stand beside her.

That night, I walked home and felt sorry that I did not have even a fraction of Aslan's charm. Could I have gained Nelly's attention then? I knew, however, that despite my looks, and I was handsome once upon a time, I would never get someone like Her.

I began to see her more often after that day. I was constantly begging Aslan to take me with him to Nelly's dorm. I wonder if he guessed that I was desperately in love with his girlfriend. A pity that I can no longer ask him about it. My friend has been dead for many years, without the time to live his life and really enjoy its beauty. Back then, we were still young and thought that the whole world would fall at our feet sooner or later.

Aslan and Nelly's relationship lasted for several years. I could see that he was not her equal and knew about his infidelity. I was sure that someone like Nelly deserved a lot more, but I could not say anything. I preferred to stay out of it. The only way I could help her was to scold my stupid childhood friend again and again for flirting and even worse with other girls. She found out about his cheating without my help. Most likely, she had suspected as much earlier but preferred to turn a blind eye to the doubts and inconsistencies in Aslan's lies. Perhaps she was in love with him and did not want to accept the truth staring her in face. Aslan was upset about their breakup for a long time, refusing to let her go, but Nelly was adamant. She would not share him with someone else and pretend that she did not know what was happening.

Despite their breakup, I continued to visit her. She was working as a school teacher by this time and renting a small room in the apartment of a nasty old woman with an equally nasty dog. Every time I came to the apartment, the dog would bark madly at me, which made me want to not just hit it, but kill it. Then I would find myself on the other side of the door and in Nelly's circle of friends, with Nelly at the very centre radiating light and incredible power. And I knew that I would put up with a thousand vicious dogs for this.

A little later, I started coming to her school and waiting until she finished work. We walked home together and then had tea but nothing else happened. For her, I was simply a "good guy", nothing more.

The New Year celebrations were approaching when I decided to propose to her. The party was to be held at her best friend's house, who had recently gotten married. I thought that I would get down on one knee in the midst of the fun, she would say yes, and her friend would rush to congratulate her, because now they would both be married ladies and we could be family friends. Of course, it did not work out that way. As soon as we entered the house, I kept looking for a way to put my plan into action but could not bring myself to carry it out. People bustled here and there, throwing me off each time. As a result, I clutched the modest box with an equally modest ring in my hand and huddled in an uncomfortable armchair in the corner.

Speaking of the party, it was quite fun. It was the first time I had seen one like it. The parties I attended usually involved nothing but boozing, but this one included contests, games and even people in hilarious costumes based on children's cartoons. I knew that it was all Nelly's idea, it was very much like her.

Then came the fireworks. I hugged Nelly tenderly and that was it. I hurriedly said goodbye and went home. I did not sleep a wink all night, cursing myself for being so indecisive. In the morning, I worked up the courage, ran through what I wanted to say in my head again and went back to her friend's house. Again, my courage deserted me, so that I did not even enter the house and walked home.

My next chance came on Nelly's birthday. Fortunately, it was only two weeks after the new year. I carried the ring around with me all this time, but we were always surrounded by other people and my idea felt completely out of place. But that day was special. I could feel it. We were sitting in quite a small circle of our closest and dearest friends, drinking tea, and having a heart-to-heart conversation. When the doorbell suddenly rang, Nelly stood up and left the room. She was gone for a while. I grew worried and sent her friend Lessie after her, who returned quickly.

"What's going on?" I asked her with a surge of anxiety.

"Oh, it's her ex-boyfriend," Nelly’s friend waved a hand.

"Which one?" I asked, tensing up.

"Otto. She went out with him after dating Aslan."

"That's odd, I never heard about him."

"Hmm, I don't know why she didn't tell you."

"Did they go out for long?"

"Quite a while. He even proposed to her."

"Why didn't she marry him?"

"I think his mother was against it because she's an orphan. Just don't tell anyone!"

My head was buzzing. I imagined this Otto, imagined him standing outside the door with a bunch of flowers, perhaps with a ring, and my dream floating away into someone else's hands. "No way," I thought and went to get Nelly back.

It turned out that she had been sitting in the hallway and stroking the blasted dog, which started barking as soon as it spotted me. Fortunately, the dog's owner appeared quickly at the noise and took the cursed animal away. As I approached Nelly, I noticed tears on her cheeks.

"What happened?" I asked.

"Nothing," she replied, wiping away the tears. "An old friend came to wish me a happy birthday."

"I see. Listen, I've been wanting to ask you for ages, but I couldn't work up the courage. Well, it's now or never! Will you be my wife?"

Nelly laughed.

"What's so funny?" I asked with a stupid smile on my face.

"Nothing. I thought you'd never ask! Have you been carrying the ring around for a long time?"

"Yes."

"So, where's the ring?" she asked playfully.

"Oh, right! I'm an idiot." I reached into the inside pocket of my jacket, pulled out the box and took out the ring.

"It's beautiful."

"Is that a yes?"

"Yes."

I slipped the ring on her finger and gently kissed her on the cheek. This was how my dream came true.

We had a lavish wedding, thanks to my mum. She did her best, even though, for no reason I could comprehend, she disliked Nelly.

We stayed at my parents' house and were given a room. Our life went on quite calmly, apart from the fact that my mother constantly picked on her new daughter-in-law. It was undeserved, I might add. Only now do I realize that there can be rivalry between some mothers and daughters-in-law, but I did not know this at the time and was terribly cross with my mother. Nelly would stay in our room all evening after coming home from work to avoid running into her mother-in-law, but this did not help much. My mother sometimes came into our room without asking and would immediately start complaining. Nelly's patience ran out one day and she went to stay with a friend for a week. I understood that I urgently needed to look for a place to live. I could not think of anything better than returning to Nelly's old room with the old lady and her angry dog. We had been living there for three months when my mother visited us and tearfully begged us to come back. She apologized for all the insults and promised that she would not say another bad word to my wife. Hence, we came back.

A little later, we discovered that Nelly was pregnant. We were over the moon. We had not had any luck for a while and were feeling quite disappointed. We were even considering undergoing some tests, but everything worked out in the end. My second dream was coming true.

My mother also settled down for a while and even gave the best food to the expectant mother. My daughter was born after what felt like an unbearably long time. I remember coming to the hospital that day and falling in love with my daughter as soon as I saw her wrinkled red face. I thought that I had never seen a more beautiful and sweet little creature. It was the natural fruit of our love with Nelly, which was so incredible and unusual. I loved my wife to the point of madness, and she loved me the same way. I became the family she did not have. I was not just a husband to her, but also her father, mother, friend, everything.

Things went well at first after the birth of our daughter. I worked while Nelly stayed home with the baby. She decided to give up work, wishing to dedicate all her time and love to our daughter. In my absence, Nelly was constantly being lectured about how she was doing everything wrong. My mum stuck her nose into everything, and naturally, by the time I came home, the atmosphere in the house was very tense. We still did not have enough money for a down payment on a house, and there was nowhere else to go, so I urged Nelly to be patient for a little longer.

One cold January evening, an old friend of my sister's appeared on our doorstep. It turned out that my mum had invited her. Nelly and I came out to dinner for the sake of decency, although we were not up to it at all. Our daughter was running a high fever, and we could not bring it down. We wanted to have a quiet cup of tea, a short conversation and return to our room. If only we had known that this whole event had completely different goals.

"Eric, did you know that Pauline has been put in charge of a whole department at our plant?" my mother asked.

"No. Congratulations, it's a demanding job," I replied.

"She's also been given a plot to build a house."

I said nothing.

"She's already building a house. By herself! Can you imagine?"

"Right," I continued, still not suspecting anything.

"You know, she has no one to ask for help but she could use a pair of strong hands. Maybe you can come by after work and help her?"

"Yes, Eric," Pauline echoed my mother. "I'm in such a pickle! So much work and I'm on my own. I remember that you are a jack of all trades in these matters!" She smiled coquettishly.

Out of the corner of my eye, I saw Nelly's face turn bright red.

"Why should Eric, instead of going home to his wife and daughter after work, should head to God-knows-who and help with God-knows-what?" Nelly asked icily.

"Well, isn't it obvious?" Mum interrupted. "Pauline is an old friend of the family. She was before you, and she will be after you."

"I see," Nelly said, standing up. "I've had enough of this. Good luck with the construction."

After Nelly left, I stood up from the table sharply and asked my mother, "What do you think you're playing at? Aren't you tired yet?"

"What did I do? You used to be good friends with Pauline, you even wrote letters to her."

"Pauline, you should go. My mother is apparently plotting things behind my back. I'll tell you right now that you should look for someone else. I'm married and I love my wife," I said the last sentence while staring into my mum's eyes. "I love her!"

As I retreated to my room, I could hear my mother making fun of my "I love her," but I did not care anymore. I saw that Nelly was crying when I entered the room. I went over to hug her.

"I'll talk to my boss and ask for his help."

She continued to cry softly.

"Please don't cry or I'll start too. I'm definitely going to sort this out."

"Why does she treat me like this?" Nelly asked, wiping away her tears. "I didn't do anything to her, I didn't say a bad word to her, and I try to be respectful."

"I don't know, sunshine."

Sunshine. How long ago that was. Indeed, I never called Nelly by her name, always sunshine. She was the only one who made me feel warm. Only her eyes illuminated my path.

"Okay," she replied, calming down. "If anything happens, we can return to my former landlady. She hasn't let anyone into the apartment after me."

"We'll see," I laughed. "Let me talk to my boss first."

"Do it tomorrow, please. I don't even know how to get through today."

Before we could calm down, there was a knock on the door. We froze, in no rush to open it.

"I know you're awake," said a voice from the other side.

"Come in," I shouted.

My mother entered the room and immediately stared at Nelly. "What was that out there?" she asked sternly.

"Don't talk to her like that," I stood up for Nelly.

"How am I supposed to talk to her? May I remind you that this is my house!"

"It is," I agreed. "but no one gave you the right to speak in that tone to another person who actually treats you kindly. She's not your daughter."

"Thank God for that. Why did they give her up then? There must have been a reason."

Oh, that was a banned move on my mother's part. She knew how painful this topic was for Nelly.

"She should be happy that she got into such a family," Mum would not stop. "We took her in, gave her shelter."

"You know what?" Nelly suddenly snapped. "I married my husband, not his mother. I won't tolerate this anymore. Thank you for taking me in and thank you for reminding me about this every single day. I just want to remind you that when we left, you were the one who begged us to come back. And yes, I really don't deserve this kind of treatment from you."

"Are you going to let her talk to me like that?" shrieked my mother.

"What's wrong with what she said?"

"If that's the case, then get out of my house. You ungrateful bitch! I took her in without a family, without a tribe. Gave her my only son. The mother-in-law is respected in other families, not like in ours!"

Nelly turned resolutely to the closet and took out her suitcase. I somehow got my mother out of the room and started helping her.

"Lily has a fever," Nelly whispered, stopping her packing.

I understood what she meant. I left the room, went up to my mother and said, "Lily has a fever. We'll leave tomorrow morning."

I was turning to leave when she spun around and hissed, "What do I care? It's her child, let her worry! You've shamed me in front of another person. If that bitch doesn't know how to behave in polite company, then she shouldn't leave the room! It's still unclear whose child it is, I've heard that she had a lot of guys before you."

"If you insult her once more, you'll never see me again!" My fists clenched automatically.

I didn't notice that she was holding a glass of water. In response to my words, she threw the water at me and declared, "Damn you and damn the day you were born!"

I wiped the water off my face and rushed back to my room. As soon as I entered, I said, "We're leaving. She won't let us stay."

Nelly saw the condition I was in and asked reasonably, "What happened out there? Why are you wet?"

"We don't have time to discuss this. We need to leave right now. Otherwise, she'll come back in here, and I don't want you to hear what she might say."

Nelly understood and, going to the crib, touched our daughter's forehead. "She's burning up. Okay, I'll wrap her up nice and warm."

We quickly packed our bags, dressed our daughter and ourselves and left the house without saying goodbye.

The owner of Nelly's former room was not surprised to see us on her doorstep.

"I knew you'd be back," she smiled. "Come in, the room is standing empty."

"Thank you, Mrs. Clarkson. You can't imagine how glad I am. We've had some difficulties. We won't cause any trouble, and we'll pay you on time."

"Oh, I'm not worried about that. But you know, there's no heating in your room. Something happened and I didn't fix it."

We were willing to accept anything to have a roof over our heads. It was a terrible night. Lily was burning up and we could do nothing to help her. Plus, the room was bitterly cold, so we slept in our jackets and under a blanket, but even that did not help. Of course, I sorted out the heating the next day, while Nelly washed and cleaned the dusty room. Lily suddenly improved and life seemed to be getting better. But my mother's words still stung.

Considering that we did not have any savings and had not previously paid for housing, the rent really ate into our budget. My salary alone was no longer enough for us. Nelly saved on everything she possibly could. We started eating less but even that did not help. I had to come up with something urgently. I searched the newspaper ads for a new job or additional earnings, but since we lived in a small town with only one large enterprise, I could not find anything other than the vacancies at this enterprise.

The lack of money caused us to fight more often. Nelly was angry at me for my slowness. She said that out of the two of us, I was the man, and I had to take responsibility for her as promised. But it did not sound like I was doing a good job of it. To avoid the fights and questions about what useful thing I had done today, I began to stay back at work. I did not want to go home. I made up excuses about extra shifts and stuff like that for Nelly. These days, I realize that I was wrong. I should have just approached her and admitted that I could not jump over my head, I could not think of anything better, but for some reason, I behaved differently.

The lie about my "shifts" came to light quickly and unexpectedly, like any other lie. My boss, apparently after receiving a tip off, discovered that instead of going home like everyone else after my shift, I would lock myself in my office and go to bed. He decided to personally intervene in the lives of the young couple and called my wife.

"I'm calling about a sensitive issue," he began. "I've learned that Eric is sleeping at work, and it's been going on for some time. I hate to say this, but if you are having troubles at home, they can always be resolved. Helen and I have been married for over 30 years and plenty of things have happened to us in that time. But I can tell you that there is nothing that can't be solved, except death, of course. If it's something less serious, then you just need to sit down and have a heart-to-heart conversation."

"What are you talking about, Mr. Knight?" Nelly asked in confusion. "Of course, we are experiencing some difficulties, but they are more of a financial nature and do not relate to our relationship. You assigned him the paid shifts yourself, didn't you?"

"You see, we don't have any night shifts."

"What?" Nelly gasped. "No additional shifts to help a young family?"

"Nelly, I think you need to talk to Eric. I probably shouldn't have called, but I just wanted to help. Well, have a nice day. I hope the two of you can figure it out."

Nelly stood with the phone pressed to her ear for a long time. She recalled all the times that Eric came tired from his so-called work, and she took care of him, even though she was exhausted after a day with the baby. It was unfair, completely unfair. Why the lies? Why?

I came home from my "shift" around midnight. I thought that Nelly was already asleep, but the bedside lamp came on as soon as I opened the bedroom door.

"You're not asleep, sunshine?" I asked.

"No, I'm not," she replied icily.

"What happened?" my heart sank with fear.

"What happened is that your boss called me."

"And?"

"And nothing! Turns out that you're not working night shifts at your workplace. Why did you trick me?"

Instead of confessing to everything, I started lying. She saw that I was lying, for she was smart and could sense the lie. Nelly got more and more irate with every word I uttered.

"Just tell me the truth. Aren't you ashamed of lying to me?" she asked. "Your boss called me. Here," she said, reaching for the phone. "The conversation was a couple of hours ago."

"Honestly, we have shifts, sunshine."

The conversation was going the wrong way. She began to raise her voice at me, and for some reason, I did the same. In the end, I got dressed again and left. I told her that I was sick of her and that my life with her had become unbearable. I hurt an innocent person, even though I was at fault. I can admit it now, but back then... I do not know who I was back then.

I could not think of anything better than to go to Aslan's and get drunk. I should have called Nelly the next day, but I knew that I would have to go home, and my night of drinking would not go unnoticed. This would mean another fight.

A couple of days later, I finally showed up on our doorstep. Nelly refused to talk to me and rightly so. I asked for her forgiveness and finally confessed that I had not been working extra shifts and had been too afraid to admit it. I told her that I had learned all this deception and trickery as a child, to avoid being punished by my mother. Nelly felt sorry for me and kind of forgave me but asked me never to do it again.

"I'm not your mum," she said. "We have a new family, we have a daughter, and I don't want her to see such poor behaviour from her father."

After such a serious quarrel, as it seemed to us at the time, I tried to be a decent person. After work, I would collect Lily and go to the park for a while to give Nelly some time to herself. It did her a lot of good. It is true that creativity is born in silence.

One day, when I returned from a walk, I found my wife on the floor with a pair of scissors. Fabric scraps were strewn around everywhere, and she was clearly making something.

"What are you doing?" I asked, barely containing my laughter.

"I'm sewing," she replied, turning around. There was a mischievous twinkle in her eyes.

"What are you making?"

"I'm making clothes for Lily. She's growing so fast that all her old clothes are too small. Also, I saw a girl in the playground wearing the cutest dress! I'll make the same for our Lily. Maybe even better! How about that?"

"That's wonderful, sunshine."

I had no doubt that she would sew the most beautiful dress. I remembered her saying that her late grandmother had taught her to sew. Nelly had loved her dearly, even though she had lost her grandmother early. This kind and positive woman had instilled in my wife the qualities that I admired greatly, namely: perseverance, hard work, faith in the future, love and care.

"Can you feed her? I'll do the machine stitching in the meantime. And then you'll steam it, okay?"

"Of course!" I agreed. I would do anything to keep her as enthusiastic as she was now.

I woke up around 5 am as usual. It was still dark outside, but our room was lit by the soft glow of a lamp. The bed was empty and at first, I wondered where my wife had gone. Rubbing my eyes, I glanced towards the window, where stood the desk that we also used as the dining table. Of course, Nelly was there. Her head was lying on the table and I realized that she was asleep. I got up quietly, went over to her and spotted the gorgeous baby dress with a full skirt hanging on the back of the chair. If I hadn't seen her sewing it, I would have thought that it was from the most expensive and fashionable store.

This dress was followed by another and another and another. Then came two-piece sets, jackets and even fur coats. Funnily enough, they were all made out of Nelly's old clothes. People turned to look at us on the street and all the mothers asked, "Where did you get such a jacket?" or "In which store can I buy such pants?" When strangers found out that Nelly had made these clothes herself, they showered her with compliments and asked for the same for their son or daughter. That was how the idea of the atelier was born. Nelly had thought about it before, back when she was a university student, but she had been a little scared of the scale of the enterprise and had no money for the start-up capital. Not that there was money now, but as time passed, her dream became clearer and more solid. She had assembled a folder full of drawings of clothes and patterns, her brand name was ready, so it was only a question of finances.

She had inherited a few things from her deceased grandparents: a couple of sets of jewellery, some medals, and other knick-knacks. I knew that even in the most difficult times, when Nelly literally had nothing to eat, she did not resort to selling these valuable objects. Now she reluctantly decided to pawn the jewellery. She pressed the rings and earrings to her lips one last time and whispered to them that she would definitely get them back a little later. She kept her word.

The mean and unfriendly neighbour on our landing made the first order. I am sure that Nelly still remembers her. It was the first order back then and Nelly had set a completely ridiculous, symbolic price that barely covered the cost of the materials. She thought she would make our neighbour's granddaughter such a wonderful dress that word of it would spread through the neighbourhood. That is exactly what happened. Orders began to flow in, the price increased, and the neighbour transformed completely, or maybe she had never been mean and we just did not know her very well.

As soon as we had some savings, Nelly rented a room and began working not only full-time, but also overtime. She brought her work home and sometimes sat up until 3 or 4 am. Her hard work paid off and six months later we moved into a spacious apartment that we did not have to share with anyone. Then we bought a new car. I will never forget its smell and bright crimson colour. All my troubles began with the purchase of that car.

Nelly's business was growing. She hired assistants and managed not only an atelier but also a fabric store. She would drive to the big city to purchase materials and did not take me with her since I had to keep an eye on the baby. During one of my wife's absences, my daughter and I were riding around the city and ran into Aslan, my long-forgotten friend, at a bus stop. I could not remember the last time I had spoken to him, and eager to talk to another adult, I invited him to our house.

"Wow, how did you do so well for yourself?!" he said in surprise, entering our stylish and cozy home.

I made a silly joke, but I did not say that it was all Nelly's work.

"And where's my favourite girl?" Aslan asked.

"She's away on a business trip."

He looked disappointed. I knew he was upset that I had ended up with Nelly. Perhaps this was why we had stopped talking.

We sat down to drink and talk about our childhood and got caught up in the reminiscence. Stirred up by the alcohol and the past we shared, we had an unexpected heart-to-heart conversation. He talked about his wife, complaining that he did not love her and would have never married her if she had not gotten pregnant. I talked about the difficulties Nelly and I were having and, for some reason, complained that she was grumpy and short-tempered.

We got really drunk that night. After finishing all the alcohol we had in the house, Aslan suggested that we go out. He had a female friend who lived nearby, and she had a pretty friend.

"You have no idea what minxes they are! They're incredible! Come on, go and get ready. Can I take a shower here?"

Why did I not say no? After making sure that my daughter was asleep, I got dressed and went out into the yard. What was I thinking, leaving my child all alone? I think that nothing bad happened that night only because someone invisible was watching over her.

It was a dark and frosty November night. The roads were not yet covered with snow, only a thin layer of frost. Before getting into the car, it felt like something pulled at my jacket sleeve, as if to stop me, but Aslan convinced me to get behind the wheel. I could not be bad in front of other people, only in front of my family, although the opposite would have been better.

We reached our destination without incident. We were surrounded by a gaggle of young women who turned out to be quite wild. Aslan quickly disappeared with one of them, while I sat in an armchair and quietly drank my whiskey. I was not going to follow Aslan's example, because I loved my wife and could not imagine cheating on her. The young woman clearly had other plans in mind. She flirted with me shamelessly until I got tired of her. I stood up abruptly and headed for the door, cursing Aslan for some reason.

The journey home made me happy but, suddenly, my brain began to shut down. I still do not remember how I got into the accident. I suspect that I simply fell asleep. I remember weaving from side to side as I foolishly turned the steering wheel. I failed to get the car under control and drove into a tree. I was not hurt at all, but our brand-new car was wrecked. The windows were smashed, a wheel flew off, and the bonnet was crumpled. To add insult to injury, the tree I drove into snapped and collapsed onto the roof.

I panicked. My heart was pounding. I instantly sobered up and imagined how tomorrow, that is to say, today, Nelly would return, and I would lie and dodge again. I knew for sure that I could not remain innocent in this situation.

When I got home, I started frantically calling car repair shops. I completely forgot about our daughter and did not even check if she was breathing. Another sign of how worthless I was.

When I got through to the only working panel beater, I explained my problem and, hearing that the repairs would not be so expensive, calmed down and went to bed.

I woke up to someone hitting me painfully in the shoulder. My daughter was crying in the background. My head was buzzing and I struggled to understand what was going on around me. When I finally opened my eyes, I saw Nelly. She was not simply yelling at me but actually screaming. My daughter was sitting in the cot, red from crying.

"How could you?" Nelly's words reached me.

"What's the matter, sunshine?"

"How dare you call me sunshine! What have you done? Why is our girl sitting in her cot, hungry and dirty? I could hear her crying from the street!"

"I fell asleep," I tried to explain.

"Did you crash our car in your sleep? You're not a person, you're a monster! I work so hard to earn this money! I sit day and night over the garments so that we have everything, but you? You just take and destroy everything! I hate you."

"I don't destroy," I replied, getting up and wondering how she knew about the car. "Did you see the car?"

"See it? Haha," she gave a jittery laugh. "I saw it. Where you dumped it. The neighbours also told me that the police came to our house. Where were you?"

"I was home."

"I'll ask again, where were you? Why is there a tree on the roof of our car? And why is the car that I worked so hard to buy smashed to pieces?"

"Lily developed a fever so I went to the pharmacy."

"Don't lie to me!" she shouted. "Don't you dare lie to me!"

"I'm not lying."

"We have fever-reducing drugs," she continued, trying to get me to admit the truth.

"I didn't find any."

"We have two whole bottles for babies. They're standing in the most obvious place. You knew this. Where were you?"

I was frantically running through excuses in my head, and I think Nelly saw it.

"Are we going to keep playing these games? Again?" she asked wearily.

"I had to drive Aslan on some errands."

"Where was Lily during this time?"

"Home," I replied, bowing my head.

"You left our young child alone at home?"

"Yes. She was asleep."

"What if someone had broken into our house? Do you have a spare child?"

"No. I didn't want to go but he asked me."

"So, you're willing to sacrifice your family for the sake of a stranger?"

"Well, nothing happened."

"Nothing happened?"

"Well, it happened but not with Lily."

"You know what? Go somewhere else! To Aslan, to your mother, to anyone. Leave."

"Nelly, please..."

"No, don't 'Nelly' me. I'm not even talking about the car or the fact that you're lying to me again! You left our only child at home alone! If you think that's okay, then you don't belong in this home. Leave."

"Please," I protested weakly. I could see that she was adamant, and my only fear was that she would leave me.

"Get out," she repeated and left the room with our child.

I did not take my things with me that day, hoping to return in the evening. But when I arrived, no one opened the door. I grew even more frightened. I blamed myself for stopping when I saw Aslan. I imagined what would have happened if I had not met him at all. Yet I did not blame myself, even though I simply could have not gone with him!

I fell asleep on the house steps. That was how I spent my night. The next morning, Nelly opened the door and let me in.

"Sit down," she told me as I entered the living room. "Do you understand the consequences and what could have happened because you were so irresponsible?"

"I understand."

"You've seen how hard I have to work. Didn't you?"

"Yes."

"Do you understand how much I'll have to work now to pay for these car repairs?"

"I understand. I'll help you with everything. I'll spend the nights with you at the atelier."

"Do you think this is so easy to fix? We'll spend a month or more and everything will be fine? This is my life! My work. Do you understand or not? This was such a slap in the face!"

"I'll never drive again. I swear on our daughter's heart."

"Don't ever swear on her heart."

So, I remained in the house. The car was taken to the panel beater, but it is a pity that the same could not be done to our relationship. Nelly did not come near me for a long time and talked to me only when necessary. But I was grateful even for that.

As time passed, peace returned to our home. I tried to be as co-operative as possible with my wife and daughter. This behaviour bore fruit and Nelly began to warm up to me again. Of course, I did not do it on purpose. I genuinely wanted to be back in her good books and for everything to be the same as before. I did not see Aslan again and did not answer his calls.

When our daughter turned two, we found out that we were going to have another child. I was overjoyed, but Nelly did not seem very happy. She was afraid to take time out of her business, aware that the pregnancy would have a negative effect on her health and function.

The entire nine months of her pregnancy were like hell. She could barely move, breathed heavily and slept a lot. She envied, without bitterness, other women for whom this magical time was truly magical.

My wife and I had a big fight not long before the baby was due, and it all started because of a pack of cigarettes.

It was a windy day, and Nelly was resting on the porch, trying to get some oxygen. The child was pressing on her ribs and lungs, indeed, on all her organs. She felt so rotten that she sometimes thought that she would suffocate. Nelly was lying peacefully on the bench when a sharp gust of wind blew a pack of cigarettes off the porch. It took her a moment to understand what it was. She struggled to her feet and slowly approached the object. Glancing up, she immediately figured out when the packet had been hidden and whom it belonged to. Her face went crimson. The fact is that I had quit smoking when our daughter was born, but all this time, I continued to occasionally smoke in secret. Nelly would mention that I smelled like cigarettes, but I always replied that other people smoked at work, and I had simply stood next to them. I do not know why I did not tell her that I had started smoking again since she had not forbidden it.

When she entered the house, she came up to me with dragging steps and asked, "Whose is this?"

"What?" I tried to play the idiot.

"You know what. Have you started smoking?"

Then I started playing the 'you smoke/you don't smoke, you're lying/you're not lying' game. When Nelly could not stand it, she grabbed something heavy from the table and threw it at me. I got angry, forgetting that I was the reason for this display of emotion (she had run out of reasonable arguments) and pushed her hard onto the couch. She hit her coccyx on Lily's toy lying on the couch and began to cry bitterly. I will never forget her face, twisted with pain and resentment. Even now, so many years later, it hurts me to think about it. I begged her forgiveness and made promises again. It was a well-trodden path. Sooner or later, my wife forgave me, even though she should not have. I took advantage of her weakness, I used the fact that, being an orphan, she had married me forever, in sickness and in health. I knew that family came first for her, even ahead of herself, so I was sure that she would never leave me.

When our son was born, something broke in Nelly. The birth was difficult and lasted almost two days. As a result, she left the hospital feeling even worse than before. I hoped that she would feel better with time and being back home, but this was not the case. My wife lay in bed for days on end, unable to not only do things around the house, but even get up.

Her condition affected the business as well. It started to falter and I had to quite my job so I could keep an eye on it. I was pretty good at first. Feeling terribly important, I drove to the atelier (our car had been completely repaired by that time), supervised the seamstresses and checked the income and expenses at the fabric store. I did not even notice when and where I started making mistakes. First, when talking to the employees and overstepping boundaries, and then when adding up the numbers. I have never been very good at maths, as well as in other aspects, so the shop and the studio began to operate at a loss. When Nelly asked for the accounting books, I fudged the numbers so she could not understand where, and most importantly by whom, the mistake was made. We had another huge fight, arguing about who was right and who was wrong. I tried to evade responsibility in any way I could, shifting the blame onto the seamstresses. A large investigation took place at work and Nelly finally discovered the problem – I had been making incorrect calculations to pay for the fabric. They sent me a smaller amount and I paid as if for a large one. Nelly was ashamed to show her face before the staff, who were openly laughing at her.

Still weak, she had to go to work and correct my mistakes herself. I stayed home to keep an eye on the kids. I was not good at this either. I would put them and their toys in the same cot and have a nap. One day, Nelly came home earlier than usual and found me asleep. Our son and daughter were sitting in the cot and tearing something up. When Nelly came closer, she saw that they were ripping up money. It turned out that while I was asleep, our daughter would climb out of the cot and wander around the house. She had somehow gotten into the closet and, rummaging through there, found our small savings stash. The kind girl had brought the find to her brother and, unaware of its value, they ruthlessly, almost fiercely, proceeded to destroy it. I was able to exchange only a couple of banknotes out of the whole wad, while the rest could not be salvaged. Unfortunately, I can no longer remember how I managed to beg forgiveness that time, not that it matters anymore.

Our children were growing, we sent them to kindergarten, and life was more or less peaceful. Nelly worked hard while I acted as her driver. I never got another job, which I did not regret in the slightest. I would be an ordinary worker there, while here, I was sort of the boss. I did not realize back then that I was not the boss, only the boss' husband. For some reason, I considered myself part of my wife's business, even though I had contributed nothing to it.

For me, the happiest memories of that time were our weekends. A fuzzy pine forest lay 10 minutes away from town and no more than a 15-minute drive from our house. We always loved going there. They say that bears used to live in the area but then disappeared. Perhaps they had found a better forest. They left behind toppled trees and their smaller brethren, the hares and the moose, which we came across quite often. Every time we rolled along the winding wooded path, I imagined a huge, powerful creature with antlers rushing at our car and my heart would skip a beat. Luckily, they never charged at us but passed peacefully by. They were probably more afraid of us that we were of them.

As we made our way deeper into the forest, we would notice the light fading, for the tall pines with their mighty boughs were all tangled together. However, a little while later we would reach a sunlit glade with the glitter of a lake hidden inside the forest. I will never forget that smell of summer freshness and pine resin.

We would always have a picnic under the same tree. After laying a blanket out on the sand strewn with pine needles, we left the children to play while we went swimming. I swung Nelly around in my arms and she laughed. The sunlight turned her brown eyes amber and they seemed to glow with gold. Was that not happiness?

Then we ran back to the children and sat down to eat whatever we had brought from home. I remember that we always brought along watermelon on such trips, and one day, we saw an ant dragging a rather impressive piece of it. The children surrounded it and I told them that an ant could carry a load 20 times its weight. I would give anything to return to my joy hidden beyond the forest. My God, why was I such a fool?

Lily was five when Nelly got into a car accident. She went to collect a large shipment of goods that winter, which she had to do personally. It was a long drive to the city of N, about 500 miles. She did not take me with her and hired a proper driver with experience.

I found out that there had been an accident when the police came to my house. I could not understand from their words whether she was alive or not. They had not taken her to the city but left her at some hospital between our town and N. Leaving the children with my mother, whom I was forced to turn to, I raced off to see Nelly. I hitchhiked the whole way and stormed into the hospital, demanding to be taken to my wife. The staff at the hospital, even though it was in a backwater town, were sensible and did not scold me for inappropriate behaviour.

When I entered the room, I saw Nelly. She was unconscious and covered in tubes. I stroked her hand and begged her to come back to me. She did not seem to hear me.

A little later, I found out that her spine was broken and her spleen was ruptured. The doctors said that it was a miracle that she had survived. The same could not be said about the driver, who was dead. I did not feel sorry for him. I knew that the accident was his fault. He tried to overtake at high speed, at a spot where overtaking was prohibited, and had driven into a truck going the other way. Nelly had miraculously survived after such a collision and, besides, there were no airbags in our car. Nowadays, they are in every car, although not everyone survives even with them.

As soon as Nelly felt a little better, I transported her back to our town. It was possible to live without a spleen, but no one could guarantee that her spine would recover. The doctors tried to be positive, but we could see that even they did not know how things would turn out. This was how Nelly became bedbound.

My father and I made her a hard bed out of planks because someone told us that hard surfaces helped with recovery. It was uncomfortable for Nelly to not only sleep on it, but even to lie on it. She was in constant pain and had little faith that she would recover, although she was `usually an optimist. I saw that she was fading away. Only our children kept her going during that time. They would tip-toe up to her bed and say, "Get well soon, Mummy," kissing her cold hands. Tears of pity would roll down Nelly's cheeks, but pity for them, not for herself.

My mother started helping us around the house. Nelly did not mind, she was actually grateful. My mother took pity on Nelly after the accident and warmed up to her. She understood what kind of person Nelly was and who had kept our family going for all these years. I now had more time to myself. Naturally, this had a negative effect on my behaviour.

After about six months, I got sick of feeling sorry for my wife, sick of listening to her complain about her pain, and I could not think of anything better than staying back at "work". In reality, I was spending time with my hopeless friend Aslan again. I started drinking with him regularly and did not notice when I had become reliant on alcohol. I could not imagine that a young man like me could become an alcoholic. I have been sober for many years but, unfortunately, no one cares about that anymore.

It turned out that drinking cost a lot of money, and I could not get it anywhere except from the cash register. So I started stealing. Stealing from my own family and employees. The hole I was digging for myself got deeper and deeper every day. Staff started quitting the atelier and it had to close. I sold all the equipment, but at least I brought the money home, presenting it as the atelier's profits. I had to close the fabric stores too. Before I knew it, only two remained out of the several that we owned. I still did not have enough money, so I started borrowing and soon owed half the town. Of course, Nelly found out about it. I stupidly borrowed money from her best friend and, knowing about Nelly's condition, she did not ask for it back for a long time. In the end, she decided to call us when she and her husband had an emergency. It was then that Nelly found out that Lessie had lent us a large sum of money, which they had been saving up for a car. Her friend was left without money, which had never reached Nelly. Another scandal, me running away from home and slamming doors. Our children witnessed these horrible scenes. I think they already understood that this was not normal. The things they saw! I do not want to remember.

The last straw came when gangsters turned up at our house because I owed them money too. Idiotically, I had borrowed money from them with interest and never paid them back, thinking that the situation would somehow resolve itself. Nelly, struggling to walk, took them outside so that the children would not be present.

I know that the gangsters felt sorry for her, but they could not write off the debt nor the insane interest. Nelly returned home in tears, stroking the walls of her house.

"Who were these people?" my mother asked.

"Gangsters."

"Oh, my God! What did they want?"

"Eric borrowed a large sum of money from them."

"Ha, I told you that this business of yours would be nothing but trouble. See what happened?"

"What does my business have to do with it?" Nelly glared at her mother-in-law. "My business was booming and making money. My business paid for this house and the car that Eric crashed."

"Then where is this debt from?"

"Oh, you should ask Eric that question. By the way, we need to put the house up for sale."

"What?" My mum clutched at her chest and dropped to the floor.

"The house is security for the loan. The interest is skyrocketing for every day of his debt."

"No, no, no!" My mum screamed.

"Yes."

A serious conversation awaited me when I got home. Nelly did not shout or make a scene but calmly questioned me about the reasons for these circumstances. I had to tell her everything or almost everything. I did not say that I needed the money for partying with Aslan. I claimed that I had made a mistake in the accounts again or something like that.

"Do you realise that you have put our children's lives in danger?"

I nodded.

"They're innocent! My children, our children."

"I understand, sunshine. Forgive me."

"I have no more forgiveness left. I'm tired. After we sell the house and pay off your debts, we will file for divorce."

"Please, no."

"This is not up for discussion."

I could see that Nelly meant it. I knew that she made decisions quickly and there would be no way back to her heart.

It did not take long to find buyers for the house. Nelly did not cry as she descended the stairs for the last time, which she had once painted with her own hands. I do not know what was in her heart, she was probably in pain, but there was no room for pain because she had to think about the children and their future.

With the money left over from the sale of the house, Nelly rented an apartment, hired a nanny for the children and focused on her health. Rehabilitation and, most likely, the harsh living conditions, forced her to recover faster. After all, she was on her own again, an orphan. She no longer trusted me or considered me her family. She also restricted my contact with the children, believing me to be a bad influence on them. It was true. They had already seen enough of my disgusting behaviour. Even though she did not want to keep in touch, I came to her building every day to sit on a bench and wait for her or the children to pass by. She did not stop me when she saw me but would keep walking. If the children were with her, she would let them spend some time with me. The children felt sorry for me, unaware that their "dear daddy" was responsible for their current living conditions. They cried and asked Nelly to take me back after such meetings. She was adamant.

A year went by. Nelly could not restore the atelier nor save the fabric stores. The damage I had done was too great. She went back to working at a school, now as a teacher's assistant, which she was grateful for at this stage. Her health was still fragile so she could not work full-time.

I did odd jobs and lived with my mother. I still could not believe that I had lost my family, so I continued turning up and tugging on my children's heartstrings. Only now do I realize that I was saving my family not for them, but for myself, for my own selfishness. I should have left them alone, because I knew what kind of person I was, but I continued to torment them, making their hearts and souls bleed with pity for me. As a result, I was allowed back into the family.

All her friends and even strangers tried to persuade Nelly against it, but she did not listen to anyone and decided to give me yet another chance. Her mistake was believing in me again.

As we strolled along the only embankment, I could see people turning to look at me. It was a small town and everyone knew how I had messed up. I felt uncomfortable. Having decided to put an end to all this and my past life, I convinced Nelly to move to another city. To the capital. I imagined new opportunities and a happy new life. I was always good at telling stories and persuaded her quite quickly. My closing argument was the gangsters and the possibility that they might appear at our door again.

On a rainy September day, we loaded our things into Nelly's car and set off. My daughter was crying, her face pressed up against the back window. She did not want to leave this beloved and familiar place. I still remember her frowning and distraught face. Poor child.

Not everyone liked the new city. The conditions we found ourselves in were very different to what I had previously described. Things were not good with housing or with work. Although it was a big city, the work situation was terrible. There were no available positions and nowhere to go. Nelly did not despair, though, and kept going to interviews every day and thinking about what we should do next. Her enthusiasm and faith in a better future inspired us all.

The only positive in this move was that Nelly managed to get the children into a very good school, in her opinion, although the children did not like it. They were always reminiscing about their old school and asking to go back there.

Our meagre savings ran out quickly and we urgently needed an income. I got a job at a factory, but my salary was not even enough to cover the rent of our horrid apartment. My God, I could not stand that squalid apartment! An old sofa, terrible wallpaper, the cold and heavy darkness. That autumn is forever etched in my memory. I remember the feeling of hopelessness and the dank cold that sank into my very bones.

By winter, Nelly had finally adjusted to the new reality and was somehow full of new ideas. She wanted to earn money, she wanted a beautiful new house, better than the old one. "Everything's going to be all right," she kept saying. She came up with a new business idea and did not waste any time before putting it into practice. Since Nelly was a good teacher, she made educational flashcards that were easy for children to understand. It did not require much money to launch the product given that she printed the cards, cut them up and put everything into the magical learning boxes herself. It really was a great idea, and I was proud of her once again. Her boxes contained not only flashcards, but also notebooks, pens and even diagrams with examples. It was a proper, full study set for young students. This was how money appeared in our family again. We began to climb out of the hole we had found ourselves in and even started saving for a place. Nelly began travelling with her product to neighbouring cities and was invited to education conferences. Meanwhile, I stayed with the children and fell back into what I had run away from. When I came home from the job I hated, I would open a bottle and sit down in front of the TV. My mood improved with every gulp, and I would start playing and joking around with the kids. The ritual would be repeated the next day. By the time Nelly returned, I would clean the entire apartment, removing even the slightest hint of mischief.

"Why don't you have any money left?" she would ask me every time.

"We spent it. We went to the grocery store, to the park."

When she opened the refrigerator, she would find it empty and give me a hard stare.

"I was eating, and I took a lot to work."

"Are you at it again?"

"No, no, sunshine. Absolutely not. I will never betray your trust again," I lied.

Before I knew it, I stopped enjoying spending time with her. I survived from one of her trips to the next. I preferred it when she was not home, because I could then drink in peace. My drinking affected not only my relationship with my wife but also my job. I was fired when they realised that I was a drinker. Well, I also stole some stuff from the warehouse. That would be more honest.

Nelly had almost saved up for an apartment when her business abruptly collapsed. A larger company had spotted her project, which was unusual at the time, and decided to simply steal it. They slightly modified Nelly's magic boxes and launched the product using all the mass media. Memorable ads were playing on TV and bright new packages stood in the very centre of every shop, even in small grocery stores. Nellie cried like a child, with big, bitter tears.

She tried to fight, contacted the authorities and the courts, but all in vain. They tried to convince her that this was not theft, but a completely different product, just similar. That was how her business ended and with it, the money in our family. Nelly fell ill after these events. It seemed to be depression, and it was only much later that we found out that she had a tumour. How many awful things could happen during our time in the city of N?! You would think that none of this is true. Surely people could not live in such a nightmare for years? I would not have believed it either if I had not faced it myself.

Here we were again, moving from one cheap place to the next, the children and all of us suffering from the frequent moves. We were burning through the apartment money because I barely earned anything. Moreover, even though my wife was ill, I did not rush home but stayed back with my friends to drink after work. She knew that I was drinking, but she did not say anything. She had no strength left for it and had withdrawn into herself. Did I want to help her back then? I do not think so. I have no idea where this callousness came from. I did not see anyone but myself or think of anything beyond the next drink. Although, to be honest, it is easy to blame everything on alcoholism, using it to hide my cruelty and dishonesty.

It was May when my father called me at work and told me that my mother was dying. I remember that I started crying. She had fought cancer for many years and my sister had supported her. As always, I remained on the sidelines. I provided neither financial nor emotional support. She knew about my misbehaviour and worried about me. Perhaps worrying about me had a negative effect on her health.

When I got home, I gathered the children and drove to our hometown. Mum was delirious when I entered the room. She kept repeating the same phrase, "go away, go away," and I could not tell if she was saying it to me or to death. She passed away two days later without regaining consciousness. I remember her stony, purplish yellow face. I sobbed over her grave. Funny how the people around me said lots of the good things about her, and that the world had lost a wonderful person. I could only snort, remembering how my mother had cursed me left, right and centre. Often without cause, by the way. I wondered if these people would still think well of her if they knew what I did.

Why is it that when a person dies, no one speaks the truth about them? I am sure that when I die, Nelly will not stand there lying over my grave. If she does come to say goodbye to me (of course, she will not come), she will probably say, "He destroyed my life more than once. Whatever I built, he broke. I would build again, and he would break it again. It wasn't just my life and the children's lives that were broken, but also myself. I was fortunate enough to be born strong, fortunate to withstand these blows of fate, but what if I wasn't? My children would have grown up in other people's families while I lay in the cold ground. I guess I understand now why his mother wanted to get rid of him. Maybe she sensed something? It's a bad thing to say, of course, but this man really was a monster. Destruction was in his blood, and maybe he didn't want to, but he did it. I feel sorry for myself, sorry for the 14 long years we lived together, which did not lead to anything good. I don't know why all this befell me, but there must have been a reason. Can I ever forgive you? I don't know, but I promise to try. If only for the sake of my soul, since it's too late to save yours."

Stupid, of course. She will not say anything, but maybe she will think about me? A long time ago, my grandmother told me a legend that all souls, who were close on Earth, meet later in heaven. She said, "We are all from the same basket. We love each other up there and we meet again in this world." It seems to me that Nelly will no longer want to be in the same basket with me, neither here nor there, nor anywhere else.

We drove back to N. after the funeral. Nelly was not home when we returned to our old, dilapidated house. The children grew very worried, yet I reassured them that Mum would be back soon. But she did not come back that day or the next. A couple of days later, I learned from a neighbour that Nelly had been urgently taken to hospital. The same neighbour had found her unconscious on the lawn in front of the house.

When I found out which hospital she had been taken to, I went to visit her. They would not let me see her because she was still very weak. She had developed appendicitis in our absence, and the doctors also found a tumour during surgery. She had to undergo two operations, suffering a lot, but she was getting better. I knew she would pull through. That is exactly what happened.

She returned home a month later. The refrigerator was empty once again and there was no money to be found. The children were hungry.

"Where's Dad?" she asked the children.

"He hasn't been home in several days."

"What?" she asked incredulously.

"I don't know."

Nelly suspected the worst and rushed to the hiding place where she kept the remaining money. Naturally, it was empty. She was too tired to cry about it. Clutching the napkin that had once held her savings to her chest, she thought feverishly about how her future. I think the decision to break up with me once and for all had come to her a long time ago, she just did not have the energy to separate. She was too busy trying to survive. Now that she had recovered, she was herself once more and could make decisions.

I came home drunk like always. I threw my shoes in a corner and was about to collapse on the sofa when I saw that it was occupied. It took me a moment to recognize Nelly.

"Have you been discharged?" I said in surprise.

"As you can see."

"Can you move over? I want to lie down too."

In reply, she jumped up from the sofa and dragged me to the kitchen by the sleeve.

"First of all, shut your mouth, you'll wake up the kids, and second, don't you dare talk to me! I don't want to hear you or see you. Take a blanket and lie down in the kitchen. I want you gone from this house in the morning. Do you hear me?"

Her response made me very angry. I was drunk and my mind was fuzzy, so I started being openly rude to her and putting her back in her place.

"If you speak to me like that one more time," I hissed slowly and ominously. "I'll kill you on the spot!"

"You? Kill me? Don't you dare talk to me like that, you thief and jerk! How dare you steal money from your own children! How dare you leave them alone in this house! Let me remind you that we don't live in a safe neighbourhood and anything could have happened to them! You're a heartless bastard. You're not a human being. I don't want to see you here in the morning."

One thing led to another, and we got into a row. It felt like she was humiliating me, although she was simply stating the facts, while I was openly humiliating her. I had done it before to break her. The things I said to her! I knew the most hurtful things to say. She certainly did not deserve this.

"I'll get married again, and the children and I will have a good life. No one will drag me to the bottom, and no one will get in my way!" I remember her words.

"Who would want you?" I laughed. "Have you seen yourself? Old (she was only 35 at that time), flabby, and with a brood of children? Nobody!"

"Who? Plenty of men would!" she argued with me. "I know who I am! I'm a good person and a good mother. I've lived my life in such a way that no one could say a bad word about me! How have you lived your life? Always wriggling out of things like a snake, always tricking, lying, avoiding responsibility. You already owe everyone you know in this city!"

I do not remember exactly what she said that made me snap and hit her. Most likely, she regretted not marrying her ex again. It was not a strong blow, more of a slap on the face. The fact remained that I had not only used emotional violence for years but had progressed to physical violence. I forgot in that moment that Nelly was not a timid person. She grabbed a metal kettle from the table and smacked me with it in reply. She hit me on my head and back, striking me so fiercely that I could not answer in kind. I do not know where this tiny woman found the strength, but she pushed me out of the house and slammed the door in my face.

I tried to force my way back into the house for a long time, I do not know why. I hope that it was not to hit her again, but neither the door nor my wife gave in. I spent the night on the porch.

The next morning, I went to work and was summoned by my boss. As it turned out, he was sick of putting up with me. He put a piece of paper and a pen in front of me and asked me to write a letter of resignation and not come to work again. Somehow, I was not upset at all. The decision had been brewing inside me for a long time, but I had not been able to put it into action. Perhaps my conscience, or the remnants of it, would not let me. As I signed the resignation letter, I knew exactly what I was going to do and where I was going to live. Home, home! Back to the people who knew me, the familiar suburbs, friends and everything else. All that remained was to collect my things from Nelly.

I heard yelling before I reached the house. Boxes were flying out the front door, and I was about to pick up my pace when I saw the landlady. She was the one shouting and throwing things.

"I want you out today!" she screamed. "You promised to pay but you never did! I don't care about your health! I have children to feed too!"

I saw Nelly following the landlady out of the house and trying to calmly explain something, to negotiate. Given that the woman's tone did not soften in any way, Nelly's approach was not working. I could see that Nelly was struggling with the conversation. I could see her trying as hard she could to buy a couple of days to pack our things. The landlady did not listen and, ignoring her tenant, stubbornly repeated, "get out right now, right now." She got into the car, stepped on the gas and drove off. That was when Nelly saw me. I will never forget her look of hatred and resentment.

When I reached the lawn, I gathered the things the landlady had tossed out and entered the house with them. The children were sitting in silence on the couch. Our daughter was calm, while our son was crying softly. Was my heart crushed with pity for him in that moment?

Nelly sat in the kitchen, smoking and staring blankly at the wall. She did not even turn around when I came in. "Did you bring the stolen money?" she said in a flat voice.

"No," I whispered.

"She'll be back in two hours. We need to be gone by then. Do you have any idea where we should go?"

"No."

"Why did you come?"

"To get my things."

"Mm-hmm. Are you going take the children's things too?"

"No, just mine."

"Do you have somewhere to go?"

"I decided to go back."

"What about us?"

"You can come too."

"What about the school? What about the loan sharks who pose a danger to us?" she sneered.

"We could find a school there, I guess." I had not thought about it at all.

She glared at me. It was hard for me to bear her gaze, so I looked away.

"You weren't planning to take us," she concluded. "You were going to go by yourself. We're supposed to manage on our own. Interesting, huh, that the children are ours, but I'm the only one taking any responsibility for them. Do you think that's fair?"

"No."

"Pack your things. I have nothing more to say to you."

"Forgive me."

"Yes, yes. I've heard that a million times. If you could just put a "Forgive me" plaster on a life you've ruined and heal it all, wouldn't that be great? But it doesn't work that way. Your apologies don't make me feel any better. I wanted to have a family with you. I tried so hard... Why do you treat me like this? I haven't caused you any harm, yet you treat me worse than any enemy. And now, having robbed us, you come for your things, saving yourself – not us, but yourself!"

The tirade could have gone on and on, she had plenty to say after all these years, but she fell silent.

I left the room and quickly packed my things. I felt like scum but there was nothing I could do. I really was just saving myself. I wanted to get away as soon as possible and forget about everything and everyone. I cried and begged for forgiveness when saying goodbye to the children. My son was sobbing, unable to believe that I was leaving. My daughter held herself together. She would not look at me, and I could feel that she hated me as much as her mother did. Everything inside her screamed that I was a traitor. I left quickly, without looking back.

I hitched rides home since I did not have enough money to buy a bus ticket or even a pack of cigarettes. The trip took 12 hours, but I did not care. I just wanted to get home as soon as possible.

Once back at my family house, I collapsed on the bed and fell into a deep sleep. I slept for two days. When I woke up, pain shot through me and my heart felt like it was bleeding. My behaviour towards my family bothered me. As I sat down to eat hot soup, I wondered if my children had eaten. I tried to drown out the question as best I could.

I went to see my friends. My old father gave me some money, so I knew that I did not need to worry for the next little while.

I drank incessantly to the point that I did not reach home and slept on park benches. Was I ashamed? Not at all. Five months passed this way. It was June when my children appeared on the steps of my father's house. At first, I thought that I was imagining things.

"What are you doing here?" I asked.

"We came to stay with you for the summer," my daughter replied coldly.

"Where's Mum?"

"She stayed back in N."

"Have you found a place to live?"

"Yes, yes. Are you going to invite us in or are we just going to stand here in the doorway?"

"Of course, come on in. I was asleep and thought that this is a dream. It's so unexpected."

"Yes, yes."

"Are you hungry? How did you get here?"

"On the bus," the son replied. He was glad to see me, I could feel it. I hugged him and he hugged me back. I will never forget the warmth radiating from his little body.

I hastily prepared something and began to ask them about their lives. My son answered willingly, but my daughter kept kicking him under the table, ordering him to be silent. I understood her protest.

For the first couple of days that the children lived with me, I stayed away from alcohol, but since when were my children a deterrent? Not for me. I continued my binges, completely forgetting about their presence. It is sad that they saw me lying in a stupor, sad that I did not spend that summer with them. Perhaps if I had cleaned up my act, I could have shown them that I was someone to be trusted, that I could be relied on. I often think back to that time. If I could go back, I would have stopped drinking, gotten a job and sent all the money to the kids. I would have taken them to my place for the school holidays, taken them to the park and for rides on the carousel. I would now have a life with children and grandchildren, instead of a miserable and lonely existence, where one day is the same as the next. Oh, if only I could go back and fix even a single mistake!

When their school holidays were coming to an end, Nelly came to pick them up. I was smoking at the entrance when a silver car, not new but well-maintained, pulled up. After parking, a young and beautiful woman got out of the car. I was so bewildered that it took me a moment to recognise my "old, unwanted wife".

"Hello," she said.

"Hello," I choked out. I was afraid to look at her. Afraid I was going to cry.

"Are the kids at home?"

"No, they went to the river."

"Okay, I'll wait."

"Will you come in?"

"No, thanks. I'll wait outside." She took a cigarette out of her purse and I offered her a light. As I held the lighter up to her face, I glanced into her amber eyes. How beautiful she was!

"Well, how are you?" she asked matter-of-factly.

"Yeah, all right. Probably not as good as you. Have you lost weight?"

"Yes. I've been busy, as you can imagine. No one was there to serve me bowls of soup. I don't have a home or a dad."

"I'm sorry," I began.

"Oh, stop it. *I'm sorry, I'm sorry*. We're past that."

"Have you found a job?" I asked quietly.

"Yes, but I didn't look for it, I went and created it myself. As always."

"I'm very happy for you. Which field are you working in?"

"Landscape design. It required minimal investment."

"Did you hire workers?"

"I'm the only worker so far."

"Don't you have to carry rocks and stuff like that?"

"Yes, that's why I lost weight. It's heavy physical labour."

"Maybe I could help you?"

"You've helped me enough! You've helped so much that I don't even know how to describe it in one word." Her tone was mild, but this hurt me the most. It meant only one thing, that she no longer felt anything for me, neither love nor hate. Nothing.

For some reason, the children returned quickly this time and interrupted our conversation with shouts of "Mum!". There was so much I wanted to tell her, even though she had heard it all before, but I did not get a chance.

The children packed their things and rushed outside to get into the car. I hugged my son goodbye and watched as the car drove away. It contained the old life that I had lost forever.

I drank and drank as they years passed. I was hardly ever home, and every time the phone rang, I did not answer. I was unable to. It was my son calling, for there was no one else. I am sure it hurt him that I did not answer or call back. In the rare moments when I was conscious and wanted to talk to him myself, he was either already asleep or at school. After a while, the calls stopped. I was almost completely alone. My friends, or rather my drinking buddies, were dying one by one due to heart or liver disease. It would scare me for a day, yet I would continue the very next day.

I became genuinely alarmed when I landed in hospital due to a heart attack. There I learned that my liver was severely enlarged and required long-term treatment. That was how I finally gave up alcohol. The longer I stayed sober, the more I was haunted by the mistakes of my past. My soul suffered and burned.

I forgot to mention another sin of mine. Living with my father, I got him addicted to alcohol too. It started slowly and quietly with just a couple of drinks. I did not even notice when my father increased the dose, which was dangerous at his age. One day, he suddenly had a stroke after drinking. He was rushed to hospital and somehow got back on his feet. Well, Ariadne got him back on his feet. She treated him for a long time and saved him. I do not know if I took it seriously. Probably not, since I let him drink again.

One day, I suggested that my father and I have a drink in Ariadne's absence. I was out of sorts and did not think about the fact that he should not have any alcohol. We drank too much, and I do not even remember falling asleep. When I woke up, the house was suspiciously quiet. I washed my face, took a shower and went to my father's room. It was empty. I called his name, but he did not answer. When I entered the kitchen, I saw his feet. He was lying on the floor, and it took me a while to realise that he was dead.

"Hey, Dad, get up!" I said, laughing.

I gently touched his feet, which were already icy cold. I turned him onto his back and saw his pale face. I started calling him, performing CPR, but to no avail. Apparently, he had died in the night while I was sleeping. This was how my other parent died. I was left all alone.

Returning to my story after my heart attack: I finally tried to take control of my life after I was discharged from hospital. I joined Alcoholics Anonymous, and these guys helped me a lot. During the day, I seemed like a normal person. I went to work, then to an AA meeting, but as soon as I was left alone with my thoughts, they would torment me, eating away at me from the inside. Perhaps the reason for my binges were these thoughts, which had tormented me before. Was that why I became an alcoholic? To leave, to forget, to remember nothing. I do not know. I self-analyse myself a lot, and perhaps if someone had helped me earlier, there would still be children's laughter in this house.

The age when I was supposed to take stock of my life has long passed and I have nothing much to show for it. I have not done anything good. Nothing. I know I have grandchildren, but I have never seen them. I know that my family is doing well. Nelly married a doctor and built a large business. I saw an article about her in the newspaper. Well done, what else can I say? She is a true human being. A phoenix. It is good that she did not break and is living with a man who suits her. Although my happiness for her is not genuine. Why lie before the end? I do not know what bothers me exactly. I guess that it is not me standing beside her in the newspaper photo.

Every day before going to sleep, I think back to the place where the sun hid behind the forest. I see two people sitting on the shore – she and I. I run my fingers through the sand with fallen pine needles, gaze into her beautiful, iridescent amber eyes, and there is no greater happiness for me. I remember everything down to the smallest detail as if it was yesterday. How I wish that I could go back and start over. There are lies there, but they can be fixed. There are no betrayals, tears, humiliation or ruined lives yet. Our whole life is ahead of us.

I imagine us living together in a nice house, and our children and grandchildren visit us on the weekends. I toss my grandchildren up into the air and they laugh uproariously. The smell of vanilla wafts from the house, and I glance back towards the window. She is standing there. She looks at me with eyes full of love and gratitude for the years of love and support, and our strong and close-knit family. But these are just dreams. A pity that I cannot fix the mistakes or rewind my life.

I have nothing more to remember and say, and no one to say it to.

The end!

A psychological portrait of the characters and the mistakes they made

1. Eric, the main character (husband, father and narrator)

Characteristics:

- A person traumatised in childhood and not loved enough by his parents. His mother rejected him when he was still in the womb and his father remained indifferent. This led to deep-seated self-doubt, fear of being unwanted and thirst for recognition.
- He is a person who seems to have a split personality: he sincerely wants to be good, and dreams of love and a family yet destroys everything he builds. He contains a destructive program inherited from his mother.
- Manipulator: he unconsciously uses self-pity as a tool to keep people beside him, especially his wife and children.
- Liar: lying has been his defence mechanism since childhood. He lies even when it is not necessary, for fear of punishment.

- Weak-willed: he often goes with the flow, does not accept responsibility for his actions, blames his circumstances, friends, mother or wife, but not himself.
- Emotionally deaf: he ignores the harm he causes his loved ones until he finds himself at the very bottom.

Main mistakes:

- Justifies his inaction with his difficult childhood, even though he is an adult.
- Does not take responsibility for his life.
- Avoids difficulties instead of solving them.
- Constantly runs away from reality, first using lies and then alcohol.
- Unable to take responsibility for his family.
- Emotional and physical abuse (towards Nelly and the children).
- Self-destructive behaviour which also destroys those around him.
- Exchanging family happiness for short-term pleasures.

2. Nelly (wife, mother and strong woman)

Characteristics:

- Strong, persistent and hard-working – she achieved success without getting a "leg up" or any family support and built her own business.
- Emotionally stable – she endured humiliation, forgave betrayal but continued to move forward.

- Loving and selfless – she put her heart and soul into her husband and believed that he could be saved.
- Inner strength – despite her suffering, she does not break even after the car accident, bankruptcy and Eric's betrayal.
- A mother who became a father to her children – when her husband betrayed them, she took everything upon herself.
- An excellent strategist – every time her life felt apart, she found a way to start anew.

Main mistakes:

- Excessive faith in her husband – she gave him chances that he did not deserve.
- Tolerance for abuse – emotional and eventually physical.
- Did not know how to abandon a toxic relationship in time – if she had left earlier, she might have saved her health and her business.
- Did not realise that love for her husband was not love but a fear of loneliness – her childhood trauma (being an orphan) tied her to him, even when he caused harm to her and the children.

3. Mother of the main character

Characteristics:

- Egocentric and cold – she did not want a child, tried to get rid of him, did not love him, and repeatedly said "go away" even on her deathbed.
- Manipulator – she made her son feel guilty and used him.

- Conservative – she thought that her son should live the way she wanted him to and that she would choose a bride for him.
- Toxic parent – instilled an inferiority complex in her son that ruined his life.

Main mistakes:

- Eric's programming is based on unhappiness. His mother shaped his feeling of uselessness. **Refusing to love her own child** broke him.
- Toxic competition with the daughter-in-law, which led to the destruction of her son's family.
- Inability to acknowledge her own cruelty and its consequences.

<u>4. Father of the main character</u>

Characteristics:

- A weak man who chose to abandon his family instead of standing up to his wife and taking care of his children.
- Irresponsible, avoided his duties.
- Careless, he thought more about himself than his family.

Main mistakes:

- Running away from his problems instead of solving them.
- Allowing his wife to be the dictator in the family.
- Did not serve as a good example of a man for his son.

5. Aslan (Eric's friend)

Characteristics:

- A person living in the moment and lacking moral principles.
- An egoist who uses people for his own convenience.
- He is jealous of Eric, but not enough to make himself a better person.

Main mistakes:

- Dragging Eric down by taking advantage of his weaknesses.
- Mindlessly destroying his friend's relationship without realising the consequences.
- Never learning from his mistakes.

6. Daughter (Lily)

Characteristics:

- Smart, perceptive and mature beyond her years – she quickly realised what kind of person her father was.
- Strong, but cold – she did not forgive her father, unlike her brother.
- Growing up with a sense of betrayal and is likely to have trust issues in adulthood.

Main mistakes:

- None – she is a victim.

7. Son

Characteristics:

- Kind, open and attached to his father – he keeps loving him despite everything.
- He is weaker than his sister and it is harder for him to survive the betrayal.
- He may repeat his father's mistakes if he does not draw the right conclusions in childhood.

Main mistakes:

- None – he is a victim too.

From my notes: This story is about an unbroken cycle of destruction that is passed down from generation to generation. The main character became who he is because of the way his mother raised him. Most likely, his mother also experienced some trauma in her childhood. The only way to break this cycle is for Nelly and her children to live differently if they draw the right conclusions.

***

"You know, Heleina, "Gishi says to me after I close the folder, 'I know it's you.' He narrows his eyes and stares at me intently.

"What are you talking about?" I pretend not to understand.

"You know. You know everything."

"Do you want to know what I know? That you have obsessive-compulsive personality disorder. Workaholic, perfectionist. I bet you had a harsh, emotionally cold father. You had to earn your father's love through your achievements. You were punished for mistakes and failures, not allowed to show your emotions. And your obsession with the truth, your desire to get to the bottom of things at any cost, appeared as compensation for the fact that this is the only way you can control the situation and feel safe". After revealing all this, I watch his reaction. He tries to control himself, but he doesn't succeed, and tears can be seen in the corners of his eyes. I've hit the nail on the head.

"It wasn't like that at all! "he says, defending himself.

"Yes, it was," I say, nodding affirmatively. "That's exactly how it was."

"Our conversation is over for today," he says, standing up. "You are free to go. We will call you back."

He leaves, and I sit motionless for a while. Detective Fraser enters the office and smiles at me, telling me I can go.

I get up from the chair, tuck my shirt into my pants, button my jacket, pick up my bag from the floor, and leave this awful place.

I drive home in silence. I feel tired again. Tired of having to go back to a place I don't want to be. Actually, these are the sins I was talking about. Am I to blame for getting rid of unwanted elements? Every time, an angel and a demon fight inside me. The demon says that they need to be gotten rid of, because these bad people not only ruin their own lives but also take the lives of others. What right do they have to do that?!

The angel tells me that everything is God's will and that God himself knows who to punish and when. And I ask the angel, "Why didn't your God help many of my clients? Why did your God allow atrocities to be committed on Earth? Why didn't he help me personally when I needed him so much?"

The angel has no answer to this and falls silent.

I remember all the people who have passed through my hands. Some were terrible, and some were good, really good. But there were still more terrible ones. And I often wonder, which are there more of on Earth, the good or the bad? Who will win in this battle between good and evil? Will evil prevail sooner or later, plunging life on earth into an abyss of grief, violence, and lawlessness? I don't want to believe that. I want to believe that someday only good, kind-hearted people who are capable of love and warmth will remain on earth. Of course, I won't be around by then.

Returning to the good people I have met in my practice. There were a couple of cases when I not only enjoyed working but also enjoyed living. Yes, my clients made mistakes, but one of them became a kind entrepreneur, and another became the best mother for her child.

A CONVENIENT WIFE

Gilly married Ken straight after high school. The marriage was not due to a pure and intense love but an unplanned pregnancy. The couple lived with Ken's parents at first. Although they disliked Gilly and were extremely displeased about their son's imminent fatherhood, they provided a home for the young couple. After the birth of their grandson, they paid the rent for quite decent accommodation, as they called it, which was actually a trailer. There was no money for anything bigger, but Gilly and Ken were grateful for it. Despite his young age, Ken took care of the family as best as he could. He worked at a hardware store and always brought his entire salary to his wife. After work, he hurried home to help his wife with their son, and life was good on the whole. They lived happily and amicably. Friends came over on the weekends and they would have a barbecue, drink beer and play the guitar. Thus did their youth pass.

Their lives had not changed by the time Ken and Gilly's son started school. They still lived in the same place and Ken continued to work for the same company. The family's income remained small but stable. Is this not happiness? Gilly stayed at home, taking care of her son and looking after the house. When Ken came home from work, she always had a rich and fragrant soup ready, as well as a main dish and, of course, pastries, which her husband adored. In the evenings, they watched movies or cartoons together, then scrolled through news feeds or social media before going to bed. Gilly liked watching how other people live, but she was never envious, she simply admired their lifestyles. Everything in the lives of these fascinating people seemed to be fictional, like a fairy tale. All their travels, jewellery and expensive clothes were so different to how Gilly lived. She had no idea where they got the money for all this, because her family's income barely covered their basic needs.

One day, there was a knock on the door. Gilly had not been expecting anyone, so she jumped. Her mother, who had not spoken to Gilly since high school, stood at the door. Nor had she seen her grandson. Before opening the door, the girl smoothed her hair and tried to hide her trembling.

"Hello, Gilly," Mum greeted her coldly. "May I come in?"

Gilly wanted to hug her, but her mother's dry tone made it clear that this was not a friendly visit, so she stepped aside wordlessly.

Once inside the trailer, her mother studied the residence appraisingly. It was worth noting that the place was clean, so Gilly had nothing to be ashamed of.

"Well, at least now I know where you live," her mother began. "Really, I'd expected as much as I told you back then."

"Yeah," Gilly confirmed. "Has something happened to make you come?"

"Uncle Jack died."

"Jack who?" Gilly asked.

"A distant relative of your father's. He lives, that is, he lived in Asia. Do you remember when he came to visit for your 15th birthday?"

"I don't," Gilly replied, "but I'm truly sorry. What happened?"

"He picked up some kind of bacteria in a river."

"That's terrible! How can you talk about it so indifferently?"

"People die every day," her mother stated.

"Well, you haven't changed one bit," Gilly shook her head disapprovingly.

"Oh, and you still look at the world through rose-coloured glasses, of course! Remember, girl, life is no walk in the park!"

"That's what you told me when you sent me for an abortion and look at me now! None of what you predicted has come true! I'm not lying in a ditch, Ken didn't leave me, and we're pretty happy!"

"Sure, you're happy. You just haven't grown up yet. Wait a couple more years, and you'll notice that you're not so happy, that your life is being spent serving other people, and you haven't achieved anything, even though you could have!"

"I don't want to continue this conversation. We're still not on the same page. I'm living my life, you and Dad are living yours. You didn't give me the support when I needed it, well, I have a family that not only supports but loves me too."

"Oh, my girl," her mother sighed heavily, " do you really think I'm saying this to hurt you? I said it back then and I'm saying it again now simply because I've lived longer than you have. I know that you can't put all your eggs in one basket! Husbands betray and children leave. You need to focus on yourself!"

Gilly didn't want to continue the argument that had dragged on from the past. She took a photo of her son from the shelf and handed it to her mother. "This is Danny, your grandson."

The woman smiled as she held her grandson's photo. "Wow, he looks so much like your grandfather. He's got the same eyes."

"Oh, yes," Gilly agreed. "And the same nose!"

"Certainly not, Dad had a beautiful aquiline nose. This nose is clearly not from our family."

Gilly pursed her lips. "Do you want some tea?"

"No. Actually, I came to give you a cheque."

"What cheque?"

"Jack left your dad some things. Your dad sold them at a sale, and decided to give the money to you. There's 200 dollars."

Gilly looked doubtfully at her mother. She was certain that Dad would not have sent Mum to do this. As if you could make this woman do anything! Besides, Gilly kept in touch with her father, unlike her mother, although not very often. He had not mentioned anything about a relative's death.

"You came here because of 200 dollars?" Gilly smiled.

"Of course not!" her mum replied, rolling her eyes. Going up to her daughter, she hugged her and said, "I've missed you. I can't stop fretting. I'm your mother and I wish you every happiness, truly. But it pains me to see where your life is going."

"It's not going anywhere. I'm living just like everyone else."

"Remember how you dreamed of becoming a doctor?" her mother asked, ignoring her daughter's words. "And then you won the interschool physics competition? I thought you'd build a career and follow in my footsteps..."

"I'm happy, Mum."

"You can't survive on happiness alone. Sometimes, life makes you look at the world differently."

"Let's hope it won't happen to me."

"Let's hope so," her mother did not sound convinced.

Her mum's visit left a bad aftertaste. Gilly still could not understand the true purpose of her mother's visit. Perhaps she really did want her daughter to be happy, but what was she offering? Gilly could not be turn back time or prevent the pregnancy, and she had always been against killing a fetus. Especially when the boy was so adorable. The apple of her eye. Her pride and joy.

By the time Ken came home, Gilly was still sitting at the table with Danny's photo in her hands.

"How are things in our kingdom?" Ken asked as he entered. "Why do you look so sad?"

"My mum came."

"I see," Ken tensed. "What did she want this time?"

"Nothing, she brought us 200 dollars."

"Interesting. Were they accompanied by a tirade about what a fool you are and how you've ruined your life and theirs?"

Gilly nodded.

"Right. Ignore her. What's for dinner?"

"I didn't make anything. We'll have to have an omelette."

"Okay. I'm not used to this, of course, but I'll forgive you this time," Ken joked.

Gilly felt down for several more days after her mother's visit but everyday life swept the feeling away over time. Gilly felt happy and satisfied with everything again.

Her 30th birthday was fast approaching. A pretty important date, so Ken decided to throw a big party. Gilly was against it for a long time, but her husband was so keen that she eventually gave in.

They were expecting many guests at the party, so Gilly decided to prepare properly. A week before the event, she had her nails done and her hair cut and coloured. It would be nice to lose 40 pounds, she thought, but she would not be able to do that in time.

When the day came, Ken sent her to a cafe to give the guests time to gather and jump out of the bushes as if completely unexpectedly and shout "Surprise!".

Gilly felt elated as she sat in the cafe, enjoying a light dessert. A tight-knit family and a cute little home – so what if it was a trailer? A sweet child. What more could she ask from the Lord? Perhaps a little more money but, really, it was time for her to find a job and take some of the pressure off Ken. Yes, that was what she would do. Suddenly, someone touched her shoulder and she jumped. When Gilly turned around, she did not recognize the person in front of her at first. A beautiful, well-groomed blonde was smiling at Gilly with her charming, pearly white smile.

"Bella?" Gilly asked.

"Yes!" the woman exclaimed joyfully and went to give Gilly with a hug. "How are you, my dear? It's been so long! You haven't changed a bit since school. You're still the same!"

"Yeah, right," Gilly smiled. "And you're as stunning as before."

"Thanks! Mind if I take a seat? So, tell me, how are you? We've completely lost you. Has family life consumed you utterly and completely?"

"Well, yeah. There's nothing exciting in my life," Gilly hesitated. "I don't even know what to tell you. Everything's good, on the whole. Ken works and our son is in school."

"He must be pretty big by now."

"Yes. He's shooting up. I actually feel sad that he's not a baby anymore. I'd rather hear all about you!"

"It all worked out just like I'd planned. I became a doctor, like I wanted to."

"Really? What is your specialty?"

"Paediatrics. Remember how much I like kids? I'm doing what I love. I'd like to get a PhD in the next few years. I'm writing a paper and conducting research."

"Wow, you're amazing. How's your personal life? Are you married?"

"Not yet, it's too early for that. There's still so much to do and so many places to see. There'll be time to get married later. You know me, I'm a career woman."

"Yes, you were number one in school."

"That's for sure! So, why are you here all by yourself?"

"It's my birthday. My husband is preparing a surprise party and sent me here!"

"Oh, congratulations! How could I forget? Our birthdays are right next to each other!"

"Yes, I remember – yours is tomorrow. Happy birthday for tomorrow!"

"Thank you. It's a pity that I'll have to celebrate on the plane."

"Where are you off to?"

"London."

"That's cool. For a holiday?"

"I wish. I'm presenting at a conference. Although I'll have time to relax too – wander through the foggy streets of Albion."

"I've always dreamed of visiting London, even since I was a child."

"Your time will come!"

"I hope so. Have you been there before?"

"Yes, many times. Actually, I've travelled to many countries. I like to travel, you know. The world seems so big when you've never gone anywhere, but once you've explored it all, it seems so small. It feels like it's at my feet at times. The world, I mean. I sound a bit loopy, right?"

"No, it's an interesting idea. Perhaps that's the way it really is."

"Oh, I didn't ask you what you ended up doing. Where do you work?"

"I'm a housewife," Gilly mumbled, embarrassed all of a sudden.

"That's right, someone has to look after the house," Bella supported her old friend. "Not everyone gets to do big things. Oh, my driver is here, I've got to run. It was so nice to see you. Happy birthday again!"

"Thank you. I was glad to run into you too. I hope you have a good flight!"

Bella left behind a trail of expensive perfume and a bitter sourness in Gilly's heart.

"Is it envy?" she asked herself. "Why don't I feel happy for her? Why do I feel so sad and sick? I could have gone to university with her since my marks were very close to hers. Whose fault is it that I got pregnant and didn't build a career? Oh, Mum warned me about this."

Gilly felt like a worthless loser on the way home. She wanted to be someone so much but she was nobody. A simple girl who got married too young, completely unqualified. Yes, she was raising a son and had built a solid and happy relationship with Ken but was that enough? She wanted something else, but life seemed to be already over, and it was too late to change anything.

As she approached the house, she put on a smile and pretended to be very surprised to see all the guests, yet Ken still realized that something had happened. He knew his wife very well and could sense her mood.

"What's wrong?" he asked when the guests sat down to eat.

"Nothing, I'm fine," she replied, not wanting to upset her husband. Besides, she was not even sure what was wrong with her.

"I can see that you're upset! What is it?"

"Really, it's nothing. I guess I'm just tired. Go and have fun with the guests, honey. Thank you so much for this party. It turned out just as you had planned."

"We had planned." Ken replied, sounding offended.

Gazing at the trailer's backyard, the guests, the balloons and the blue sky, it suddenly felt so unbearable that Gilly wanted to burst into tears in front of everyone. "Is this how it'll be for the rest of my life?" she thought. "A smelly trailer that we can barely afford, buying only discounted products, and not being able to go on even the cheapest trip?" Bitterness quickly turned to anger, and she began to blame Ken because she needed to blame somebody. As she watched him, she was filled with hatred. This man was responsible for her ruined life and wasted youth.

Late in the evening, after everyone had gone and they were cleaning up the backyard, Gilly seized on something minor and started a huge row. It was a shock to Ken, because they did not fight more than once a year, and even then it would be over nothing. Ken was doubly hurt because he had worked hard to arrange this party and prepared a small but lovely gift. "Why is she doing this?" he wondered.

"What's the matter with you, Gilly?" Ken asked, swallowing the hurt. "Tell me what happened. You're not mad about these plates right now, are you? Did something happen in town?"

"I met Bella."

"Who's Bella?"

"My high school friend. Or rather, my high school rival."

"And?"

"And she's achieved so much over these years. What have I achieved? Nothing! I have no formal education, no profession – all I'll ever do is take care of you and Danny! But he'll leave home sooner or later and I'll be all alone! While other people are striving for something, we continue to eke out a living and can't even afford a small house! Not to mention something else." Gilly buried her face in her hands.

Ken sighed heavily. "Gilly, I don't have a profession or an education either."

"Yes, you're still working at the same job where you get paid pennies. We have to change something!"

"What, right now?" Ken tried to make a joke.

"Right now," Gilly replied firmly, gazing at him with eyes full of tears.

Ken did not continue this conversation, which seemed silly to him. He did not like that Gilly was thinking about change. In his opinion, with God's help, they lived neither well nor poorly. He had seen worse things happen to others.

Gilly, on the other hand, clearly did not think it was silly. From that day on, she grew silent and distanced herself from her family. She no longer watched cartoons and other nonsense with them in the evenings, did not laugh as hard or join in the family games. After they put the child to bed, she would take a chair out into the courtyard and stare at the sky for a long time. Ken tried to talk to his wife, to understand what was going on with her, but how could she tell him when she could not figure it out herself? Endless thoughts raced through her head. Something was changing inside her, she was reflecting on her life and the results did not please her in the slightest. The joy drained out of her life and neither her son, nor her husband, nor food pleased her. She felt like she had lost something and could not find it again.

One night, staring at the dark ceiling and listening to her family snuffling beside her, Gilly repeated the same thought, "Lord, I don't want to anger you, I'm grateful to you for the roof over my head, for our daily bread and that everyone is alive and well. Yet I'm missing something. I don't want to ask you for more than you've already given me, but I'm wondering if I was only born to be the mother of this child and the wife of the man you sent me. I know it might be arrogance, but I'm desperate for something bigger. I want to become more than what I am today, you see? It feels like a fire is burning inside me and if I don't do something worthwhile in my life, I'll burn to a cinder. I don't know, Lord, I can't even explain how I feel to you. Please send me a sign if I'm worth something and where should I turn next?"

Of course, she did not receive an answer and her heart continued to fret.

One day, mindlessly scrolling through her phone while Danny slept, she suddenly came across a video of a young woman decorating gingerbread. Gilly thought it would be nice to make such biscuits for a holiday, such as for Halloween, which was just around the corner. She got up from the sofa and went into the kitchen to check her cupboards. She did not have enough ingredients for gingerbread and would have to go to the store. As soon as Danny woke up, she dressed him and herself, and they wandered through the empty streets. They chatted along the way. Gilly loved listening to her son and finding out what thoughts lurked in that little head. They talked about different things, but Gilly always reminded her son that he should study hard, grow up to be a good and decent person, graduate from university and then find his calling, and not end up like his mother. She hoped her son would meet a kind person to build a strong family with.

Holding her son's hand, she suddenly felt a surge of love and happiness again. It felt like they would turn the corner and something magical would be waiting for them there, maybe a celebration.

Everything was going well in the store until Danny got stuck in the video game console department. Gilly knew that her son had wanted one for a long time, and it upset her that she could not afford to buy it for him. As they walked back home, she thought that maybe her mother was right in some ways. In fact, she was mentally agreeing with her more and more lately. Gilly thought that her mother had the same conversations with her as a child and had dreamed that her daughter would live comfortably, rather than struggling to make ends meet. She probably imagined her daughter's wedding at an impressive venue, her daughter wearing a beautiful dress and having a nice house, a car and savings... not this, when there was no money to buy her son what he really wanted.

"Oh," she sighed. "Enough. We'll make it somehow."

Once they were back home, she let Danny watch cartoons and went into the kitchen to bake the first gingerbread cookies in her life. She became absorbed in the process, pushing the previous thoughts out of her mind.

"Danny," she yelled, "come and see the glaze I'm making. The colour is just magical."

"I don't want to," her son replied.

"Oh, well then," Gilly said, not at all upset.

Everything seemed to be going well. Gilly was sticking to the recipe and thought that her gingerbread would turn out to be as good as the girl's in the video, if not better. No way. The gingerbread got burnt and the glaze was too runny. Gilly was upset, of course, but she did not give up. Taking a knife, she began to scrape the burnt spots from her creations, hoping to hide them under the glaze. Alas, this did not make the biscuits any better.

Gilly was still in the kitchen when Ken came home.

"Whoa, what's happening?" he asked, smiling.

Entering the kitchen, he saw Gilly with smudges on her face and burst out laughing. Gilly laughed in reply.

"Did you decide to burn down the house?"

"Something like that. I saw a girl making fancy gingerbread biscuits today and I thought I could do the same."

Ken chuckled again when he approached the baking tray. They looked quite ridiculous, even ugly.

"That's alright, dear. They'll turn out better next time. If at first you don't succeed... You're good at everything else! Very good."

"There won't be a next time!" Gilly said firmly.

"Never say never," Ken supported his wife, biting into a gingerbread biscuit. "They taste pretty good, by the way."

Gilly broke off a piece from her husband's biscuit and bit into it with difficulty.

"You can break your teeth on them!"

"Yes, you can. But it's still delicious. We just have a bad oven."

"Don't try to make me feel better."

"Absolutely not. You need to try again, that's all. Can you at least show me the video of how they were supposed to turn out?"

Ken laughed again after watching the video.

"Yes, these are exactly like hers!" he concluded. "Even better."

She slapped him playfully on the shoulder. "Don't laugh at me!"

"I won't." He kissed her on the forehead and went to hug Danny.

Gilly tried to recreate the video the next day, and the next day, and the next. She got better each time. The gingerbread biscuits were now soft, but she still needed to work on the decorations. Gilly did not know why she needed to perfect them and did not consider what it might lead to. She posted all her unsuccessful attempts on a social media and laughed openly at herself. Some supported her and some even insulted her. Gilly was hurt by such comments, but afterwards, she thought that she was not the one with the problem, but rather the person who wrote those nasty things. Perhaps something bad had happened to them or maybe they were in pain.

After weeks of practice, she finally created something similar to what she had seen. During her endless attempts, she fed her gingerbread not only to all her neighbours and Ken's colleagues from work, but even to complete strangers.

One day, she was asked a question in the comments: would she like to sell her gingerbread biscuits? Gilly had never considered it since it seemed ridiculous. She believed that her creations were quite terrible and, moreover, of no interest to anyone. Nevertheless, after thinking about the question for a long time, she created a separate account from her personal one and even wrote a catchy and funny introduction.

"Well, you can never tell," she concluded.

Slowly, people began to subscribe to her account. Gilly was happy to see each and every one. She actively liked them and always wrote only nice things.

In December, when the planet's biggest holiday was only two weeks away, she suddenly started receiving orders. Well, that was not quite how it happened. It all started with the first order, placed by quite an unremarkable girl. Gilly saw that she had a lot of subscribers but did not think about what it could mean. Gilly completed the order with diligence and love, and without any ulterior motive. The gingerbread biscuits sparkled with brilliant festive colours in a white, homemade box. Gilly also tied them with a fancy ribbon left over from a bouquet Ken had once given her. The customer must have noticed the presentation flaws, but this was not particularly important. She liked what Gilly had done and wrote a big thank-you post, tagging Gilly. Orders began pouring in from that moment on, so that she had to work even at night. Luckily, Ken helped with everything. He thought that his wife's hobby would end sooner or later and did not suspect that danger lurked in all this for him personally.

When she had earned her first and, as it seemed to her, big money, Gilly felt over the moon with happiness. She was glad not so much for the money itself as the fact that she had earned it herself. It was a real achievement for her. For the first time in her life, she went shopping with her own money and bought whatever she wanted. Yes, these were small purchases and inexpensive gifts for the family, but these were her gifts, obtained with her own two hands.

Gilly thought her little hobby would come to an end after Christmas, but the orders kept coming. This led her to the decision to expand: to make cakes, pastries and fragrant fresh bread, rather than the stuff sold in the shops. Somehow Gilly was certain that her products would not only be delicious, but beautiful too.

In the first few months, almost all her earnings were spent on baking materials and other bits and bobs. Ken did not mind. He was still amused by his wife's hobby and was waiting for it all to come to an end. But it did not stop, instead, it only gained momentum. As time passed, Gilly's business grew and so did she. Her small success and own money awoke something in her that shocked even her at times. She could only wonder where this or that quality had come from. She developed a commanding tone and became more confident and businesslike. Before this, she thought that she would never amount to anything and would continue to live in a trailer and raise children. Yet she was becoming a self-sufficient woman, a somebody. She changed her style, her hair and wardrobe and even became interesting. Not a mouse, as she told herself.

"I'm not just the mum of a little angel now, I'm a woman who is capable and can even provide for her family."

After officially registering her brand, Gilly rented a small room and hired a couple of assistants. The orders just kept coming. She could only marvel at how many weddings and birthdays took place in their city.

The larger her business grew, the worse her relationship with Ken became. He did not like his wife's new image and the changes in her. Their quiet and measured life was over. He still believed that this situation would not last forever, although his wife annoyed him more and more with each passing day. He did not want to come home and hear about how she did this or that. For some reason, he found it unpleasant. He was sick and tired of her stories.

"You've changed," he said. "And I don't like it."

"What don't you like? Having money in our bank account? Do you know that we'll soon have enough for a house deposit ? Or that we have the money to buy Danny whatever he wants?"

"That's enough, I'm sick of this conversation already. Our life used to be better, and I want everything to go back to the way it was."

"Have you thought that maybe I don't want to? I only have one life."

"Well, so do I."

"I understand, but I don't want to keep living the same way. We're human beings and I think, no, I'm sure that we're meant to advance as we go through life. What do you think I should have done next, now that Danny's older?"

"Have another baby."

"I knew you'd say that. How? We could barely afford one child."

"And yet we survived somehow and didn't starve to death. I don't understand when all this happened in you. When did you become like this? It's true what they say – money changes people. It's changed you for the worse."

"I haven't changed, Ken," Gilly concluded calmly. "I simply grew up, that's all. People tend to change throughout their lives. By the way, I read that it could be a 30-year crisis. That's what the psychologists call it."

"Not your psychology again! I get it, you've become the smartest one here. Give it up already! If you hadn't run into your classmate back then, none of this would have happened."

"Exactly! It wouldn't have happened. Thank God I met her, otherwise, I would have continued wasting my life."

"So, you believe that the years you've spent with me have been a waste?"

"You're not hearing me. Please understand what I'm trying to say. I was happy in that period of my life, but it's time to change and do something bigger. I wanted to be someone once upon a time, but then we found out that we were having Danny. I simply didn't get a chance to find out who I am and who I want to be. I know now."

"The great gingerbread maker?" he sneered.

"Yes, a great one," she was offended now. "I have nothing more to say to you. It's like we're living on different planets."

Despite the clear differences that were becoming more obvious with Gilly's inner growth, she still hoped to preserve their marriage and continued loving Ken. She remembered all the good things that had happened in their life and how hard her husband had worked for their sake.

The discord with her husband worried her, but with the business growing and generating a substantial income, there was no time to sort it out. New bakeries were opening around the city, and the range of products and number of staff were growing. Aware that she lacked competence in many matters, Gilly took more and more courses. She was constantly learning something new and she loved it. Her success brought her satisfaction, although she was often tormented by remorse at night. Having found herself as an identity, she began to lose herself as a mother. She no longer had time for her son. Gilly could only dedicate 15 minutes a day to him for a short chat and a song before bed. Of course, that is not enough, she thought. On the other hand, her son now had the opportunity to attend a good university and choose a profession, which she had been deprived of.

As Gilly achieved more and more, the gap between her and Ken grew and grew. She began to notice how limited her husband was. Moreover, he refused to do anything about it.

"Maybe you should try your hand at the bakery?" she suggested once again. "You could find out how it all works and become a manager later on."

"I don't want my wife as my boss, and I don't want people to laugh at me."

"No one is going to laugh at you. I think it looks funny now. We have a whole chain of bakeries, but you still work as a salesperson at the hardware store."

"Can't you just leave me alone? I'm sick of these conversations. How can you keep pressuring me?"

"Ken, I'm not pressuring you. I just want you to become more important."

"Why, so I can be your equal? Am I not good enough for you now?"

"How can you say that? Where does this aggression come from?"

"It's not aggression. We had a normal life before, but devil knows what it has turned into. You're never home, there's no food in the house, the place is a mess and our child isn't being looked after."

"So, you were satisfied when I was a stay-at-home drudge? Was it convenient for you?"

"Yes, it was convenient!"

"Well then, I'm not a convenient wife anymore. And either you accept it or you don't. There's no other option. Look at how we're living nowadays! We have everything! The house renovations are almost finished. Our house that I made..."

"With your own two hands," Ken said sarcastically before she could finish.

Gilly did not know how to respond to such rudeness. These conversations were not going well, and Gilly could sense that the expected consequence was just around the corner.

As soon as the house renovations were completed and their things were packed, Ken made a declaration that Gilly had been prepared for but not really expecting.

"I'm not going with you," he said sullenly, packing a box of Danny's things.

"Why?" Gilly asked.

"I don't want to."

"What about Danny? What about me?"

"I'll come and visit Danny, and you're fine without me. You have a business to run."

"This again?"

"No. You know, Gilly, I've met someone at work. I'm sorry, but try to understand me. Really, it's not about her, it's about us. We've grown apart and you don't want the same things I want anymore.

Gilly burst out laughing. "To live in poverty?"

"What does poverty have to do with it? We weren't beggars, I was earning a salary."

"And who is she?" Gilly instantly changed the topic.

"She works with me."

"And I was wondering why you were taking more care of yourself!"

"You should have realized what your absence would lead to!"

"You're blaming me for your infidelity?"

"Yes, you. If you had been at home, I wouldn't have felt so lonely. You're the one who abandoned us."

"I didn't abandon you, I was building a future, a safety blanket for us."

"Me, me, me. Say it a hundred more times in case we haven't got it yet!"

"You could have done well, too. I suggested that you join the bakery many times. I said you could go and study. You could respect yourself, and I could respect you."

"That's the thing. I already respect myself, but you don't respect me anymore. How about we stop discussing this for the hundredth time?"

"And why should I respect you? It's true, you've supported this family for years, and good on you for that. But when it was time to take the next step, what did you do? Nothing! You don't want to!"

"I don't. I like living the way I live now."

"Great. So be it. Where will you bring your bride? Here?"

"That doesn't concern you."

"Ken, I can't believe this is happening."

"Gilly, can we not? We have a son."

"Yes, we have a son. So, what will you tell him?"

"I've already told him. I said it like it is. I said that Mum and I would no longer be together, but we'll still love him the same."

Gilly could no longer listen to him and dashed out of the house with a gaping wound in her heart. She wandered the streets, trying to calm down. Who would have thought that when she opened a new door, she would be closing the old one? Who knew? In truth, what would she have chosen: to live as before and chafe at her shackles, or for things to remain as they are now? Her thoughts were interrupted by the phone ringing in her pocket.

"It's Mum," came the voice on the phone.

"Hi, Mum. Has something happened?" Gilly tensed.

"No, I just wanted to say that I'm proud of you. Very proud of you. Well done. This is exactly what I meant ages ago. For you to be your own master, standing on your own two feet."

"Thanks, Mum."

"I frequent your bakery, by the way. It's delicious."

"I'm glad. Sorry, I've got to run, I still have some work to do here."

Gilly hung up and burst into tears. Yes, her mother's words were nice, but she was crying from bitterness more than happiness. Her heart ached as she approached the trailer, which still twinkled with the fairy lights that they had hung up years ago. This chapter of her life was closing forever. She sank down into an old chair and looked up at the sky. Everything was the same, but Gilly herself was different. Ken's attitude to her had changed too. He did not love her anymore and, frankly, neither did she. What had she lost? Her past, her husband and her love for him. Yet if she looked at it from another angle, she had lost something and found something else, namely self-love and self-respect. This was important too.

Could she live without Ken? Gilly knew that she could. Did she regret choosing something else instead of a quiet family happiness? No! She had become an important and necessary person, not only for her family, but for herself and others too. She was making people's lives better. Her baking brought joy to customers, which meant endorphins of happiness; her bakeries gave the staff the opportunity to live this life, pay for purchases, kindergartens and other needs. She was not stingy with salaries, paying them generously for their work, because she knew first-hand what it was like to live without having money for basic things. So what if Ken did not need her? It was no longer so important. Yes, her soul was on fire from the failure of their marriage, but she knew that she would survive because she knew herself, knew who she was and that she could take care of herself. And who knew what the future held?

A psychological portrait of the characters and the mistakes they made

1. Gilly (main character)

Characteristics:

- The initial role as the "housewife"

She got married right after school without fulfilling her intellectual potential (she wanted to become a doctor and participated in interschool competitions);

She initially wears "rose-tinted glasses" and is content with a quiet and modest life with Ken and their son.

- The prolonged stagnation and sudden push

Her awakening ambitions coincide with her 30-year crisis. Seeing her mother and then friend Bella serves as the catalyst for change.

She begins to wonder if she has wasted her life and never became anyone, which triggers an internal crisis.

- Finding herself through a creative pursuit

At first, baking is just a hobby, which later results in financial success. The rapidly growing demand spurns Gilly on to further growth.

- The internal conflict between the love for her family and the desire for self-realization

The desire for growth leads to less time for her husband and son, which causes feelings of guilt and anxiety.

Nevertheless, Gilly does not back down, aware that she is finally doing something important for herself.

- The resulting shift and new values

Willingness to sacrifice the old family set-up for the sake of her own fulfilment.

She feels pain from the breakup with Ken but understands that life goes on and that she is capable of more.

Main mistakes:

- Ignoring her desires for a long time: she spent years in homemaker mode, which led to internal dissatisfaction and the resulting "explosion". It would have been better to look for development pathways earlier (courses, part-time work, etc.), without bringing the situation to a head.
- Insufficient communication with her husband: when Gilly realized that she wanted more, she should have actively involved her husband in her plans, looked for a compromise and building a new life together. Instead, she immersed her-

self in the business and gradually distanced herself from Ken.

2. Ken (husband)

Characteristics:

· A faithful but "stunted in his development" spouse

Took responsibility for his family after graduation and gave all the money to his wife. At the same time, he did not seek career growth or additional education. He was comfortable with a stable but low-income lifestyle.

· Conflict with internal stereotypes

He was used to Gilly being a housewife, who cooked him dinner and waited for him at home. This was familiar and convenient for him.

When Gilly decides to do something different and break out of her cage, he is not ready for the change. He reacts with irritation and passive resistance.

· Resentment and a sense of loss

He sees his wife moving ahead, while he is left on the sidelines. He realizes that their former closeness is being lost.

Instead of trying to grow together (as Gilly suggests), he seeks solace in another woman, blaming Jilly for triggering these changes.

· The role of the traitor

In the end, he leaves Gilly for another woman, while claiming that Gilly left him first (by becoming absorbed in her work). This looks like a weak attempt to save his ego by making excuses.

Main mistakes:

- Refusal to grow together.
- Insufficient attention to his wife's emotional state. He does not notice that her "30-year crisis" is a signal for change and that he should support her, instead of trying to sabotage her.

3. Gilly's mother

Characteristics:

· A tough and pragmatic woman

She previously suggests that her daughter has an abortion to avoid "ruining her life" with an early marriage. She believes that you should always bet on yourself.

She is cold, on the one hand, but she wants the best for her daughter and believes in her abilities, on the other hand.

· Late remorse and support

Main mistakes:

- Lack of empathy: she should have been kinder to her daughter and supported her in her youth. The "I know best" attitude led to alienation.
- Being late with the praise: she only said "I'm proud of you" after Gilly had achieved everything on her own. If she had acted earlier, Gilly and her mother could have reconnected and helped each other.

<u>4. Bella (Gilly's school friend)</u>

Characteristics:

- The embodiment of the opposite fate

Successful and driven, without a family but with a career.

She seems to be living the "perfect life", eliciting conflicting feelings in Gilly and regrets about her own path.

- A catalyst for change

She does not do anything wrong but unwittingly gives Gilly the idea that life could be different.

Her vivid presence makes Gilly think about her missed dreams and opportunities.

Main mistakes:

The character does not really have any mistakes. She serves as a contrast, reflecting a different life scenario. She acts as the "trigger" for Gilly's self-development.

Life is all about change. Gilly transforms from a woman who marries young and lives a modest life to true maturity, in which she (sadly) loses her family as it currently is. Yes, Gilly is left without a husband, but she finds herself and makes an informed choice. Gilly's story shows that you can grow and change even with a small hobby. You should remember that by changing yourself, you change not only your life, but your established relationships as well, sometimes. It is this moment that is the main contradiction and the main drama in such situations.

I'M NOT YOUR MOTHER

"Shut up! Just shut up! I don't want to hear another word from you," she was almost shouting as she opened the gate to the front yard.

He trailed behind her with grocery bags, mumbling under his breath.

She turned around abruptly and asked, "What are you mumbling about?"

"Nothing," he replied sullenly.

"Do you have something to say to me?"

"No."

"Dear God, Alex! Come on, I'll have my own son soon and I can't be responsible for someone else's too! It's time you grew up."

They entered the house in silence. He was thinking that she had gotten mad at him for nothing again, and she was thinking that she might have made the wrong choice once upon a time.

Natasha began dating Alex after ending a painful relationship with her ex. Perhaps she wanted to marry him out of spite, or perhaps she just wanted to get married and finally have some stability. Her mum was also pressuring her, and all her friends had long been married.

They met at work and she had not paid any attention to him at first – he was that unremarkable. A little while later, when they were assigned to the same project, she began to notice many positive qualities in Alex. He was quiet and calm, which was exactly what she needed after her previous relationship. It had been a volcano of passion, which she was incredibly tired of after six years together. Being with Alex was so peaceful, like basking in the sun on the shore of a tranquil lake.

He quickly moved into her apartment – she insisted on it. Natasha was tired of being alone, of living far from home and kin, but now she had a family of sort. She was also the one who had proposed marriage. They were smoking on the balcony one day when she suddenly suggested, "Let's get married?"

"Let's," he agreed without hesitation.

Alex was head over heels in love with Natasha. She was an unattainable star and yet here he was, standing next to her, even living with her. She was his.

It was a modest wedding with only 20 guests – their closest friends and family. On their very first night as a married couple, they had a terrible argument. When Natasha entered the hotel room, she immediately sat down to count the money they had been given. Alex had expected something else and, of course, was offended. It probably did not look good on her part but, on the other hand, they were behind on their rent, which Alex somehow did not think about. It was the first red flag, but Natasha knew nothing about red flags and had never heard of them back then.

Life went on, they attended parties and met up with friends but preferred spending time together at home. They bought various snacks and watched new movies or TV series.

Three months after the wedding, Natasha discovered that she was pregnant. Well, not quite discovered. She had been waiting for it. Her dream was finally coming true. Alex, however, was not ready for children and was completely against the idea. Natasha had brought it up more than once, but his answer was always the same, "Let's find our feet first and then think about it."

"Alex, I'm already 30. The clock is ticking," she laughed. "This way, you might never be ready for children. What if we never find our feet? Anyway, as practice has shown, it's actually easier to achieve everything with children, because you're doing it for them!"

"No, Natasha. Not yet. By the way, did you take your pills?"

"I did," she said, hurt.

She had stopped taking the birth control pills ages ago, deciding to take matters into her own hands. For some reason, she knew that she absolutely needed a child. Every morning, she asked God to send her a child, and God had heard her prayers.

In the morning, Natasha did a pregnancy test while Alex was still asleep, but it showed only one line. Disappointed, she went back to bed. When she woke up a couple of hours later, she went into the kitchen, made coffee, and decided to take another look at the test. When she took it out of the trash, she could not believe her eyes. The second line glowed there very clearly. Natasha's heart was in her throat. She hurried back to the bedroom and woke Alex up.

"Good morning, my love," he whispered drowsily, holding out his arms for a hug.

"I'm pregnant," Natasha burst out gleefully.

Alex woke up at once and a fake smile appeared on his face. It looked silly.

"Aren't you happy?"

"I am."

Natasha could see that he was lying.

"How did it happen? he asked, reaching for the test.

"God sent us a baby."

"Weren't you taking the pills?"

"No."

"But what are we going to do with a child?" Alex asked with a hint of anger.

"Other people have them somehow! And in much worse conditions, I must say."

"Natasha, I don't even know what to say."

"Alex, it'll be fine. You can't see the future now, but you're mistaken. In five years' time, all the difficulties will be forgotten. We'll have a son or daughter – I'd prefer a daughter – and we'll be living happily."

"You always do whatever you want!"

"And you don't want to be responsible for anything. At the rate that you're moving up the *career ladder*," she emphasized the last two words, "we'll never be ready for parenthood. I know what needs to be done, that's all. Really, this wasn't the reaction I was expecting."

He hugged her and tried to convince her that he was happy, although he was mostly convincing himself.

Natasha quit her job, and they lived on Alex's modest salary and the money Natasha's mother sent them. There was not enough money, considering that the lion's share of the budget was spent on rent. Natasha realized that they would not last long this way and suggested that they move to her hometown. It was cosier and smaller than the capital city they lived in, and most importantly, they could live in lush nature and eat environmentally friendly food that was so important for Natasha's growing baby.

Nevertheless, Natasha cried while packing her things. She knew that her decision regarding the move was correct, but she was sorry to leave this part of her life.

After filling the car to the brim, they set off. Natasha drove the entire 800 miles. By this time, she did not trust Alex with her car or her life.

They drove into town late at night. Alex liked it. Lights were on everywhere and the streets were clean and looked after. When they reached their destination, Alex noticed that Natasha had a very nice house. It was a peach-coloured seven-storey building. The block was surrounded by a wrought-iron fence, and a colourful, large playground stood in the courtyard.

"Do you like it?" Natasha asked.

"Well, yeah. I can just see us walking around here with a pram."

They spent a couple of hours carrying their belongings into the apartment. The apartment was dusty and dirty but freshly renovation, and the furniture were new. Natasha had lived there for less than a year after purchasing it. The apartment was actually a present from her mother. In their culture, it was customary to take care of children, buy them cars and apartments, and generally help in every possible way.

A few days later, Natasha was referred for pregnancy care and became a frequent visitor to the hospital. Everything was fine with the baby, thank goodness. In week 20, Alex and Natasha found out they were having a boy. Natasha was disappointed as she had always wanted a girl. For a long time, she refused to accept that she was having a boy and called her baby bump "Ella".

Alex got a job at a prestigious car dealership, selling cars. Well, he tried. Things were not going well, for some reason. Once again, there was not enough money, despite their own apartment and help from Natasha's family. Natasha became cross with Alex. She felt that she had provided Alex with everything he could dream of: a family, a cosy home, delicious dinners, an attractive and comfortable environment, yet he could not achieve anything even under such conditions.

"Maybe you're doing something wrong?" Natasha tried to help him. "Maybe you're not talking to the clients the right way? You had some success in your last job."

"Well, that was my last job," Alex would snap. "Don't confuse the last place with this one! That was the capital, but here we're surrounded by hillbillies!"

"At least these hillbillies have money, which they've earned!" Natasha would reply indignantly. "If you're so clever, why are you serving them instead of them serving you?"

The relationship deteriorated quickly. Natasha realized that it was mainly physical attraction that had previously held together. Once she fell pregnant, the connection disappeared and all his flaws became visible, overshadowing his good qualities. Natasha discovered that she did not respect her husband – there was no reason to. The more time passed, the more she realized that she had married a child. Despite looking like an adult, inside he was a boy who had yet to grow up. Natasha did not know if she could raise a man in him, but still she hoped and believed that she could.

"Have you considered getting a side job?" she asked one day. "I've looked through the ads and there are some very good vacancies."

"I don't know," Alex replied reluctantly.

"It's only temporary, until I'm back in the game. You get off early and you leave home late. Why don't you have a look at the ones I've highlighted?"

"Well, all right," he said grudgingly.

Natasha could see that he did not want to change anything. His life was very comfortable. He brought home his meagre salary, which was never enough, and had no idea that all this time, they were living on handouts from Natasha's mother.

One day, Natasha began another conversation about improving their financial well-being.

"You know, I've been thinking, why don't you change your line of work?"

"To what?"

"Start making something yourself, for example."

"Like what?"

"I don't know, you could open a small printing centre, take passport photos for people. I've already had a look, the start-up capital would be small, so I think we could manage. We could also print the photos and put them in beautiful boxes tied with a purple ribbon. What do you think?"

He had no thoughts. Alex did not want to change anything. There had already been too many changes that he still had not processed, and now – a new business. The only thing he had ever wanted was for Natasha to be his. He had not considered the responsibility that came with it.

Natasha thought that everything was bound to change. She hoped that as soon as she gave birth and got back on her feet, she would start a business and get Alex involved. Once he saw that things were going well, he would become more ambitious and strive for something.

When she was two months away from giving birth, Alex was invited to a corporate party in another city. Natasha did not want to be left alone, but she understood that Alex needed to strengthen ties with his colleagues, so she let him go. He was gone for three days. Yes, they stayed in touch, but she was the one who called him. It seemed to Natasha that her husband was glad to be free as a bird, and it hurt her feelings. One evening, she called him again and he answered from a noisy place that was not his hotel room.

"Where are you?" she asked warily.

"We're at a bar," he replied cheerfully.

"Hmm, interesting. Isn't it a little late to be out? And why didn't you tell me?"

"What's there to tell? The boss invited me, so I couldn't refuse."

"Alex," said an unfamiliar female voice, "come and join us!"

"Who's that?" Natasha asked indignantly.

"That's Lisa, my work colleague."

Natasha hung up the phone. He called her back a couple of times but that was it.

Alex returned home the next day, smelling of alcohol. Natasha felt disgusted. It reminded her of a horrible memory from her childhood – the reek of her own father, whom she had not spoken to since her parents' divorce.

Of course, she threw a well-deserved tantrum. She said that he had not gone to a corporate event to drink, but to bond with his colleagues and impress his boss.

"I was left home alone!" she shouted. "You weren't going there to party!"

"I wasn't partying," he defended himself. "So what if we went to a bar and had a couple of drinks? So what?"

"Nothing! You're not listening to me, as usual! I don't want to look at you."

Natasha slammed the front door and went outside. Wandering around the town, she thought, what has happened to her life if she did not want to return to her own apartment?

Coming home when it was growing dark, she found Alex sleeping on the couch, wearing the same clothes he had arrived in. He was snoring loudly with his mouth open and drooling onto her clean new sofa. Natasha had never felt more revolted in her life. After this incident, Natasha started sleeping in a separate bed.

Natasha's birthday was fast approaching. She had disliked this day ever since she was a child and did not plan on celebrating it, but she was still looking forward to well wishes from her loved ones. Waking up on the special day, she walked into the kitchen. There were no balloons or flowers, not even a festive breakfast, which she was used to from past relationships. Alex was sleeping on the couch and, apparently, had no intention of congratulating her.

Natasha turned on the coffee machine and began cooking her own breakfast. The noise woke Alex up.

"Good morning," he said.

"Good morning," she replied through clenched teeth.

"Why the bad mood, birthday girl?" he asked.

"Nothing, everything's fine," she reassured him, not wanting to start the day with complaints again.

"Are you going to congratulate your mother?"

"Of course! It's a family tradition. You're not going to congratulate me?" Natasha could not hold it back any longer.

"I will, just a little later. I ran out of time yesterday."

"You were home," Natasha said in surprise. "Was it so hard to get up early and at least inflate a couple of balloons?"

"I told you, I ran out of time. And where would I have hidden these balloons?"

"You could have hidden them in the kitchen."

"You would have heard me. I'll have everything set up by the time you get back."

Natasha went to visit her mother in a bad mood. Unlike her husband, she had prepared in advance, with a gift, a bouquet of flowers and balloons for her mother.

Her mood improved a little while she was at her mother's house, and she tried to calm down and find an excuse for Alex on the way home. When she entered the house, she found a bouquet of flowers and a card with a single line: "I wish your family happiness. Alex."

"That's strange," Natasha thought, "why your family and not our family?"

Natasha felt like her list of complaints could not get any longer until she discovered her husband's texts to Lisa, his work colleague. Yes, it was probably Natasha's fault, she should not have gone poking around in his phone, but there they were. Natasha thought that Alex loved her, which meant that he could not be chatting with other women. To her surprise, she discovered that their messages had nothing to do with work. They were flirting

– he sent her his photos and she sent him hers. He was writing her compliments, and they appeared to be spending all their time at work together. Natasha was very hurt by this. Especially now, when she was in such a vulnerable position and had gained over 40 pounds. Natasha dug deeper and, opening the chat with Alex's mother, saw that he was constantly complaining about his wife. He wrote that Natasha was constantly demanding something from him, that he was tired of living like this but could not leave Natasha because he had lost his former life and former job because of her. He wanted to go back and had no desire to live in this, as he put it, backwater. His mother felt sorry for him and insisted that he return to his hometown. She wrote that he had a home where he would always be loved and accepted.

Natasha had not finished reading it all when the bathroom door opened. She quickly closed all the tabs and tossed the phone back on the couch. Her heart was pounding and there were tears in her eyes. She was a good wife: she always greeted Alex after work with her make-up and hair done. There was always a hot, delicious dinner on the table, and his shirts and trousers were perfectly pressed. She tried so hard for him, she really did. And what did she get in return? Getting paid back with what she definitely did not deserve?

She was silent for a couple of days, claiming that she felt unwell. A storm raged inside her. The child, sensing his mother's state, was also unsettled and kicked very painfully. She called Alex when she had gathered up the courage for a talk.

"I need to talk to you," she began seriously.

He was all ears.

"Alex, I looked at your phone and read your messages."

"What did you read?" he immediately tensed up.

"All of it. First of all, how can you flirt with another woman when you have a wife and are about to have a baby?"

"I wasn't flirting. She's the one who writes to me!" he defended himself.

"Don't lie, I can't stand it," she continued coolly. "Second, how can you complain about me to your mum when you've got such a good life here? You don't even know where the money comes from, do you? Do you think we live on the $400 you proudly bring home and still manage to use for drinking all the time?"

"You know I'm still on probation!"

"I told you to find a part-time job. You need to quit this job if it's not working out. You've got to do something, instead of leeching off my mother. Alex, we should get divorced. And this isn't just my "hormones" playing up, I'm serious. I've thought long and hard about it and I just don't see another way out. Our relationship has turned into a mother-son relationship, and I don't want to be your mum, I want to be your wife."

Alex did not answer and seemed to be considering her words.

"Well? Don't you have anything to say?" she wanted him to promise that it would never happen again, that he would be a good husband to her from now on, but this was not what he said.

"Natasha, let's not rush into anything. If you don't like me texting Lisa, then I'll block her. We weren't flirting anyway. She just writes to me. And I didn't exactly complain to my mum. She started telling me to come home all of a sudden, saying that life in my hometown is much easier and that I have a place there. Of course, I have no plans to return there. There was a reason I left when I was 23. It's even more of a backwater than this one. And I'll quit my job and find something else. You shouldn't be getting stressed in your condition."

"I'm not stressed – I just can't live like this anymore. Our relationship isn't working out. It's nothing like what I wanted."

"Look, it's going to be okay. You need to calm down. How can you talk about a divorce when we're about to have a baby!"

It was Natasha's turn to stop and think. She had no idea how she would manage alone with a child, so she decided to give their family another chance.

On a cold and rainy October night, Natasha woke up from a strong click. She realized that her water had broken. Jumping out of bed, she ran to the bathroom to check. Yes, indeed, the time had come.

"Alex," she panicked, "my water broke!"

"What?" he asked, baffled.

"My water. Get up!"

"What should I do?" he asked sleepily.

"You're asking me? You said that you read the book I gave you!"

"I read it, I read it," he lied. "Just a minute."

He staggered out of bed and went to get dressed. Natasha went to the shower to wash her hair. She struggled to dry it as the contractions were getting stronger. Although she had prepared for childbirth and had read plenty of books, she went completely blank at this crucial moment. She forgot how to breathe properly, forgot what the time between contractions should be.

It was drizzling outside when they left the house. Natasha was filled with fear as she climbed into the taxi. She had been eagerly awaiting the baby's arrival, but now she dreaded going to hospital. To make matters worse, she had previously stumbled across various videos about women not surviving childbirth or their long-awaited children dying by accident.

"It will be fine," Alex reassured her, not worried about his wife at all. He obviously did not realize what she would soon have to go through.

Once at the hospital, Alex escorted Natasha to the ward and went home. Natasha insisted on it. She did not want Alex to witness the event. Maybe if he had stayed, he would have understood what women go through when they give birth to a new human being.

Natasha's labour was very tough. She bitterly regretted refusing the epidural anaesthesia, eager to experience all the delights of childbirth. She changed her mind after a painfully long time.

"Give me something," she begged. "I can't stand it."

The pain relief the nurses gave her did not work, and she still felt excruciating pain. It felt as if her insides were being stirred with a large metal spoon. After nine hours of labour, Natasha gave birth to a baby boy. Tears of happiness flowed down her cheeks – not because she was now a mother, but because this hell was finally over.

When the already clean baby was placed on her chest, she looked at him for the first time. He was a charming little boy, or maybe it just seemed like that to her. He had pale skin, blond hair and a small button nose.

"Edgar," she whispered and kissed her son gently on the forehead.

After putting her son in the cot, Natasha texted her mum and Alex, took a shower and finally lay down in bed on her stomach.

Alex arrived late in the afternoon. He looked odd. Natasha noticed the change in him at once but could not understand what had happened to him.

"You're very silent. Is something wrong?"

"No, no, it's fine. I just can't believe that I have a son. We have a son."

Natasha did not believe him. There was a chill coming from Alex but now was not the time to focus on her husband. She had to think about her son.

When they were discharged home a couple of days later and she was left alone with the baby, without the help of the nurses, Natasha was terrified. The child cried incessantly or, rather, screamed. Natasha was not ready for this.

"Alex, you need to get home right away!" she shouted into the phone, calling her husband at work. "He hasn't stopped crying for two hours. There's something wrong with him."

"Maybe we should call a doctor?" he suggested.

"Oh, my God! Always with your "maybe"!"

"Well, what can I do to help? I'll try to leave work early."

Yes. Try. Once again, the problem did not concern him. She called an ambulance for nothing, as the doctors later explained to her. Edgar was simply suffering from colic, and it was completely normal for him to cry like that. He was prescribed some medications, which, as Natasha later found out, did not work. That was all.

Edgar was asleep by the time Alex came home from work. The house was a mess, used diapers scattered everywhere and a mountain of dishes in the sink.

"Let me sit with him," he suggested, "and you take care of the chores."

He took the child and sat with him in front of the TV, while Natasha went to clean up the house.

Life with a baby turned out to be much more difficult than Natasha had imagined. Alex was at work, not that it did much good, while she took care of the house and the child. In the first two weeks after having the baby, Natasha felt like she had aged ten years. She barely slept and barely ate. Each night, she had to get up five times to feed Edgar. He did not stop feeding for hours and then screamed because of stomach pain.

One night, Natasha woke Alex up and asked him to put socks on Edgar. She could not do it herself as she was feeding him.

"Where are the socks?" Alex asked in a displeased tone.

"In the dresser."

"Which drawer?"

"The first one," Natasha replied in a whisper.

"There aren't any socks here."

"There are. Green ones. Check again."

"I found them."

Then Alex could not put the socks on the little feet, fiddling with them for at least 10 minutes. Natasha was fuming.

"Can't you do anything right?"

"I can," he snapped.

"How dare you speak to me like that?" she was indignant. "I feel sorry for you, so I don't wake you up when he wakes up, and you can't even put his socks on!"

"Then I can't. Calm down."

"Calm down? He's your son, too. Do you have any idea how tired I've been? More than you. At least you get a break at work, but where's my break? I should be resting this soon after the birth, not cooking, washing and cleaning up. You come home from work and lie on the couch with him instead of doing the housework! You're useless. How long are you going to keep this up?"

Alex stood up from the bed abruptly, picked up his blanket and left the room. As a parting gift, he swore at her. Natasha felt as if a bucket of ice water had been poured over her. This was unacceptable in her family and for her in particular. She had never heard Dad treat Mum like that.

"What did you say?" she gasped.

"What you heard. I've had it with you."

Natasha was left alone in the room with the baby in her arms. She did not leave the bedroom in the morning to avoid running into Alex. She had no energy left to argue or sort out a relationship that no longer seemed to exist.

She thought long and hard during the day and concluded that Alex had to leave. She realized that she could no longer put up with what was happening in her own home. She wrote him the following message:

"Alex, I've been thinking and realized that I can't do this anymore. As I've said before, you need to grow up, but you never did. I can't and I won't be responsible for two sons. You should listen to your mum and return to her, especially since you've both decided that I'm a terrible person. I wish you every happiness, and I'm sorry that it turned out this way. I was hoping you'd change, but I guess it's true that people don't change. I don't want our son to grow up and see such a disrespectful attitude towards his mum. I certainly know that I can’t forgive you. They were terrible words, and I can understand if they were addressed to a man, but to a woman, your wife, who recently gave you a son? No, I can't accept that. That's all."

She saw that he had read her message and waited for his reply, but none came. In the evening, he came home in silence as she sat watching TV. Approaching her, he turned the TV to silent and spoke. "I thought about what you wrote, and I agree with you. I'm leaving."

Natasha thought she ready for this, but she had not expected him to agree so easily.

"What about Edgar?"

"It was your decision, and the responsibility is yours too."

"Hmm. I see."

"I can't take care of you. I'm not ready for this. I knew it as soon as I saw him. I know you'll say that I'm a grown man, I'm 35 years old and everything, but I just can't."

"And how am I supposed to live alone with a baby? With no financial support? All the money that Mum gave us is long gone..."

"I don't know. You'll figure something out."

"And when are you leaving?"

"Tomorrow."

"Have you already bought a ticket?"

"Yes."

Natasha had nothing left to say. She would not hold him here. She could see that nothing could stop him, and that the child was her problem alone.

The next day, he took his remaining salary and came home early to pack his suitcase. Natasha even helped him pack his things. She could not believe that he would leave just like that. He took all the expensive gifts she had ever given him, too.

When his things were packed, Alex went to Edgar's crib, picked him up and said, "I hope you grown up to be a good person. Forgive me."

"Alex! How am I going to cope on my own? You can go to my brother's house and stay with him for a while, since we can't be together, but still help me with the baby. At least I can find a job then and get back on my feet. There's one dollar and one last diaper left at home."

Alex did not answer. He put the baby back in the crib and headed for the door.

"Do you realise that this will ruin whatever good is left between us — even for the sake of our child?"

"I understand," he replied, opening the door.

He left without saying goodbye. Natasha remained standing in the hallway, listening to the descending lift.

Strangely enough, she felt quite calm when she went to bed and woke up in the morning. To her surprise, Edgar slept soundly all night without waking up. After getting ready, she fed her son, dressed him, dressed herself and stepped outside with the pram. Large flakes of snow were falling from the sky, and she felt very peaceful. When she reached the right building, Natasha unbuttoned her down jacket and took out the jewellery she had wrapped in a napkin. There was a diamond engagement ring, a chain, and a few sets of gold earrings. After pawning her pieces at the pawnshop, Natasha went to the supermarket. She bought diapers and groceries and came home with a calm heart. She could do this. On the way, she reflected that she was in a much better position than some other women. She had her own apartment, she was relatively healthy, and she had a family, which was the most important thing. However, she did not tell her family that Alex had left her. She did not know what she would do next or how she would survive, but she was certain that everything would turn out fine. She believed it.

When Edgar was two months old, Natasha enrolled in a makeup and hairdressing course. Her brother looked after Edgar during this time. Having learned the tricks of the trade, she began to visit clients in their homes. There were not many at first, but over time, Natasha became a well-known figure in the city. She raised her prices and no longer took on every bride. She was good at her job and worked hard. The customers were satisfied and thanked her.

There was enough money for everything, and Natasha even managed to get a babysitter. She secretly followed Alex's life, which was sickening to watch. He returned to the city where they had met and spent time with his old friends, travelling to expensive resorts. Natasha was very hurt. Hurt that she was the only one who cared about this gorgeous, healthy child and that she alone bore responsibility for him, including financial responsibility. Life was hard. No one saw her crying at night from frustration or her tears of exhaustion.

When Edgar turned two, Natasha decided to move to a warmer region, with glittering waves and palm trees swaying in the breeze. Life bustled and sparkled in the new city, but not for her. She felt down, sad, lonely and scared. She did not know that this happened to everyone at first. She did not know that this city would become her home with time, but now it was a strange place full of strange people. Sha wanted to go back for a long time, but something held her here.

It took a while to get her life in order.

Her professional skills were not in demand in this new place, for there were plenty of other make-up artists. Natasha had to come up with something else. The city was expanding rapidly, and people were moving here from all over the country. Natasha promptly got a job as a real estate agent. She was good at it and knew how to charm people. For the first time in her life, she had plenty of money. She began to enjoy life, spending money on herself and Edgar, and sending money back to her mother. They moved into a spacious apartment, its windows overlooking the water. In the morning, Natasha loved to make coffee and look out at the white-caps churned up by the blue sea current.

Edgar had started first grade when Natasha began dating her dentist. He was a good, kind, mature and self-sufficient man. He admired everything about Natasha, especially her sharp mind. He could listen to her for hours and admired her. Natasha liked him, but she did not consider marriage, even though he had asked her more than once. She did not want to let a stranger into her house and close to her son, even though she saw that Edgar gravitated towards her boyfriend. It seemed that he missed having a father figure after all.

Speaking of his father. One day, Natasha and Edgar went to show a properly in a newly built luxury building. The clients were running late, so Natasha decided to go to a cafe to pass the time.

They sat down at a table, ordered, and started fooling around while waiting for their order to arrive. After a good long laugh, they had a delicious lunch, and Natasha was asking for the bill when she suddenly felt someone's intense gaze on her. She had not brought her glasses with her, so she could not make out the other person's face. It took Natasha a moment to realize that it was not the waiter approaching their table.

"Natasha!" a familiar stranger addressed her.

Natasha stared at his face and could not believe her eyes. Alex stood before her. Frankly, he looked bad, wearing cheap, not very clean clothes and with a creased, puffy face.

"Hello," she said calmly.

"Hello. It's good to see you."

"I don't know if I can say the same."

"Is this Edgar?" he asked, nodding towards the child.

"Yes," Natasha snapped. "My son."

"And mine, too."

Natasha glared at him and replied, "He's my son. The son I've taken care of and been responsible for all these years. The son I stayed up all night with, and these aren't just words, I really did stay up all night. He's my child."

"Well, I can see that everything turned out well with you."

"Yes, everything is fine, thank God."

"What are you doing here?"

"We came in for lunch. What about you?"

"I'm here with a friend for a couple of days. How long are you here for?"

"We live here."

"Oh, right."

There was silence.

"I hope you're well." Natasha forced out. "Are you working?"

"Yes, things are fine. I'm working at my friend's company."

"Doing what?"

"I'm a courier. I deliver this and that."

"I see. Talk about career growth."

"Right," he laughed awkwardly. "And you're still the same smartmouth, I see."

"It's what life made me." Her phone rang. "Well, we have to go."

"Shall I walk you out?"

"There's no need," she replied, paying the bill.

He followed them out anyway. He was startled when Natasha took out her keys and a nearby car beeped loudly.

"A Mercedes?" he was surprised.

"Yes, I've always wanted one. Edgar, get in the car. Well, I don't know what kind of meeting this was but, in any case, I wish you the best."

"Can we meet again?" he asked hopefully.

"We'll never meet again. We made our own choices, and we bear the responsibility for them. I managed. Goodbye."

She drove away from the cafe with a roar. She saw his hunched shoulders and dull gaze. Perhaps he was thinking about what could have been, or perhaps he was not thinking about anything. Natasha did not care anymore. She had a life to live and a son to raise.

A psychological portrait of the characters and the mistakes they made

1. Natasha

Characteristics:

- An active person with high expectations

Before meeting Alex, she was in a painful relationship that ended badly. She suffered serious emotional damage and decided to "heal" by quickly marrying someone else, as if shutting the door on the past.

She craves stability but also sets quite a high bar: she wants her partner to increase his earnings, grow and make decisions. She is not afraid of change (for example, moving to another city) and knows how to quickly organize her life.

- Wants to tightly control everything (she proposed to Alex herself and decided to have a child despite Alex's repeated "no".

Important: this pattern develops when a person experiences situations in their youth when their family and loved ones lost control (illness, lack of money, divorce, or parental abandonment). This leads to the subconscious idea of "I'll never a situation get out of control again".

It may also be due to unrealistic expectations and a heightened sense of responsibility instilled by a person's parents, such as pressure to do well at school and behave perfectly.

The next possibility may be the inability to rely on others. Perhaps there was a lack trust in one's partner in the family. Perhaps Mum and Dad fought, or Dad failed to show that he was responsible, etc.

The tendency to control everything is often due to a combination of personal traits (anxiety, perfectionism) and life circumstances (for example, passive parents or early traumatic experiences). Together, it creates the scenario of "either I decide or everything will fall apart".

How to loosen tight control:

1. *Understand the root of the problem. Remember what caused it the first time.*
2. *Develop self-awareness. Ask yourself the questions of why and what for. What am I afraid of? Why am I controlling this particular situation?*
3. *Learn to delegate and trust.*
4. *Learn to ask for help. Accept that you can't (and shouldn't) do everything on your own.*
5. *Allow yourself to make mistakes.*

- The unmet need for a strong man

Natasha's past relationship was quite fiery. Now she wants a "safe harbour", but she does not consider that Alex's quiet nature could mean passivity and a lack of growth.

She becomes irritated when Alex doesn't develop and doesn't take responsibility, preferring to remain in his comfort zone.

- The principle of "I'm not your mother"

Natasha feels that Alex acts like a child. Once she has her own child, she is not prepared to "carry" someone's else adult child.

- The ability to quickly deal with difficulties

She doesn't develop an addiction or become depressed after the breakup. She changes her living environment and tries to build a career.

Main mistakes:

- Getting married for the wrong reasons

She chooses the quiet Alex after a difficult breakup, without considering whether they are suited to each other in their values and goals.

- Ignoring red flags

They quarrel over money on their wedding night. Natasha rationalizes everything: "we need money," but does not wonder why she is the only one concerned about their problems.

· Pressure and harsh criticism

Uses derogatory comments to complain ("you're not a man");

The mindset of "if you don't grow, then I don't need you" is a harsh stance that leaves no room for compromise.

· Insufficient cooperation when raising the child

Natasha plans and organizes her son's life without involving her husband. Therefore, Alex is pushed out of the family system.

The mother-son dynamic in their relationship is partly her fault as she adopts the "I know better" position, leaving no room for her husband to take the initiative.

2. Alex

Characteristics:

· Passive codependent personality

Calm, doesn't like to take initiative and tends to go with the flow.

· Avoids difficulties

He demonstrates apathy if any problems arise (relocation, the need for part-time work): "I don't know, I don't want to, I don't like it".

He withdraws in moments of conflict, such as spending the night on the couch and chatting to Lisa.

- The need for support and an easy life

He is happy that Natasha, the "star", notices him, and so feels that he is in an advantageous position. However, he does not consider that such a woman might need a more mature man.

He finds it convenient that Natasha's mom pays for everything and that the household runs smoothly but doesn't want to put in the effort to meet Natasha's expectations.

- Emotional immaturity

May swear and speak rudely in stressful situations.

Doesn't know how to sympathize with a pregnant wife or newborn child, instead saying "I'm not ready".

Texts another woman and complains to his mother, i.e. he seeks pity and support from outsiders instead of solving the problem with his wife.

Main mistakes:

- Agreeing to take a serious step without considering the consequences.
- Lack of self-development and unwillingness to look for a fulfilling job.
- Emotional infidelity/flirting with Lisa.
- Shifting the blame onto others.

3. Lisa (Alex's colleague)

Main mistakes:

- Flirting with a married colleague.

***

These are the stories I am proud of, because I was part of them, helping these women become the best versions of themselves and overcome all adversity.

YOU HAVE OBSESSIVE THOUGHTS

Finally, I'm home. I close the door and undress right in the hallway. I want to take a hot shower and wash away today. Leave it in the past. I don't want to think about it or remember it anymore. I know that Gishi and I are facing our final battle, and it makes me nervous.

Many years ago, I was already under suspicion by a detective. And where is he now? I have a proven plan, and I'm sure it will work this time. Gishi turned out to be a weakling. His wounds from the past still hurt, and that's bad for him because they can be used against him. By me, of course.

After a shower, I settle down on the sofa and turn on a mindless TV series to give my brain a little rest. But it doesn't want to rest; it's thinking through our next plan of action, down to the smallest details.

The next day, I go to work again. Only this time, before leaving the house, I turn on the camera. I know that sooner or later, Gishi will find his way into my house. Most likely, given his diagnosis, that's exactly what will happen.

On the way to work, I analyze his personality and the motive for his future crime. Will it be breaking and entering, theft, stalking, or all of the above?

If Gishi fails to prove my guilt, namely that I am the maniac, he will perceive it as his own fault. "You're not good enough again," he will hear his father's voice say.

He won't be able to stop, he won't be able to let me go, because that would mean he failed, and that is unbearable for him. I know how you think, Gishi!

You doubt your guess, you start checking the facts and yourself, wondering if you made a mistake somewhere. You think you missed something, and that there is irrefutable evidence of my guilt in the files and in my folders.

You search and search, losing your peace of mind and your already restless sleep. You are in a constant state of tension, afraid of making mistakes, and it is exactly like your relationship with your father.

But you are not driven by a search for the truth, but by an attempt to restore order in your soul. And of course, none of this is about professional duty.

Come on, Heleina, tell me what's really going on!

There's a little boy inside you, and he thinks that if he does everything right, he'll finally be loved. The trap has closed.

In the office parking lot, I notice an old car. It doesn't belong to any of my employees. I deliberately drive closer so that I'm level with the window of the driver I already know.

"Good morning, Detective Gishi," I shout, opening my window.

He turns away and pretends to look for something in the back seat.

I repeat my good morning and wait for him to turn around.

"Good morning, Miss Pascal! "he replies, turning to me.

"Do you have any more questions for me?"

"Yes," he replies, trying to sound as confident as possible.

"Well, you can come to my office, and we can discuss everything in a more pleasant setting."

I know he didn't want to come to my office at all. He wanted to follow me, and I had cleverly thwarted his plans. He already hates me for it.

I go into the office without waiting for Gishi. Throwing my bag on the sofa, I go to my fancy coffee machine and brew the detective a fragrant cup of coffee. I put a spoonful of sugar in the coffee, pour in some cream and a little milk. This makes the coffee mild and quite pleasant. I put some cookies and candies on a plate next to it. I'm sure he loves sweets. As a child, he was probably watched closely to see what he ate and restricted in many ways.

When Gishi enters my office, I invite him to sit down in the chair and serve him hot coffee without asking if he wants it. I deliberately let him know that I am in charge here and he is just a subordinate.

"You didn't sleep very well either, detective? " I ask solicitously.

"No, I slept well," he lies.

"You look tired. Have you been checking yourself again?"

"Check myself for what?" he asks defensively.

"For the mistakes you've made, of course. You came here today to follow me, didn't you? You don't have any evidence, so you decided to find it another way. You know how it is: sometimes people just want to be recognized. Even if it means persecuting innocent people."

"Do you consider yourself innocent?"

"What do you consider me guilty of?"

He rolls his eyes.

"Not those tricks again!"

"No tricks, just a simple question. You and I are similar, very similar, we just have different methods of survival."

"We are not similar at all! I am on the side of truth, and you are on the side of what?"

"The truth?" I can barely keep from laughing. 'Is it really the truth?' I ask, staring intently at him. "As I already told you, you're not chasing the truth, you're chasing what you were deprived of as a child—recognition." And even though, presumably, your father has long since passed away, you continue to fight him internally. Apparently, he died before your brilliant career began. You do have a brilliant career, don't you? I ask this question deliberately, because I know that he never achieved anything significant in all his years of work. At least nothing outstanding or substantial, that's for sure.

Watching his reaction, I realize that I'm on the right track. I'll crush you mentally, even without using hypnosis, which is what Eleanor really fell for.

"My career may not be brilliant, but one thing you can't take away from me is my professional instinct. I spoke to Eleanor yesterday, and she still insists that she was subjected to some kind of interference."

"What kind of interference?" I ask, raising an eyebrow.

"It's unclear. At first, she was adamant that it was hypnosis and said it was you."

"And what does she say now?"

"Now she says you have nothing to do with it. The thing is, she's been having seizures."

"Hmm, strange, probably due to stress. What kind of stress? "I ask, pretending not to know.

"She says she's burning up."

"Oh, my God!" I explode. "So, a mentally unstable woman is giving dubious testimony, and you start suspecting me?!"

"Didn't you know she was unstable?"

"When she came to see me, she was fine! We don't know what triggered her behaviour. Maybe her husband said something to her that morning or something else. You looked at my records, you should know that she was fine."

I can see that he doesn't believe me. Intellectually, he understands that I am right and truly innocent, but his heart tells him otherwise.

He's leaving me with nothing. In the days that follow, he'll check every little clue again, search for my relatives again to establish my identity. But he won't find anything, because absolutely everyone I'm related to is dead.

The following days pass quietly, but one evening, when I'm late coming home from work, I receive a notification on my phone that there's movement in my apartment. I take out my phone, open the camera, and see Gishi. I don't let him know right away that I know he's there. I give him a chance to rummage through my things.

Finding nothing in the bedrooms or my study, he goes into the living room, where a folder with his name on it is lying on the coffee table in plain sight. He slowly approaches the folder and shudders at my voice coming from the camera.

"Mr. Gishi, I didn't expect to see you in my house. Were you rummaging through my panties? I hope you managed to grab one before the police arrived?"

My laughter echoes through the apartment, and Gishi leaves the scene of the crime. After his escape, he will probably tell one of his close colleagues about the break-in, perhaps Fraser. She will certainly try to help him, speaking with a voice of friendship and support.

Two hours later, my phone rings.

"Hello," I answer.

"Good evening, Miss Pascal, sorry for calling so late. I know you've had an unpleasant incident, " Fraser says to me.

"What are you talking about, detective?" I ask, puzzled.

"It's about my partner. I don't know how to explain it."

"Did something happen to him?"

"Of course. He was at your place. He broke in."

"No one broke into my place, Detective Fraser, "I say with complete confidence.

"What? He claims he broke into your apartment two hours ago."

"Oh," I sigh, "it's started, hasn't it?"

"Started what?"

"The progression of his illness. I told him about it when he came to see me for a consultation."

"A consultation?"

"Yes. He came to my office a week ago. He was very tense, so I made him some coffee, gave him some candy, and we talked about everything that was bothering him." I may be meddling in something that's none of my business, but if Gishi is important to you, I advise you to take some action.

We say goodbye, Detective Fraser apologizes again, and I reply that everything is fine. The "distrust" machine is set in motion. Now Fraser will divide everything Gishi says in half and not trust him 100%. What's more, now every time Gishi talks about me, he'll be digging his own grave. It won't be long now.

For the time being, I distance myself from driving Gishi crazy and go about my business, but by the time Gishi's condition is more stable than not, I make my way to his house. His home is shabby, clearly that of a bachelor. An old, worn-out sofa, a coffee table covered with letters and papers, and a small refrigerator. That's what's in the living room. There is no bed in his bedroom, only a mattress covered with a dirty blanket. On the wall in front of the bed hangs a board where he writes down all his thoughts. I read his notes and realize that he is a good man, on the right path.

There is nothing more for me to see here. As I leave, I spray his pillow with my perfume and leave a note on his table with a single sentence: "You are not good enough." This is a phrase he has known well since his early childhood.

Now all I have to do is wait for him to come home, smell my perfume, and see my message. He'll know it's me. He'll frantically search his tiny apartment for something else, but I didn't leave anything else. Then he'll find the empty bag, put my note in it, and the next day he'll go to the police station to have my fingerprints taken and my handwriting checked. Of course, the note will be empty the next morning, because I'll sneak back to his place while he's asleep, and he won't check his main piece of evidence before leaving for work. In the days that follow, I will make him paranoid. I will stand under his windows so that he can see my silhouette, I will call him on his phone and remain silent. I'll sneak into his house again so that he won't feel safe anywhere. And since

I already know that he can no longer control himself, it won't be long before he bursts into my office. It will happen after he sees that his board is gone, that his meticulously and even lovingly collected notes are gone.

Two months have passed since our personal meeting, and now I finally see him again. He bursts into my office. A client is sitting in the office, but Gishi doesn't care. He grabs me by the throat, stares at me with wild eyes, and repeats, “I know it's you,” while choking me. People rush into the office, trying to pull him off me, while I cry dramatically and play the victim. The police arrive at the office, handcuff Gishi, and I say only one sentence as I leave: “You are always to blame for everything.”

This is followed by a lot of red tape with statements and other legal issues. Gishi is sent for treatment. What is his condition? He agrees with everything he is accused of, he easily agrees to undergo treatment, he is broken. He considers himself guilty of everything. He begins to replay all the moments of his childhood, all the mistakes he has made. Moreover, he blames himself even where he is not at all guilty. He blames himself for not being able to protect his mother from his father, who most likely abused her as well as his son. He blames himself for not being able to make his wife happy, devoting himself entirely to his work. He will begin to blame himself for attacking me and will also begin to doubt himself and his assumptions. He will start to think that all his notes and guesses are false until he receives a bouquet of orchids with a small card inside. The card will say, “You were right.” This does not make him feel any better, because with each passing day, he is gradually slipping further into a vegetative state due to the sedatives.

Did I satisfy my thirst for thrills? Probably yes, more than no. I was curious to see what I could do. It's a pity that he turned out to be such a weakling! Perhaps deep down I wanted him to get the better of me and even put me behind bars. I often imagined my life in prison. The work there would have been much more interesting than the work I do here.

WAS I BORN OR WAS I MADE?

I have two new clients I'm writing their files and staying late at work. I don't want to punish them, there's no reason to. Life has beaten one of them up without my help, even though she's a good person. And once again, I am convinced that life is unfair. Right, Angel?

Was I Born or Was I Made?

This tale happened many years ago, when I was in my final year of university. As I was young and inexperienced, I dreamed that my work would change the world for the better. I still have not achieved this much, and I no longer have the desire. What can I say, we all tend to fall victim to youthful idealism.

At the time, I was writing a term paper called "Are criminals born or made?" and, luckily for me, I could hear about it straight from the horse's mouth. My aunt Jane, who worked in prisons, often told me creepy stories of crimes committed, as she thought, by people who were not inclined to crime at all. Therefore, I called her as soon as I had chosen the topic for my upcoming paper. She was happy to help me. Thanks to her, obtaining permits and the other paperwork went like clockwork and, a week later, I travelled to a neighbouring state to begin my research. Had I known then how deeply it would affect me, for the rest of my life, I would never have gone and would have chosen an easier topic. But it is what it is.

Having reached the small town and left my things at the hotel, I immediately went to the prison. The people working there greeted me warmly – I was a cheerful girl and they liked it. The atmosphere was quite decent for such a place. Everything was clean and tidy, everyone was busy with their tasks, and only the orange uniforms and bars served as a reminder that this was no holiday retreat.

I spoke to many prisoners. Nearly all of them seemed like pleasant members of the human race – until I found out the reason why they were in prison.

I take a dim view of illegal substances and believe that this criminal offence is tantamount to murder, since someone may die from an overdose. Once there, however, I realized that illegal substances were the least of my worries. I remember one man in particular. He was getting on in years, but his face still reflected the beauty of his youth. He was clever, well-mannered and polite. He clearly did not belong in this place.

"What has he been imprisoned for?" I asked my aunt once.

"He killed his wife and children."

My eyes widened and I blurted out, "No way! Him?"

"Yes," Jane smiled sadly. "You can't really trust anyone in here. They might look harmless, but you have no idea what's going on inside their heads."

"How did it happen?"

"He claimed temporary insanity, but I don't believe it. He was cheating on his wife, and she found out about it. She threatened to take the children and the house and said that he would pay her alimony until he become a beggar, and so on. He shot her while she was sleeping and then killed the children. He wanted to kill himself, too, but people like him care more about their lives than the lives of others."

"Why kill the children?" I asked, shaking my head.

"Who knows? May they rest in peace. You be careful with him and don't listen to what he says. He's a charming devil! Stacks of women come here to see him."

After that, I stayed away from him and avoided even glancing his way. I was so disgusted with him that I could not look at him.

Before coming to this place, I was sure that psychotherapy was my calling. I liked what I was doing, I liked understanding people's motives, feelings and ways of helping them. Prison, however, with its stories of life, death and ruined lives, made me question whether I had made the right choice. Every time I heard a case, a chill ran down my spine, and then I felt a rising hatred for all living things. It was also the first time in my life when I began to doubt God. I was constantly haunted by the same question: why does God allow such monsters to be born and why must others suffer at their hands? I have now found answers and rediscovered religion, but back then, my soul was in utter chaos. Yet that is not what my tale is about.

One day, Jane called me into her office and said, "Ava is heading to the women's prison. Do you want to come with her? There's a woman in there, whose case might be useful for you."

"Is it an interesting case?"

"Not for your paper. For your life."

"Okay, why not?" I agreed and set out the next day.

It was a sunny morning and the sky was a brilliant blue. The sun rose slowly, bathing the ears of corn in a warm light. A light breeze drifted through the slightly open window, and it felt like everything was still ahead of me – joy and happiness and my entire life. I was in a good mood.

Upon reaching my destination, I went to the warden, with whom Jane had already made arrangements. I got acquainted with the case and wrinkled my nose. There was nothing interesting in there – just another domestic murder.

"Oh," I sighed, "what a waste of time."

There was nothing to be done – I was already there, so I decided to go ahead and talk to the prisoner. They left me sitting in a dark office with bars, where I waited. After a while, an incredibly beautiful woman was brought into the room. She was not wearing any make-up, and her hair was tied back in a bun, but none of this diminished her beauty. Nature had clearly been especially generous with her.

"Hello," she greeted me meekly and held out her handcuffed hand.

"Hello," I replied, not holding my hand out in return. "Have a seat. I'm Diana."

"Nice to meet you. My name is Paris."

"That's a beautiful name."

"Yes, my mother was from France. Well, she still is."

An awkward silence fell between us.

"I was told that you were writing a paper," Paris began first.

"Yes, I'm sorry. Let's get started. I'm writing a paper about crime, particularly murders, and what motivates people to do it. That is,

I'm trying to understand whether murder is genetically predetermined or whether it depends on certain external factors."

The woman chuckled. Her laughter was quiet and intelligent.

"I'm sorry," she apologized, "but this is really funny."

"What's so funny about it?"

"You think that killers carry a particular gene? Yes, I agree that there is a small percentage of people who kill for pleasure – psychopathy and sadism can be hereditary. For the most part, however, it is circumstances or other people that make monsters out of us, not our genes."

"Are you familiar with the statistics?"

"Yes, I read a lot on various topics. I used to be a teacher, you know," she said thoughtfully.

"Can you please tell me your story?"

Paris shook her head and then covered her face with her hands. Smoothing her hair, she gazed up at me, and I saw something strange in her eyes. I was not sure, but it looked like fear.

"My story?" she asked. "My story. I replay this story every day in my head and, you know, it drives me crazy sometimes, and I literally start banging my head against the wall of my tiny cell."

"If you don't want to talk about it, then I can leave," I said sympathetically.

"No, no. I think I should tell it. Maybe I'll be of some use to other people, to women, this way."

"Then let's get started," I smiled at her encouragingly. "When were you born? And who are your parents?"

"I was born into a wonderful, kind family. My father was a violinist, and my mother was a pianist. They met at the music academy. We lived modestly but amicably. My parents gave me all they could since I was their only child. You know, there were never any fights or quarrels in our family. I didn't even know that you could grow up in any other way. My dad loved both my mum and me, and he was affectionate, calm and quiet. He turned any tricky moments of life into a joke, and no matter what happened in our lives, we always remained positive. He went through life laughing – this phrase really applies to him. As a child, and even as a teenager, I never caused them any trouble. I was a good girl. I only had one serious argument with them, when it was time to choose a university. I wanted to become an actress, but they insisted on what they thought was a more serious and respectable profession. I don't know... I wonder what would have happened if I had followed my heart and gone to study in another city. Would I have ended up here or would everything have turned out differently? This is my point of return to the past."

She fell silent, staring at the wall, as if reliving what she had said earlier. With a heavy sigh, she continued, "After some thought, we decided that I wouldn't follow in their footsteps. I had no talent for music, so I chose to become a teacher. I don't know if I liked it or not. I loved children, but I wasn't strict enough. I was a pretty good teacher, and the children treated me well. Sometimes, though, they played pranks on me that brought me to tears, and I couldn't punish them or complain to their parents. It felt awkward. My dad felt ill in my fourth year of teaching – he was diagnosed with rectal cancer. It was too late to save him as it was in the last stage. The doctors operated and removed the tumour, but the metastases spread and three months after the diagnosis, he was gone. Mum and I were left alone. It was like a light had gone out in our lives without him. The house grew so quiet, and we stopped laughing. At all. While my work served as a distraction for me, my mother really struggled. She talked to him all the time, as if he was sitting next to her, and at times I thought that she had lost her mind. It was at that vulnerable moment in my life that I met my husband. He was the father of my most well-behaved student. I had never met such polite children before. His mother, on the contrary, was very loud and vulgar, and I wondered how such a clever and kind boy could come from such a family. As I later found out, his parents were divorced and shared custody of their son. While I saw his mother all the time, his father had only recently appeared in his life.

"I'm Rick Martinez," he had said back then. "Gregory's dad."

"It's nice to meet you. I haven't seen you around before," I replied.

"Yes, I was living in another city on a contract. The contract is over, so I'm back and I'll be picking my son up from now on."

"I see," I replied. That was the end of our conversation.

He did pick Gregory up every day from then on. Every time he came to pick up his son, he gave me the most charming smile. Before I realized what had happened, I was looking forward to seeing him at the end of my workday. At that point, I had never been with a man – if you know what I mean – and I had never truly been in love either. A student crush does not count. I suppose I fell for him... or rather, for the idea of him. I thought he was a good father, and he always looked great and smelled amazing. He looked like a real, rugged man, just like in the movies.

One day, I had left the school and was heading to the bus stop as usual. I did not have a car and did not know how to drive. It took me a while to realize that a car was following me. When I turned around, I could not see the driver's face. I had picked up the pace when the car pulled up to me and I saw Gregory's father in the open window.

"Miss Whitty, fancy meeting you here!" he said.

"You scared me to death, Mr. Martinez," I replied.

"Come on, it's just me. Are you heading home?"

"Yes."

"Get in, I'll give you a lift!"

This was my second mistake. I should have refused his offer, I should have noticed that he never even got out of the car, continuing to talk to me through the window. It shows a lack of for a woman. My father would have never done that. But I got in the damn car, and he drove me home. We talked about all sorts of things on the way. I found out that he had a rotation job that involved oil rigs – a field I knew nothing about. He said some beautiful things, and I discovered that he was quite knowledgeable, even about painting. I was pleasantly surprised. When we pulled up in front of my house, we did not say goodbye for a long time. I found him fascinating to talk to. He was something new in my boring little life.

As soon as I stepped inside, my mother bombarded me with questions of who he was and where had I met him. She was worried that I did not have anyone in my life. While all her friends' daughters were married, and some already had children, her daughter continued to live with her and did not date anyone. Of course, Mum did not want me to leave the nest, but her desire for my happiness outweighed her own.

The next day, when I left the school, his car was already gone. I felt a bit disappointed. It was not until I reached my house that I saw him. When he spotted me, he got out of the car with a bouquet of red roses. I had never received such bouquets before. And then? Then I started making mistake after mistake. Countless mistakes over the years.

I married him after a beautiful courtship. It happened quite quickly. If I had gotten to know him better, perhaps I would not be sitting here right now.

I soon discovered that I was pregnant. According to my mother's beliefs, everything was working out the way it should be: a wedding, children and a happy life. There was a wedding and children, but my life was far from happy. I quickly learned that my husband had a terrible temper. At first, it did not touch me – only his son, who stayed with us every weekend.

It turned out that Rick was beating his child, and cruelly. When I first saw a big man like him swing his fist and strike a small, defenceless child on the head, I shuddered. Tears ran down my cheeks and I ran to the child's defence.

"What are you doing?" I shouted at him.

"Mind your own business!" he answered. "Get back!"

I did not leave. He swung at me, but I did not budge and continued to cover the silently crying child with my body. To my shock, the boy did not sob, even though the blow he received had been strong. I found out later that his dad had raised him that way. I should stay out of it, he told me, a nine-year-old boy. He did not want me to get hurt because of him.

"Why did your mum and dad get divorced?" I asked him.

"They were arguing and fighting all the time," he replied calmly, as if this was the norm. "Mum kicked him out and wouldn't let him back in anymore. She said she'd kill him if he ever came near her again."

Well, I would have said to myself today, that is another red flag! Run, run! But I did not run.

I was still working when he hit me for the first time. I think I was seven or eight months pregnant. He showed up at school unannounced and saw me talking to the father of one of the students. I thought nothing of it at the time. It was just a normal conversation between a teacher and a parent, and besides, I was heavily pregnant. I came home as usual, where he was waiting for me. Without saying a word, he walked up to me and slapped me across the face as hard as he could. He had suspected me of being unfaithful. He shouted that I was a harlot and even though I was carrying his child, I was still flirting and batting my eyelashes at other men. For me, who had never experienced anything like it, not even insults, let alone physical abuse, it felt like madness. You know, because no one had ever struck me in my life? I did not know what to do or how to react to it. I think that instead of sending girls to music or dance classes, we should enrol them in martial arts. It would be more useful, considering how much violence is perpetrated against women.

I did not tell my mum about it. I really did not want to upset her, although today, of course, I think that I should have. Yes, she would not have been able to protect me – she is weak – but she could have sheltered me at least. I am sure she would have never let me go back to that monster.

Thus, my life turned into a nightmare. He was constantly jealous, so I could not go anywhere or talk to anyone. Whenever he took me out to a cafe or restaurant, he would beat me up afterwards. He was constantly seeing things that were not there. I tried to talk to him, to explain, but it was all in vain. He could not hear me during those fits of rage. The next day, however, he would become as courteous as before. You are probably thinking "Why didn't you leave?". I do not know myself. I was no longer working, we had a son growing up, and I wanted him to have a full family, like I once had. At the time, divorce seemed like something terrible, like a death that broke people's lives, including the children, because they suffer so much. If someone had told me back then that divorce is normal, that children are healthier emotionally if they survive their parents' divorce rather than suffer constant domestic violence, I would have surely left him. My little son witnessed such awful things in my marriage that I do not know what he will be like with his wife. I pray that he will not end up like his father.

Violence, violence.... Such a simple word. But what does it really mean? Physical pain? You know, it is very painful when someone hits you, strangles you, tries to kill you, or uses your body in the most depraved way. So much adrenaline is released into the bloodstream, such horror and fear that strikes your very heart. You start to fear that it will happen again. You break down mentally and spiritually. You no longer exist as a human being. There is only a small, defeated animal, paralysed by fear. You cannot run and you cannot stop it. I was also on the back foot because he was well off and I was not. If anything happened, he said, he would hire the best lawyer and take my son away from me. I knew that if he took the child, he would beat him just like he beat Gregory. I could not let that happen. My advice to you? Always keep money in your own account. Always. Money is your protection for a rainy day. If a woman has money, she has freedom, including the freedom to choose.

My son was six years old when it all happened. Rick came home from another shift, tired and angry as usual. I was preparing dinner for his arrival. I did not think he would arrive that early, so there was nothing but soup in the house. I was chopping meat, and my son was drawing at the dining table when Rick came in.

"Why are you using pencils at the table?" he asked our son sternly.

"I'm helping mum," my baby replied.

"Welcome home! We're glad to see you," I chimed in, sensing that something was wrong. "Baby, go to your room."

Just as my son got up from the table and gathered up his pencils, Rick saw a mark from one of them on the white table. He grabbed our son by the hair and started pushing his head into the table, where the mark was.

"What's this?" he shouted. "Do you know how much this table costs? Do you know how hard I work so you can live like this?"

My son started crying. This infuriated Rick even more.

"Stop crying! I said, stop it! Are you a weak little girl?"

I went up to my husband and begged him to let our son go. "I'll wash the mark off, it's just pencil!"

"Get out of here! I'm disciplining our son!" he pushed me hard, and I fell back onto the stove, where the meat was frying. The frying pan tipped over my back, but in that moment, I did not feel the pain from the hot oil. All I could see was my son's face, contorted in pain. I remember that I felt calm in that moment. My heart was not racing, and I was not in a rage. I went up to my husband and stuck a knife in his neck, which I had been holding in my hands. He did not understand where the pain had come from. Releasing the boy, he clutched at his neck, blood spurting from the wound.

"Run to your room, baby. Quickly" I ordered my son and watched my husband slowly slide to the floor. I bent down and delivered more blows to him. Twenty-seven, to be precise. Like a compressed spring in physics, I had been wound up to my limit. My patience had run out, albeit in such an unhealthy way, as psychologists would say. That's all."

I sat dumbfounded. So that is what happened to this woman. I crossed my arms and covered my mouth, unable to utter a word. We sat in silence for a long time.

"And then?" I finally asked.

"I rang my mum and asked her to pick my son up. When she arrived, I said only one thing: sorry. Then came the trial. I was sentenced to life in prison, with the right to parole after 25 years. If there had been one blow, I could have blamed it on a fit of passion or self-defence, but there were 28 of them."

"How old is your son now?"

"He's sixteen."

"Are you in touch with him?"

"Yes, of course. My mum and he come to visit me all the time. He grew up to be a good boy. He plays the violin like his grandfather."

She fell silent again. Our time was coming to an end, but I did not want to part with her. I wanted to comfort her somehow, to help her.

"It's going to be okay," I told her. "You have to forgive yourself for all the mistakes. It could have ended worse. You have a son and he's alive."

"Thank you," she said, her smile weary and understanding. "Thank you for your kind words. You know, I've been here for 10 years, and every day and every night of these 10 years, I mentally return to the past and try to change it. My God, if only it could be changed! I would give anything. Even my soul. I have a rich imagination. Sometimes, I imagine the devil appearing in my cell and saying, "Will you give me your soul if I take you back to the past?" "Yes, yes!" I shout in reply. But the devil does not appear. Perhaps my soul already belongs to him for what I did. Even though I experienced unthinkable things – assault and abuse – I realize that I had no right to take someone else's life. My cellmate says that I might have saved more than one woman from the same fate, but I don't believe her. I know that I have sinned, and I have to live with it. Well, going back to your question of whether people are born with this gene. Tell me, was I born a monster or did I become one?"

I sat at the table for a long time after Paris Martinez was taken away, unable to move.

It was getting dark when we returned home. It was the same sky and the same fields, but I no longer felt the goodness of existence or happiness. The next day, I hurriedly completed my experiment and returned home. I wanted to forget what I had seen and heard as soon as possible. I still had to write the paper, though. I completed it on time and got excellent marks.

Years passed. I married a nice man, but that woman's story kept haunting me. I was always trying to spot red flags in people and relationships and avoid them whenever possible. As per her advice, I always kept my money separate from my husband's. Of course, I could see that he was not like the man in my heroine's story and yet...

I quit psychology. I could not live through people's grief with them anymore. I really wanted to help them, but when I dove too deeply into their problems, I fell into despair and bitterness.

I opened a kindergarten, trying to spend more time with children, to give them warmth and care. I never had children of my own. I could not, but I did not particularly want to. Many, many years later, I found out that Mrs. Paris Martinez had finally been released from prison. Her son and his children were there to pick her up. I want to believe that she has found her peace and forgiven herself for all the mistakes she had made. Unfortunately, I cannot know for sure.

A psychological portrait of the characters and the mistakes they made

1. Main character (the young woman writing a term paper)

Characteristics:

· Young and impressionable

She is enthusiastic and believes that she can change the world for the better.

Has recently joined the profession and has not yet acquired the psychological defence mechanisms and self-preservation skills.

· Interest in the psychology of crime

She has an initial simplistic view that the problem can be solved through "nature vs nurture".

Confronted by real cases for the first time, she begins to realize how deep the issue of violence runs and how difficult it is to engage with such stories.

· Strong empathy and emotional engagement

She is deeply shaken by the contrast between how charming some prisoners are and the terrible crimes they have committed.

After meeting Paris, the character understands that she gets too deeply drawn into someone else's grief and does not know how to maintain an emotional distance. As a result, she leaves the field of psychology.

Main mistakes:

- Underestimating the impact of tough stories.
- The "I can help everyone" attitude: youthful idealism ignores the fact that working with criminals requires long-term training, experience and emotional resources. When confronted with real tragedies, she realizes that she is not cut out for this work.
- Excessive self-identification with the victims: Paris's story hurts her deeply and she leaves the profession, unable to preserve her mental health.

2. Aunt Jane

Characteristics:

- A seasoned employee of the system, who witnesses terrible stories all the time.
- Has a realistic view of people

Main mistakes:

- Insufficient psychological care of her niece
- She should have introduced her niece more slowly to the serious cases.

3. <u>Nameless man (who killed his family)</u>

Characteristics:

- Courteous and polite
- A typical charming criminal, capable of pulling the wool over someone's eyes or evoking their sympathy.
- The cold-blooded murder of his wife and children indicates a high level of aggression
- He is a symbol that you cannot judge a book by its cover. A charming devil can turn out to be a monster.

3. <u>Paris Martinez (the woman who killed her husband)</u>

Characteristics:

- A girl from a good family, without a difficult past or trauma.
- Marries an abusive man capable of extreme violence.
- A victim of domestic violence.
- A person whose accumulated aggression spills over due to the long-term abuse inflicted by her husband.
- She feels guilty for killing her husband. She understands that she acted harshly and cannot forgive herself, although she know that she was saving her child.
- While protecting her child, she lost her freedom.

Main mistakes:

- Ignoring red flags

Even before her pregnancy, she witnessed Rick's aggression towards his son from the first marriage but did not leave him.

- Did not ask for help.
- Put up with it for too long. She should have left at the earliest signs of violence from her husband.

4. Rick (Paris' husband)

Characteristics:

- Physically aggressive, hits his own child.
- A vivid example of a domestic abuser with tyrannical traits, who craves total control and does not tolerate disobedience.
- Jealous, short-tempered and prone to sadism.
- Appears successful and seductive. Initially wins Paris over his charming gestures and presents himself as a high-status man.
- Controls their finances.

Main mistakes:

- Criminal behaviour: violence, tyranny and complete disregard for his family's feelings
- He chooses the path of violent domination instead of seeking help from specialists.

LIGHT OF MY LIFE

Life seemed was so bright and beautiful to me when I was a child, and only now do I realize that it is not true at all. It came to me quite recently that the illusion of life's incredible happiness and joy had been created for me by my parents, as surely other parents who really love their children do.

Although we were not well off and did not have many toys, my sister Errin and I were very happy. We had a warm home, which always smelled of something flavourful and delicious, the love of our mum and dad, and most importantly, the certainty that everything would be fine.

Mum always tried to give us delicious meals, to show her love for us through food. In the evening, when Dad came home from work, our little gang would throw ourselves into his arms. He would kiss my mother first, for he loved her very much, and then kiss us. My most vivid memory from childhood is lying in my new mouton coat on a sled in front of the TV. I even remember the show we were watching. Mum was knitting, keeping one eye on the screen, while dad was winding balls of yarn for her. No one scolded me for the sled in the middle of the room, no one shouted "take off the coat, you'll ruin it, it's only for going out". Nothing like that ever happened in our childhood.

Now that I am an adult — quite old, some might say — I often think back to when I was little, when I was loved and cared for. Oh, if only you knew how much I would like to return to that time and how infinitely tired I am of the life I am living now. I heave a sigh as I get out of bed because a new day has come. And yes, I know it is a sin. I know that I should say, "Dear Lord, thank you for the new day", but I cannot say it because his gift (life) has not brought me any joy for a long time. How can it? I live in a hovel with bare walls, and my clothing consists of a pair of jeans, some blouses and my work clothes. There's a bare mattress on the scuffed floor, and a tiny, barely functioning TV in the corner. This is what my life is now. Sometimes, I wonder if my parents are looking down at me from heaven and shaking their heads disapprovingly. They probably are.

One day, standing at an intersection, I tried to end it all, but a man appeared beside me at that very moment, seemingly out of nowhere. I could tell by the look of him that he was homeless. He started talking to me and unexpectedly said something that stopped me in my tracks. He had asked me, "Do you know that if you don't go through all the hardships that God has prepared for you on this earth, you'll never meet the ones no longer with you? You'll forever remain in Purgatory!" I often think about him and wonder who he was. A madman or a guardian angel who had unexpectedly descended from heaven? Could it be that I am still needed for something on this earth? Perhaps I could still be useful?

And if my journey is not yet over, how can I find the right path again? I have lost all meaning in life. Where is my path now?

So many thoughts run through my head. There are only questions that I cannot find the answers to. I also think about what brought me to this point in life. Was it betrayal or the loss of my parents in my youth? I often ask myself "what if?". If they had lived, I would not have had to grow up so fast. That is the first thing. Secondly, people would still betray me, of course, but such is life. However, if I had had my family and a shoulder to cry on — would I have suffered as much, or would it have been a little easier?

Betrayal. What does the word mean? The proverbial knife in the back? No, it is more painful than a knife, piercing every cell in your body and every corner of your soul. I guess no one knows how to live with it. The consequences of betrayal can be very different, and perhaps my case is not the worst, for I am still breathing. I often talk to myself, reflect and analyse past events. It helps me to stay sane and find some relief. The only question I ask myself every single day is how to keep on living. I do not know the answer. Perhaps it will come with time, or perhaps it never will.

My parents always dreamed of going to the ocean and saved diligently for the trip but as so often happens, they kept having to dip into their little dream chest and start saving all over again.

"Errin needs new boots," Mum would say.

"Take it from there," Dad would nod at the small, battered box above the TV.

First it was the boots, then it was something else, and so on and on. As we grew up and became more or less mature, Mum and Dad's dream remained unfulfilled. One day, when I was already 16 and Errin was 11, Dad came from work looking deliriously happy. He literally glowed.

"Pack your things," he shouted from the doorway. "We're going to the ocean!"

"How?" Mum gasped, unable to believe it.

"I won the lottery!"

We laughed, thinking that Dad was joking, but he was serious. He took a ticket out of the breast pocket of his jacket and approached my mother.

"Goodness, it's true!" Mum was surprised.

"Well, are we going?" My dad asked triumphantly.

Mum hesitated.

"Don't you think it would be better to save this money for Catalina's education? Or we can get a new car since ours is on its last legs."

"No way!" My father protested. "When I bought this ticket, I made a wish for this trip. And when, if not now? Life is passing us by! Catalina is 16, and we were planning to go when she was about 5 years old. Pack your things! It's decided."

The house was a beehive of activity for the next couple of days. Things were flying everywhere as everyone debated what to take and what to leave behind. Errin kept rushing from one room to the other, packing everything that she thought might come in handy for the trip. I was not thrilled with the whole plan. It was the summer break, filled with long evening walks with my friends, and besides, I did not want to go because of my boyfriend. At the time, I was dating the most popular boy in our neighbourhood, and I was convinced that as soon I went on the trip, he would be stolen by

Alicia, my main rival at the time. Those were the kind of silly problems I once had.

The only question was how to persuade my parents to let me stay home alone. I dragged my feet for a while, at least two or three days, but one evening, almost on the eve of the trip, I cautiously approached my mother.

"Mummy," I said, "you know, I don't really want to go with you."

My mother looked at me in surprise.

"Please just let me finish. I know it was our dream and all that, but I'm going back to school in 3 weeks, and I'd like to spend this time how I want. I want to stay here, hang out with the girls and do nothing. Do you see?"

Mum smiled and nodded.

"You know that you can trust me," I continued, "and I promise that there won't be any parties or disasters in the house. Do you believe me?"

"I believe you, sweetheart. Of course I do." She sighed. "Oh, I would love you to come with us. It would be great to spend time together while we still have it. You'll be off to university soon, and then Errin, and we'll be all alone."

"What are you talking about, Mummy?" I asked, putting my arm around her shoulders. "I'll never leave home. I'll live with you, and I'll even bring my husband to you!"

"No, thank you!" Mum laughed. "Am I supposed to look after your husband too? All right, I know you're responsible and I trust you. I know that nothing bad will happen to you, but what are we going to tell Dad? This stupid excuse won't work on him. Okay, I'll think of something. Off you go."

My mum and I were always on the same wavelength. I hugged her tightly and skipped back to my room. I fell asleep in happy anticipation.

The next morning, after loading all their things into the car, my parents gave me final instructions. Dad was a little hurt and spoke more coldly to me than usual.

"Don't bring anyone to the house, eat regularly and come home on time!" Mum was saying. "I'll call you every day. Right, what else, what else?"

"Mummy, I remember everything you said. It will be fine."

"All right then. My heart feels heavy, as if we're leaving forever," she said, giving me a parting hug.

I waved goodbye to them and went back inside, turning the music on full blast. I was strangely glad to be alone. In the evening, I went to hang out with my friends but returned home at the agreed time. It was around 10 pm and I was waiting for my mum's call since she had promised to ring me regularly. But the call never came. I was worried but not too much, thinking that they were probably exhausted after the long drive and had collapsed into bed and fallen asleep as soon as they had arrived at the hotel.

The phone did not ring the next day either. I spent the whole day by the telephone, yet it remained treacherously silent. I did not go out that evening and fell asleep on the couch beside it. My mind kept running through all sorts of unpleasant scenarios, and I did my best to push them away.

The phone finally rang the next morning at around 6 am and I jumped up, startled.

"Hello," I replied in a voice that was not my own.

"Catalina, is that you?" Errin was crying.

"It's me, it's me. Why are you crying? What happened?"

"The nurse let me call you but only briefly. I'm going into surgery soon. I just wanted to hear your voice."

"What happened?" I shouted, my nerves strung taut.

"We were in an accident."

"Where are Mum and Dad?"

"I don't know, and they won't tell me. All I remember is that Dad was covered in blood, but I didn't see Mum at all."

"Which state are you in? Which hospital? I'll be right there!"

"We didn't get far. We're in N."

"What do you mean, in N?"

"Catalina, they're taking the phone away from me! Please take me home!" Errin said before hanging up the phone.

I ran around the apartment in a panic. I could not think straight. The only word pounding in my head was *accident, accident...* Once I had calmed down a little, I began to pack. I took out a travel bag and started putting canned food and sweets in it, probably thinking that my family was not being fed in hospital. I also took several pairs of clean socks, I do not know why.

I reached the hospital quite quickly with the help of my best friend's father. We had been friends since we were 2 years old, and we also lived on the same street. I had no one else to call. Mr. Tuohy helped me at every step — I probably would not have managed on my own. He not only found the right hospital, but also the room Errin was supposed to be brought to after surgery. We found out that her spine was broken, but they would not tell us anything about my parents. We had to wait for a doctor.

After an endless period of waiting, a very old man approached us. He was not wearing a white coat, so I did not immediately realize that he was a doctor.

"Are you related to Miss Steinberg?" he asked wearily, shaking Mr. Tuohy's hand.

"Yes, we're neighbours. Mr. Tuohy," he introduced himself, "and this girl is her older sister, Catalina."

"Nice to meet you. Errin's condition is stable and in a couple of hours, when she has recovered from anaesthesia, we will transfer her to the ward."

"What about..." Mr. Tuohy asked but did not finish when he saw the doctor purse his lips.

Mr. Tuohy understood everything at once, but I kept staring at the doctor, hanging on to his every word.

"The crash was too severe. The father died on the spot, and we fought to save the mother's life for 20 hours. Unfortunately, her heart gave out. Please accept my condolences."

I snapped out of my daze at these words. "What's he saying, Mr. Tuohy?" I asked, wide-eyed. I looked from the doctor to my friend's father and could not accept what had happened.

"I'm very sorry," the doctor replied, putting his hand on my shoulder.

I burst out laughing and my wild laughter echoed through the hospital corridors, scaring not only those present but even myself. I do not really remember what happened next, as I was given some kind of injection.

I woke up to someone's touch and it took me a moment to remember where I was. For a second, I thought that I was home and everything that had happened was nothing more than a terrible nightmare.

"Go back to sleep, dear. I'm just adjusting the blanket," a nurse whispered to me.

That was when it hit me — it was all real.

"Do you know where my sister is?"

"She's fine. She's on this ward, not far from here."

"I want to see her. Can I?"

"You know, if someone sees you wandering around at night, I'll get in trouble."

"Please, I'll be quiet."

The elderly woman took pity on me and escorted me to Errin's room.

Errin looked even smaller than she was, lying in that big hospital bed. My heart was pierced with sorrow, and I was struck by the magnitude of the tragedy that had befallen us. I tried my best to be quiet as promised, but tears choked me. I sank into a chair in the corner of the room and rocked gently, as if lulling myself to sleep.

"Don't think, don't think," I ordered myself, but my thoughts would not obey me. Bright memories of Mum and Dad, our lives and our home flashed before my eyes. I could not believe that it was all gone.

The funeral service passed peacefully. My father was buried in a closed coffin, so I could not see his face for the last time. Nowadays, I think that it was probably for the best. He remains alive in my memory. I did see my mother. I remember the cold stillness of her face, looking stern. She did not look like herself at all. Where had the warmth and tenderness gone? Had they vanished together with her soul?

Our few relatives began to argue even before the ceremony was over. It was not until much later that I found out that Errin and I had been the reason — no one wanted to take us. In the end, we went to live with our father's mother. Dad had hated her, and he had good reason to. She was a bad person and a bad mother. A greedy, cruel and quarrelsome woman. As it later turned out, she did not take us out of the kindness of her heart, but so she could control our meagre inheritance. Needless to say, we did not see a single cent.

Our life went from bad to worse over the next three years. I held myself together somehow and endured it, but Errin was in a very bad way. During the treatment, and even after, once she was back home, Errin still hoped that she would be able to walk again someday, that things would miraculously improve. But the more time passed, the clearer it became to her that she would be bedridden and disabled for the rest of her life. I tried to convince my sister that her life was not over, and things would turn out fine, but she did not believe me.

When she was a teenager, I became a source of irritation for her since I could walk, and she could not. I must say that I felt unfairly guilty. It seemed to me that if I had gone with them back then, nothing bad would have happened. We would have been lucky somehow.

I did not finish high school because my grandmother pushed me to find work, claiming that our inheritance money was long gone, which was not true, of course. Ironically, she was not bothered by her own son and my dad's brother, who constantly drank, threw tantrums and stole things from the house. Fine.

I found a job, although all I could get was waitressing. The pizzeria I worked at belonged to an old Italian man. He was nasty in every way and greedy to boot. He not only cut employees' salaries but sometimes took their tips as well. I would come home from my shift at 11 pm, tired and angry. My situation was grim. We had no parents, no home and no future. I must say that I was never a naive fool to dream of a prince on a white horse, coming to whisk me away. I always relied on myself, even at a young age.

I was 19 when I got a job as a house painter. This is the only thing I am grateful to that Italian man for. That year, we, the wait staff, renovated his pizzeria for the promise of a "manager's bonus" that never came. We plastered and painted the walls and some of us even laid tiles. On the last day of the renovations, a woman entered the pizzeria. It was a lucky break in my life — divine providence, as they say. I was sanding the wall in that moment. I worked fast since I still had a lot of energy back then.

"Guys, I can see that you're closed, but can I bother you for a glass of water?" the woman asked. I did not even turn around to look at her because I was so absorbed in my work.

She was given a glass of water and one of the waiters started talking to her. It turned out that this lady was a regular customer, but I had never seen her before. She knew the Italian man and was not at all surprised that he had "hired" us instead of a team of workers.

"He won't pay you!" she declared, putting the glass on the table.

"He promised, Ms Wilkes!" Tom said.

"I bet you that he won't pay."

"It's a deal!" Tom replied eagerly, holding out his hand.

"What will you pay me with if you lose?" The woman laughed. "You're working for free, and he'll take your tips! It's not a fair bet."

When she left, she gave a tip that was clearly disproportionate to the cost of a glass of water. Before stepping outside, she turned around and asked Tom, "Who's that working in the corner? A waiter or a specialist?"

"A waitress, Catalina."

"All right, look after yourself, Tom. See you at the opening."

The opening was a week later, and Ms Wilkes came to our pizzeria with ten other ladies. They ate, laughed a lot and were surrounded by an incredible atmosphere of cheerfulness. I kept wanting to turn around and gaze at them. Tom served them, but when it was time for the bill, Ms Wilkes called me over.

"Katarina, if I'm not mistaken?" she asked.

"Catalina, with an L."

"I visited you a week ago and this place was not as beautiful as it is now."

I smiled sweetly.

"My point is, I saw you working back then, and when I came in today, I checked the results of your work. The seams are smooth, and the paint is laid down perfectly. Anyway, do you see that sultry brunette at the end of the table? She's leaving us for the joys of motherhood. I'd like to offer you her place. We have ten women in the team, and there is no shortage of work. The salary is decent by all standards."

I gasped when she named the amount and could not believe that I was getting a job so easily.

"Come to the office tomorrow — the address is on the business card — and we'll make it official. Insurance and everything."

I took the card from her hand, mumbled my thanks and ran into the back room. My heart was pounding, and I did not know what to think. All my wishes and dreams flashed through my head. I imagined taking Errin with me and living in a nice little house, which I would slowly but surely renovate.

This was the beginning of a new chapter of my life. I quit the pizzeria that very evening and kept the tip for myself this time.

As I approached the house, I heard Errin crying and rushed to her. I smelled the reek of alcohol as soon as I entered the house. As I ran up the stairs, I saw my uncle standing in the doorway of the room I shared with Errin.

"We took you in, but you're never grateful, you little jerks," he shouted, throwing a pack of cigarettes at her. "You're an invalid, a freak. Who would ever want you?"

"Get away from her, you filthy animal," I shouted, taking a run up.

Before he could turn around, I knocked him down and sat on top of him, snatching the bottle out of his hands. Smashing it on the floor, I brought the jagged neck of the bottle to his throat and hissed, "You come near her again and I'll kill you, you bastard! I've got nothing to lose. I'll kill you. I'll slash your whole face and body, cut off your fingers one by one and watch you writhe in agony. Got it?"

I could tell by his eyes that he understood me perfectly, and he sobered up at once. Not that I was a dangerous person, but I would do anything for my family or what remained of it. And he knew it or could sense it somehow.

From that day forth, he did not come near me or Errin, and Grandma never mentioned the incident even though she must have known about it.

I worked as hard as I could for Ms Wilkes. The first few weeks were hard since I was unaccustomed to the smell of paint and other things, which made my head spin. But my head spun even more when I got my first paycheck.

It was not just money I had now but a future. We had a future. That was probably when I truly became an adult. I worked during the day and tried to sort out our life in the evenings. I not only bought new furniture for the house, but also groceries.

"You only drink on weekends and do it quietly — no more causing a scene," I said to my uncle once I felt stronger. "And tell

Grandma to start cooking! I can't be standing at the stove after working all day."

And so my life got better. When I turned 21 and had a decent amount of money saved up, we moved out of my grandmother's house. It was a rental apartment, but it already felt like home. I made our little nest as cozy and charming as possible, and our home was always filled with wonderful smells again. I found a good carer for Errin, who also cleaned the house and cooked our meals. It actually turned out cheaper than when we lived with my grandmother, who had been a real drain on my finances.

I will always remember our life in that duplex fondly. For the first time in years, we felt like our life resembled the one we had known with Mum and Dad. At times, it felt like they might step through the door and appear beside us at any moment.

The years went by. I continued to work hard, saving money for our own house. Errin also made progress. She learned to hold a spoon by herself, although there was no question of sensation returning to her other limbs. Not that we expected it. This was already a huge achievement. She even tried to paint sometimes. I bought her the most expensive watercolours and brushes, and her face glowed with joy. In those moments, she really looked like her younger self. We were happy together. Although I thought of her as my child, she was also my friend. My one and only friend. I did not need anyone else. I did not want to get married and could not imagine someone else living with us. This was why I never tried to meet anyone and declined whenever someone asked me out.

However, everything changed soon after I turned 30. My team was working in a fancy suburb for the first time, and we had lunch at a number of different places. We wandered into an eatery one day. The other girls ate quickly, but I was very distracted that day and slow with everything: I washed my hands for a long time and then could not decide on what I wanted to order. Our lunch was nearly over, and we had to get back to the site, but I had barely started eating.

"Don't wait for me, I'll finish and catch up to you," I told them, remaining to finish my meal in proud solitude.

I even remember what I was eating that day. Chicken wings in barbecue sauce. I did not look like a lady at all. Although, what kind of lady would walk around in overalls splattered with paint?

"They must be very delicious," someone said as I tore another piece of meat off the bone.

I glanced at the person who said this and laughed, imagining how I must look at that moment.

"Very," I admitted.

He asked something else, I do not remember what and asked if he could sit at my table.

"Did you eat all that?" he joked, looking at the empty plates left behind by my colleagues.

"Yeah," I replied.

That was how I met Andrew. If someone had told me that I would have a relationship with this guy, I would have called them crazy. He was so not my type. He was tall, thin and kind of awkward. He had thin blond hair, blond eyebrows and pale, almost faded eyes. Yes, he certainly was not handsome. As I said, I had no intention of getting married, and I certainly could not imagine marrying someone like Andrew. I was a tall, attractive blonde with dark blue eyes. I had a curvy body that was often admired by both men and women. I knew that I was attractive.

And this seemingly unprepossessing guy scored such a beautiful woman. As I found out later, he was working class, just like me. He worked as an electrician near my worksite. He was in his 30s too and lived with his sick mother, whom he was looking after. Just like I was caring for Errin. Perhaps this is what brought us closer. It is hard for me to talk about his good qualities now, but it would not be fair if I did not acknowledge that he was funny, kind and decent back then. He is probably still decent, although not for me anymore.

It is hard for me to say exactly how he won me over — maybe it was his sense of humour or maybe his caring nature. Surely, caring for his sick mother had sharpened his empathy. He could sense exactly how I felt and when. He never had much money as he earned a lot less than I did. Nevertheless, he never came over empty-handed. He brought Errin fruit and always brought me flowers. Cheap ones, but I appreciated them all the same.

After some time, we got married and I could no longer imagine a life without him. We moved his mother to our house, so there were four of us. In the evenings, we had dinner together and watched movies, sport matches and played games. I do not remember if I was happy back then. I think that I was, but was I really, if I do not remember feeling happy?

Our city was growing rapidly, and so was I. I felt cramped with Ms Wilkes as my boss, and some might say that I acted ignobly, but I decided to leave her and start my own finishing company. Some of the staff came with me, and that was how my company came into being. Even though I was now the director, I kept working onsite. Life was tough at the start because there was very little work. Ms Wilkes did not forgive me for my betrayal and spread various rumours about me, so clients were reluctant to trust us. Slowly but surely, I built up a customer base through my impeccable work. My credibility grew, as did my income.

I finally bought a house like I had always dreamed of, where every member of our family could have their own room. Andrew and I did the renovations ourselves. Every corner of this house was created with our own two hands, nourished with our love and hard work. Every corner was meticulously thought out down to the smallest detail. We lived there in peace and harmony for five years.

I was nearly 40 when I had finally had the chance to think about children. To be honest, Andrew kept bringing them up, but until then, I did not have a moment to myself. It was all work, work, work. We had to pay the mortgage, buy furniture and pay for Errin's and my mother-in-law's medical treatment. Once we finally stopped and caught our breath, we began to pursue what my father once said was my true purpose — becoming a mother.

We worked hard at it, but every month on a certain date, my body informed me that the work had been in vain. I would be deeply upset and hoped for the next month, yet each time we were met with disappointment. When I finally decided to see the doctor, I heard what seemed to me the worst thing at the time — "You have infertility".

Andrew comforted me for a long time and even suggested adoption, but I decided that if God had deprived me of children for some reason, then there was no point in trying. Yes, it hurt that I could not give my husband what he wanted, and I felt like damaged goods for a while, but life went on and the pain of my infertility grew duller.

Just as we started to recover emotionally after my diagnosis, Andrew's mother grew worse.

"Quit your job," I suggested to him. "A family member is always better than a carer."

So, he ended up staying at home, and after his mother's death, I felt awkward telling him to return to work. There was no real need for it either, since his salary did not affect our finances. We lived on my earnings anyway.

I still do not understand when it all happened. When he quit his job and had more time on his hands? I keep thinking about it, yet I cannot identify the moment when I made a mistake. Or maybe it was not my mistake or my fault at all?

We had been married for 17 years, and I thought that we were living our best life. A cozy house, prosperity, a living and almost healthy Errin, a dog and a cat. There was nothing more to ask the Lord.

At that time, I was working less on building sites and spending more time doing paperwork at the office. On the day my world was split in two, the office was quiet and there was not much work — just the usual red tape. I was not in the mood and really wanted to be home. I imagined coming home and asking Andrew to grill some steaks. We would pour ourselves a glass of red wine, have a quiet dinner and watch a movie in the evening.

I did not call him on the way home, assuming that he was busy cleaning the house, as he always did on Wednesdays, and therefore would not hear the call.

When I reached the house, I decided to enter quietly. I imagined slipping inside and shouting "boo" to scare my husband and sister. I used to do this all the time, and we always laughed together afterwards.

The house was quiet, except for strange noises coming from upstairs. I tiptoed up the stairs. The noise was coming from Errin's room, and I no longer wanted to scare anyone. I already understood what was happening.

When I opened the door to her room, I saw Andrew and Errin. He was lying on top of her and passionately kissing her neck.

Errin saw me first. She screamed and tried to cover her body with a sheet using her good arm. I stood rooted to the spot. Although I saw everything with my own eyes, I could not believe what was happening. My brain refused to process this information. I shook my head from side to side like a horse chasing away flies.

I finally snapped out of my stupor and ran out of the room, dashing down the stairs. Andrew ran after me. He was grabbing my hands and trying to explain.

Sure, sure, I got it all wrong, honey.

Run. Run. Run.

I dashed out of the house and ran as fast as I could. I ran as if my life depended on it. Tears choked me and I could not get enough air, but I kept running. I was almost struck by a car at one of the intersections, and only then did I collapse in the middle of the street. People gathered around me, offering to help and pulling me off the road. Strangers sat me down on a bench and asked questions about how I was feeling that I could not answer. I wanted to scream at them to leave me alone, but since I had not reached that level of madness yet, I tried to convince them that I was okay. When I was finally left alone, I could not even cry. My head kept spinning, but oddly enough, my thoughts were sharp and clear.

'When did it start?' I thought. 'Does it matter?' an inner voice replied immediately.

For the first time in my life, I felt the true sting of betrayal. While I had somehow survived the death of my parents — this was the end, and I did not know how to live with this betrayal. I still do not. It is bad enough when it is a stranger, but your closest family member, your sister? The one who grew up in your arms, the one who survived only because of you. What would have happened to her if not for me? After all, I had spent my life making sure that she had everything! Not only food on the table, but a home and a family too.

The tragic death of my parents, the lack of money, the terrible conditions at my grandmother's house, the hard physical work, infertility, and now the loss of the last people I held dear. Was that not enough, Lord?

I never went back to that house. The next day, I came to the office, cleaned myself up, took a shower, put on clean clothes, and started calling all my former partners. I do not know where my composure came from.

"I'm leaving and selling my business. I need the money urgently, so I'm willing to accept a below-market price. It's a profitable business, as you know," I said in a voice not my own.

I found a buyer for my company the very same day. He knew that I had never lied in my life and always acted honourably and conscientiously, so he agreed to the deal without hesitation.

When I left the office, I saw Andrew. He was waiting for me. I wanted to keep walking but could not help coming up to him.

"How long has this been going on?" I asked the only question that interested me.

"Twelve years," he replied, looking down.

Twelve years. A lifetime. They had been lying to me for twelve long years. And living at my expense, although this only struck me recently. In that moment, this worried me least of all.

"Why?" I looked into his eyes and asked. "Why?"

He started babbling that he did not know how it happened and that they did not mean to fall in love with each other. He said that he loved me too and did not know how to break this vicious circle.

"I didn't want to hurt you."

Of course, you did not want to, dear, but you hurt me anyway. Hard to call it a hurt when it was something bigger and more inexplicable.

I walked away, not wanting to hear his voice anymore. A couple of days later, when the deal was completed, I packed my things in the office and rang my sister's number. She did not pick up for a long time, probably wondering whether she should answer or not. When she finally answered, I told her, "It would have been better if you died back then. I hate you."

I knew it would hurt her to hear those words, but I wanted her to experience as much pain as I was feeling. She started sobbing, but I hung up and threw the phone away.

I did not take the car or anything else. I decided to bury that life and everything I had. That was how I ended up in this big and bustling city.

When I arrived, I rented the first place I came across, in quite a rough area as it later turned out, and got a job as an ordinary painter.

I still have money left over from the sale of my company, so I could buy myself a beautiful house, a car and fashionable clothes, but I do not want to. There is nothing I want. I do not want to get up in the morning, I do not want to breathe, I do not want to live. I go to work not because I need the money or for any other reason. I just know that I have to go there. What is the purpose of it? Nothing, really. The problem is that I cannot live, and I cannot die.

I stopped noticing the time. It seems like it was only December, but now May is here. My life has lost all meaning. I seem to be living in wait for something. The end, perhaps.

I often write letters to Errin that I do not send. I always start with the same question, "How could you do this to me?" The worst part is that I hate and love her. Happy moments from our lives treacherously pop up in my memory. I remember that ill-fated hospital ward where my little girl lies broken, and I feel sorry for her. At times, I look for excuses and think that maybe it is a good thing that Errin got involved with Andrew and experienced a man's love. She had nowhere else to get it.

I wonder about their life and imagine Errin watching movies and drinking wine with my husband. I imagine our house and remember every nook and cranny. In my mind, I wander down the corridors and reconstruct every detail — here is the rug with the red diamonds and here is the lamp. I look up and there is the ticking clock. This makes me feel truly miserable. Longing permeates every cell of my body and soul. I miss something that no longer exists.

'It is gone forever. Forever. You don't have a home or a family anymore. You're all alone — old, sick and unwanted by anyone.'

Yes, some might say that there are people in this world much worse off than I am, but I am my own closest person. And yes, humans are selfish beings. I am in pain, I feel sad. Me, me, me.

I thought I would be alone forever until a seemingly sad situation changed everything...

About a month ago, I stayed back at work and was returning home in the dark. The streetlights were on everywhere, and for some reason, my heart felt so comfortable, as if it sensed something from the past. The lights had looked the same on the street where I used to live. It was a warm, summery day, and the air was filled with the fresh scent of flowers.

Everything proceeded as usual, and I was about to cross the road when a dog jumped out of nowhere in front of me. I had no time to flinch in surprise before the unfortunate animal was hit by a speeding car. The dog flew into the air and landed on the asphalt with a thud.

One would have thought that the dog would be dead after such a blow, but I saw its heaving ribs as I ran up to it. Something clicked inside of me as if I was suddenly engaged with life again. Cradling the dog in my arms, I hailed a taxi and was at the veterinary clinic in 15-20 minutes.

"It's a goner," said the callous vet nurse.

I glared at her, refusing to believe it. I knew the dog would survive. At least, that was what I wanted to believe.

As soon as the young vet examined the animal, he decided that it needed emergency surgery. I promised to pay any amount to save it.

"It's not your dog, is it?" The vet asked with obvious surprise.

"It's not. The thing is, I should have stepped out into that intersection instead of this dog. If it hadn't been for the animal, the car would have hit me. It kind of saved my life. Maybe this dog is an angel or something. You know all those stories?"

The vet looked me up and down, apparently determining my place in society and my mental state.

"I'm a house painter and I was returning home from work," I began to explain myself for some reason.

"Okay, don't worry. I'll do everything I can."

So began the long hours of waiting. I switched between going outside and waiting inside the clinic. Despite all the discomfort: worrying about the dog's fate, the stress, the time, a sleepless night, I never wondered why I was here.

'I wonder if it saved me or not. Or am I looking for hidden meanings where there are none again? What if it is God after all, whom I've begun to doubt lately, to my great shame.' I wondered. 'Somebody in this world still needs me. Who? Well, this dog, for one.'

After five hours of surgery, the vet came down to me. It was already light outside.

"It'll live," he said wearily. "But the rehabilitation process will be a long one."

"Thank you, doctor. I'll get it better. When can I take it home?"

"In 10 days, at best, if there are no complications."

"When can I visit?"

"Come back in a couple of days."

And I came. I visited every day that the unfortunate animal remained in the hospital.

"Dog," I said as I gazed at it through the bars, "get well, dog. I'll take you home and we'll live together. I'll buy you a bowl, delicious food and everything you need. You'll like living with me. Just get well."

And the dog recovered. I didn't give it a name and just called it dog or doggy, depending on my mood.

My life got better with it, and I seemed to get better too as I slowly returned to myself. I no longer came back to an empty house, to stew in unpleasant memories of the past. Now I had a person, and I thought of it as a person, who waited for me to come home and rejoiced at my arrival. I told the dog about my day, and the animal listened attentively, as if it understood everything. I gradually noticed that the dog and I were very similar. It was big and shaggy like me, with the same wounds on its body and soul.

I slowly started losing weight since I had to walk the dog every morning and evening. I also began cooking for the animal and for myself. I even bought a stove and gradually made the place feel more like a home. This was how an accident turned into positive change for me. I hope it was the same for the dog. I cleaned it up, washed and trimmed its fur. Of course, it was still a mutt, but now it was clean and well-groomed.

My birthday fell on a working day. I did not tell any of my colleagues, but I was planning to celebrate with my dog. It was my friend and my current family. On the way home, I stopped by the store and bought us a variety of snacks. As I approached the house, I almost dropped my shopping when I saw a painfully familiar face. It was very old and thin, but it looked like it had once belonged to my husband. I stared at him, unable to look away. When I spotted a child in the man's arms, I calmed down, certain that I had made a mistake.

'Where would Andrew get a baby?' I thought, turning away.

Before I could get the keys out of my bag, I heard my name being called. "Catalina," the voice repeated softly.

I turned around and studied the face more closely. I had not seen him in three years and heavens, how he had changed! And where was the baby from?

"Andrew?" I asked, wanting to make sure that I was not going mad.

"I've really changed, huh?" he asked me with bitterness in his voice.

"What are you doing here?"

"I've been looking for you, and I've finally found you. I need to talk to you."

"I have nothing to say to you!" I replied proudly, turning to the building entrance, even though I knew that something terrible must had happened if he had been searching for me.

"Errin is dead," he said.

"What?" I collapsed on the steps, unable to believe it.

"Here," he whispered, holding out the baby.

"Huh?"

" She died giving birth to him."

"What were you thinking? Didn't you know that she couldn't give birth?!"

"She really wanted a baby."

"When did this happen?"

"Four months ago."

"Did you bury her properly?"

"Yes, next to your mum and dad."

And then I started crying. The betrayal and resentment were gone. All that remained was my little girl, who used to rejoice when I came home from school. I could not believe that her life was over so quickly and that I was truly alone now.

The baby's crying interrupted my stream of painful thoughts.

"He's hungry," Andrew explained.

"Have you got any food for him?" I asked, wiping away the tears with my sleeve.

"Yes, the formula is in the backpack."

"Well then, let's go to my place. You can mix it up in there. I've got a dog, though, is that all right?"

"Yes, it's fine."

"Is it a girl?"

"A boy. Angel."

My goodness. Angel. What a beautiful name. Were you the reason for my life?

We went up to my apartment. I set the table while Andrew fed the baby. My bitter tears dripped onto the sandwiches. Once the baby had settled down, Andrew laid Angel on my mattress, surrounding him with a rolled-up blanket.

"So he doesn't fall off," he smiled guiltily.

Sitting down on the stool beside the small coffee table that I had set, he looked down, rubbing his hands. I knew this habit of his and knew that he wanted to ask me something.

"You didn't just come here because you wanted to tell me that Errin had died?"

"No."

"You need something from me?"

"Yes."

"Then tell me already," I cried, losing all patience.

"I'm dying."

"You're joking. You're joking, right?"

"No. It's exactly the same as it was with my mother. The terminal stage. I found out too late."

"Could it be a mistake?"

"No.

"How long?"

"No more than six months."

I was silent, struggling to process the news I had received in the last hour.

"I want you to take custody of Angel."

"But I don't know what to do with a child."

"We don't have anyone except you. Do you want him to be taken in and raised by strangers?"

"And you want me, a woman in my 50s, all sick and broken, to care for your child? If you two hadn't orchestrated all this, none of it would have happened!"

"Catalina," he whispered, covering my hand with his. "I know. I agree with every word you say. Please forgive me. It's all my fault. But as you can see, I've already been punished. Angel is innocent. I want to die in peace, knowing that you will look after him."

Andrew knew that no matter how much I baulked and accused him, and no matter how much I cursed, I would take care of the child. He knew that for sure.

They stayed with me while I handed in my job resignation and ended the lease on the apartment. After everything was settled, we got in the car and set off.

On the way back home, holding little Angel in my arms, I thought once again about how strange life could be. It was always throwing something at me that I did not feel prepared for. What was it that life wanted from me — to finally give up and die, or to fight my way out of this whirlpool and learn to appreciate what I had been given? And who came up with these wild and twisted life scenarios? God? The universe? People themselves?

The dog's head rested on my shoulder, and I could hear its soft breathing. It looked dutifully out the window and was probably thinking the same thing that I was thinking.

A psychological portrait of the characters and the mistakes they made

1. <u>The main character and narrator — Catalina</u>

Characteristics:

- Grew up in a loving and comfortable home, where her parents created a sense of absolute safety. The warm atmosphere left a lasting impression and formed an internal point of reference of "how it should be".

- After the death of her parents, she has to grow up quickly and take responsibility for her younger sister. Catalina does this not out of a sense of obligation, but rather out of a deep love, continuing her parents' mission.
- A hard worker and an altruist, she devotes all her time to work — first as a waitress, then as a painter, and eventually as a business owner. Meanwhile, her own emotional needs are relegated to the back seat.
- As she emotionally hits rock bottom, she unexpectedly saves a dog hit by a car. This act seems to remind her that caring for the weak is in her nature. By saving the dog, she also saves herself.
- Despite past events, she agrees to Andrew's request to care for the child. This is a new challenge for her. She also retains the ability to forgive and take responsibility for someone left all alone.
- She carries two deep internal wounds:

1. The death of her parents. Subconsciously, she feels guilty for not going with them that day. "If I had been there, this would not have happened." This guilt transforms into the habit "I want to save everything that I have left".
2. Her sister's and husband's betrayal. This event shatters her core belief that family members do not do this to each other. It destroys her faith.

Main mistakes:

- Neglecting her own desires. When you take care of others all the time, you forget about yourself and ignore the threats (for example, a 12-year-long affair between your husband and your sister).
- Lack of open communication with her sister. Catalina is so focused on financial matters that she lacks the chance to discuss what is happening with Errin emotionally and how she is coping with her disability.
- The drive for self-isolation after the betrayal. Instead of seeing a psychologist or, for example, going to church and talking to someone there, she escapes to a new city, plunging into depressed solitude.

2. Errin (younger sister)

Characteristics:

- Is affected more than her sister as she not only loses her parents but also ends up disabled. These psychological traumas pile up on one another, depriving her of any chance at independence.
- She constantly feels dependent on her sister, her money and her decisions. Over time, this can lead to hidden resentment ("I'm nothing but a child to her, someone to look after").
- She subconsciously envies Catalina's strength and health: "You can do anything while I'm bedridden".
- Psychological loneliness despite external support. Catalina provides for all her physical needs, but on a deeper level, Errin cannot open up to her.
- The need to feel like a woman and receive attention.

Main mistakes:

- A secret affair with her sister's husband, which is a serious breach of trust. Yet, perhaps in her mind, it was the only way to discover herself as a grown woman.
- Becoming pregnant despite the contraindications. The desire to experience the fullness of life turns into a tragedy.
- Silence. She never tries to tell her sister that she feels a lack of love, attention and more. Instead of honest dialogue, she takes a desperate, "forbidden" step.

3. <u>Andrew (Catalina's husband)</u>

Characteristics:

- A man with little backbone, who leads a parasitic existence at his wife's expense (her money and her house). He lacks integrity by becoming infatuated with his wife's sister but still loving Catalina.
- He wants a comfortable existence and a family, yet he is also attracted to Errin, apparently feeling needed and special to her. He lives a double life instead of bringing clarity to the situation.
- Passivity. He does not dare to openly date Errin but does not break off the relationship with her either. He drags things out for 12 years.
- He realizes his mistakes only shortly before his death.

Main mistakes:

- Duplicity: he deliberately deceives his wife.
- Irresponsibility: he stops working and expects his wife to provide for them.
- Immaturity and self-justification. "I didn't want to hurt you" — in reality, he hurt Catalina more than he could have ever imagined.

Note: despite the traumatic events in our lives, we have to keep living!

In today's world, where there are fewer and fewer good, kind and honest people, you must stay afloat. Do not abandon those who need you — keep going, even if it means crawling. This world needs you.

AND FINALLY, I WILL SAY THIS

It is nighttime, I am driving home from the office again and thinking about something again. Returning to the question of whether I am a good person overall. Am I good or bad? Should I be removed from this world, just like everyone else?

Yes, I have done many bad things, many nasty things, as it may seem to an idiot like Gishi, but if you look at it from another angle, maybe what I have done and am doing is good, even if it looks bad?

I often torment myself with these thoughts, and sometimes, realizing that I am still a negative character, I want to delete myself immediately, but remembering my foundation, my hand stops immediately. Who will it go to? What will happen to the people who need my help? It's not just a hotline, but also many other socially significant projects. How many people have we helped stay alive, how many people have we saved from hunger and cold?

I sigh heavily. Despite the fact that I have helped and continue to help thousands, I know that my place is in hell. This fact does not upset me at all, but only a little. I believe that my life on this sinful earth has been my personal hell, with all its suffering, torment, terrible people, vile stories, and other nonsense. In general, I think that life is more painful than pleasant. Although this may not be the case for other people, perhaps I am just unlucky? Who, in fact, is lucky: those who have a home and money? Those who are at the top of the world? No, they are not lucky either. They cry just like everyone else, only the conditions in which these tears flow are a little better. But no one is immune to grief and suffering. Some, like me, learn this in early childhood, while others, who are lucky enough to experience unconditional love, learn it later. By the way, I still don't know which is better: to learn the truth about the world from the very beginning of life or to live for a while in the illusion that life is beautiful?

Life itself may be beautiful, yes. And the world around us is beautiful, but people... What are people doing here? Who made them this way? God? I'm not sure of anything anymore.

www.ingramcontent.com/pod-product-compliance
Lightning Source LLC
Chambersburg PA
CBHW070610310726
48982CB00001B/37
* 9 7 9 8 2 1 8 7 9 5 9 8 6 *